INK AND ORE

HAYLEY WHITELEY

First published in the United States on January 23, 2024 by Storm Hollow Press.

Print ISBN: 979-8-9890476-0-4

E-Book ISBN: 979-8-9890476-1-1

Developmental Editing by Kim Long.

Line Editing by Emily A. Lawrence of Lawrence Editing.

Cover by Stefanie Saw of Seventhstar Art.

Map by Rachael Ward of Cartographybird.

For all the ordinary people
from ordinary places
who dream about making a difference.

ICEMARK GLACIER
FROZEN WASTES
FIR KELT
YULE VALLEY
LINDEN
THE NORTHERN MOUNTAINS
BAR KUR
KLOSTERN
HALSTAT
A'SLENDERIA
SLONDE RIVER
CLON KILLY
BALLYNACH
FORMER BORDER OF DREZCHY
AFDOT
FORT DONOUGH
FORT CAJETAN
JINENSIN
FORMER BORDER OF DREZCHY
TIBEDO
BEIRA BAIJA
PIZEMAC

ROSKEBORG
SEVERN ISLES
NEW
DREZCHY
VINCENCIM
TRAIN LINES
POLITICAL BORDERS
CAPITAL CITIES
CITIES AND TOWNS
FORTRESSES
THE CONTINENT OF
KERAFIN
AND
NEIGHBORING LANDS

1

Brenna

"Someone shot the king."

"When?"

Brenna Malley's mind raced as she listened. Her boss, Mrs. Teague, was smacking the newspaper in her hands as she discussed the morning's headline.

"Says here it happened just this morning, during a parade in the capital."

Brenna could only assume the shot was an accident. After all, the citizens of Bar Kur loved the monarchy. Her country was all about tradition, and no one embodied their traditions better than King Stefan XIV. He had been on the throne for thirty years—far longer than Brenna's own seventeen years of life—and she couldn't recall ever hearing a word against him.

"Is that the suspect?" asked Orla, another chambermaid around Brenna's age.

Mrs. Teague nodded and whacked the paper again for emphasis. "A foreigner, from Tibedo."

Brenna craned her neck over Mrs. Teague's shoulder. Below the headline was a grayscale mugshot of a withered-looking man. He had the typical Tibedese traits of copper-brown skin and black hair, but his other features were unusual: an oblong face that ended in a pointed beard and round, impossibly closely spaced eyes. Beneath the picture, a name was printed: *Inigo Farro.*

It took Brenna a moment to peel her eyes away, but when she did, Mrs. Teague snapped, "Get back to work," and left the room.

Brenna resumed raking a pillowcase against a washboard, grimacing as the lye burned her hands. In the year she had worked here so far, she hadn't even slightly gotten used to it. After secondary school, she took a job at the Royal Kelt, a hostel in her hometown of Fir Kelt, a tiny village in the remote northeastern corner of the country. She thought it would be fun talking to guests all day in the lobby, but it ended up being a job where she did nothing but wash bed linens.

"Did you figure out if you could go to the festival with me and Katiel?" Brenna asked, referencing her invitation from their last shift together. Orla had never taken her up on her attempts to socialize in the past, but she figured it never hurt to offer.

"Sorry, won't be able to make it," her coworker replied, not sounding very sorry at all. "But your friend from A'slenderia is going, you say?" Orla pronounced *A'slenderia* slowly, as if she had rarely heard of the country right next to theirs.

"That's right!" Brenna chirped. "She goes with me every year."

Orla turned up her nose. "Why would a foreigner want to attend the Bar Kur Day Festival?"

"Wouldn't you want to go? It's always fun." She smiled, choosing to ignore the way Orla said 'foreigner'—like she was saying 'criminal' or 'vagabond.' Brenna was used to this when she explained that her lifelong best friend was A'slenderian, though she didn't understand it. Sure, Bar Kur had lost the last war to them, but that was over a hundred years ago. No one alive today even remembered it. "Plus, she comes to sell wool at the marketplace with her da."

She paused, waiting for a reply, but it seemed Orla was ready to let the topic drop. With no other conversation starters up her sleeve, Brenna went back to scrubbing. Meanwhile, she couldn't help but notice, Orla wasn't washing anything and didn't look like she had any plans to start.

Luckily, her brother, Henred, was coming by later to keep her company on the walk home from work. Usually, Henred's penchant for bringing up politics annoyed Brenna to no end, but today she looked forward to discussing the news.

Before she knew it, the morning shift was over, and Henred was tapping his toe while he waited for her in the Royal Kelt lobby. In the tiny mirror above the coat rack, Brenna was struggling to dislodge her itchy work headscarf from her bushy hair.

"You," Mrs. Teague snapped from behind the reception desk, "take these letters and burn them on your way out, won't you? No one ever claimed them, and I'm tired of them clogging up my desk."

"Sure thing!" Brenna snatched the handful of letters from her boss's hand and stuffed them into her satchel, then scurried out the door at the dismissal. Henred filed out behind her.

The hostel was located off the main square, a large, unassuming plaza surrounded by quaint, stone-faced shops and cottages. Brenna often took her lunch break in the empty square, but today the place was abuzz with people preparing for the festival. Volunteers flitted about, adorning booths with pennants of pine and emerald and sage—everything in shades of green, the Barkurian national color.

"I'm guessing you heard the news about the king today," Henred said when they started walking. Henred looked a lot like Brenna—stereotypically Barkurian, with red hair, fair, freckled skin, and a sturdy, somewhat stocky build. He lacked Brenna's large eyes, though, and most of the time, her large smile as well.

"I think he'll be all right," Brenna said, shuddering at the alternative. "I'm just glad they didn't cancel the festival."

Henred scowled at her. "That's what you're worried about? The country could go to war over this."

"You think we might?"

"If the king dies, then yes, I think we will. Attacking our sovereign is an act of war." He puffed up his chest. "And if we do go to war, I'll be the first to volunteer."

Brenna wished her brother were joking, but she knew he wasn't. Henred was constantly talking about turning eighteen and being old enough to join the Barkurian Army. Normally she encouraged him to fulfill his dream of becoming a soldier. When the Continent was at peace, he could serve in the army by guarding the royal family in the capital or providing relief after a rice field flood. During wartime, though, he might actually see combat, a thought Brenna hastily put out of her mind. It was unthinkable to even consider him getting hurt. "The papers said he would recover."

"I guess we'll see." Henred shrugged. "I think we're about to have another Ten Years' War on the Continent."

"But that war was about magic and the wielders gaining too much power," Brenna protested. "This is nothing like that."

"You don't seriously believe there was real magic involved in that war, do you? They signed that treaty almost two hundred years ago." Henred gestured to the gas lamps lining the street, a recent invention that illuminated the main road in their small town. "People back then would call gaslight and steam engines magic. However the so-called wielders were gaining power back then, I think it was something else. Something that might be starting again."

For once, Brenna didn't know what to say. History classes had taught her that there were very few of the alleged sorcerers, even before the Kerafin Pact banned the practice of wielding magic and banned the wielders from having children. She knew people of the past didn't understand science and technology the way modern people did, but even so, she couldn't believe Henred's theory. If wielding had never truly existed, there would be no need to outlaw the practice now. And anyway, she didn't see what any of that had to do with the king being shot, regardless of her brother's wild ideas.

As they made their way home, the cobblestone pavers gave way to a narrow dirt road. The walkway cut through lush green rice fields, the likely inspiration for the country's national color, and led straight to Galvey Manor. The estate, belonging to their elder sister Derenta and her husband Jay, served as the Malleys' residence since Da passed away three years prior and Mam couldn't keep up with rent payments for the quaint cottage Brenna grew up in.

Derenta seemed to enjoy their company and their help with baby Stefan, but Jay made it obvious that he loathed having his wife's family living with him. Brenna had been a child when her sister married the statesman, and back then, she'd admired him almost as much as Henred did. Now that she lived under his roof, though, her brother-in-law had become intolerably strict, and she was looking forward to the day she saved up enough money to move out.

When they arrived back at Galvey, a fire burned in the hearth despite the fair summer weather. Derenta had a roast reheating for lunch, as usual. The second they walked in, Henred launched up the stairs two at a time, despite his short stature. He sometimes kept to himself for a while after working the fields—a habit that left Brenna bored to tears with no one to spend the afternoon with—and today seemed to be one of those days.

She followed him up, planning to solve a word puzzle in her room while she waited for Katiel to arrive. Henred's hand was on his bedroom door, about to swing it shut, when he noticed her behind him. "Shouldn't you burn those letters before you forget? The ones Teague gave you?"

Brenna opened the flap of her satchel, hesitating as she looked between the letters in her bag and the fire in the hearth below. "I don't think I'll burn this group. Parchment's been so expensive lately, and you know how many letters me and Katiel send each other."

Since their houses were a whole day's ride apart, she and Katiel exchanged letters constantly. It had all started eleven years ago, when they were both six, and Brenna spotted the strange-looking girl selling wool and cheese with her father in Fir Kelt's main square. Katiel's blond hair was tied in funny teardrop-shaped loops next to her ears, so naturally, Brenna had to talk to her. At first, the A'slenderian was painfully shy and could barely speak Endran, but after years of writing back and forth, the girls had become inseparable.

"What do you mean, 'how expensive it's been?'" Henred asked, pulling a face at her. "You aren't seriously going to use the letters for parchment, are you?"

"I do it all the time." Brenna shrugged. "I just mark out the side that's been used and write to Katiel on the other side."

"I'm pretty sure it's illegal to read other people's mail."

"Well, I don't read it before I mark it out, obviously!"

At that, Henred rolled his eyes and shut the door.

Brenna headed to her room and grabbed her pencil and last week's paper, but the anagrams proved more elusive than usual as she became lost in thought. She tried to reassure herself that the king would be fine and that Henred was just being Henred and exaggerating. There was no way this would lead to a war, and even if it did, that would be something that would impact the capital or bigger cities.

After all, nothing that happened in Ballynach would affect her little town at the edge of the country.

2

Brenna

The next night, lanterns glowed against the dark sky as night fell over the festival. Banners dotted with tiny Barkurian flags and shamrocks zigzagged between the buildings on either side of the Fir Kelt town square. To Brenna's right, endless rows of market stalls sold handicrafts and treats, and to her left, the local brass band played a jaunty Barkurian folk song with gusto. The dancers' heels clicked to the beat against the cobblestone pavement, echoing the tune across the square.

She, Katiel, and Henred were watching from beside the dance floor, Brenna straddling an awkwardly large, wrapped fruitcake between her arms.

"Why even keep that thing?" Henred laughed as she nearly dropped it for the third time. "You know it's going to be foul."

"Because the cakewalk was the only game I won this year," Brenna said, sticking her tongue out at him for good measure. "I can't win anything when I'm playing against Katiel. She is the luckiest person on the Continent." Katiel had won a frosted cake that actually looked appetizing, plus prizes at darts, ring toss, apple bobbing, and even Wielders, a complicated card game themed after the game's namesake. "Katiel can win at anything."

"Would you like me to give you the pig?" Katiel teased, pulling from her satchel an ugly felted pig she had won from apple bobbing. "Believe it or not, I *am* willing to part with it."

Brenna laughed, and her friend giggled back in her usual close-lipped way. Katiel often tried to hide her teeth because of a crooked canine, but she was actually exceptionally pretty, with blond hair always worn in some style of braids and delicate features that looked elegant against her tall frame. Katiel had a slight, clipped accent in Endran, since she grew up speaking the regional mountain language of Aslen at home with her family, but no one ever had a problem understanding her. If anything, the lilt in her voice made her sound distinguished, even when talking about silly carnival games.

"Or maybe Katiel is just better at games than you, Brenna," Henred joked. Brenna cringed as he wiggled his eyebrows. "Now, if you'll excuse me, a slow song just started, and that means I am going to ask someone to dance."

Brenna, Katiel, and the unappetizing fruitcake watched Henred clumsily approach a girl on the dance floor, who shockingly agreed to dance with him. "Poor thing," Brenna muttered about the girl, which sent Katiel into another giggle fit. Then Henred and his partner were off, lost in the throng of couples, all moving identically in the song's required steps.

She couldn't help but notice that most of the other girls were wearing a curled, half-up hairstyle. Katiel had offered to do Brenna's the same way, but she hated the feeling of having her hair up, so she had declined in favor of her usual loose, messy waves. Though now that she found herself standing on the sidelines, she wished she hadn't declined, no matter how distracting the itch would've been.

Katiel had fashioned her own hair into a braid crown and wore a lacy *dirndl* in the same shade of cornflower blue as her dress. The style was distinctly A'slenderian, which was how Katiel always dressed, a contrast to the ruffled, plaid cotton dresses or skirt-and-waistcoat sets worn by the Barkurian girls. In her plain, taupe-and-white gingham frock with a simple square neckline, Brenna felt underdressed.

Orla was on the dance floor, too, chatting with some of the other village girls their age. Brenna should have known she'd attend. She probably lied because she didn't want to be seen with foreigners at the festival. The Barkurian boys might fancy A'slenderian girls enough to ask Katiel to dance, but Brenna had been called odd enough times to know that not everyone in town approved of her friendships with foreigners.

The song ended as Dakier walked up beside them, giving a curt little wave. Brenna ditched the fruitcake at the last minute, setting it down on a random barrel next to her. The band, to her annoyance, started playing another slow tune.

Dakier was a Tibedese immigrant who worked for Katiel's parents on their farm in A'slenderia. He was the same age as her and Katiel, and tall, with almond-shaped eyes and a copper complexion. He wore his silky, black hair almost to the shoulders—longer than most men did—but Brenna was not sure if that was typical in Tibedo or individual preference.

"Has the marketplace closed for the day?" she asked him by way of greeting.

"No, but sales are slow now that everyone's dancing," Dakier said. "Mr. Salzbruck told me to take the rest of the night off. 'Enjoy my youth,' and all that."

Brenna chuckled in response. That was a direct quote, knowing Katiel's father. She was about to say something about how dull the formal dancing was, thinking Dakier would agree, when he turned to her and cleared his throat. "Would you like to dance?"

She tried to keep herself from looking too shocked. Even though she was completely shocked. She snuck a glance at Katiel, who nodded several times in encouragement.

He extended his hand out in front of him, palm facing up. Certain she could not speak without stammering, she placed her hand in his as her answer. Then, out of nowhere, he lifted her hand to his face and pressed his lips to her knuckles, holding eye contact throughout the movement.

She really could not speak now. She did not know boys actually kissed your hand, given that her romantic experience up to this point was nonexistent—though it wasn't for lack of trying. Suddenly, the slow dance didn't seem so bad.

He led her to the middle of the floor without letting go of her hand, and they took up the pose the song required, clasping one set of hands out to the side and placing the others on one another's shoulders. They mimicked the steps everyone else was doing, tracing simple squares with their feet while turning in a broad circle.

"You know, I wanted to say." Dakier cleared his throat. "With your dress and your hair and everything, you look really beautiful."

Brenna blushed, her fingers reflexively darting up to her cheek. "Really? I feel so out of place. All the girls I used to go to school with are here and so dressed up."

"Are you kidding?" Dakier smiled his wide-open smile. "You're the most beautiful girl here."

Brenna's jaw dropped. No boy had ever said anything like this to her before. He didn't look away as she met his dark eyes. The place where his fingertips grazed her upper arm was burning hot.

Dakier appeared panicked. It must have been her lack of response. "I mean, I didn't mean to be strange. Forget I said anything," he stammered. "You're not—you're not that beautiful."

"Wait, what?" Brenna's face fell.

"That's not what I meant." He unclasped his hand from hers, opting to press his palm against the nape of his neck instead. "Sorry, I just don't want to seem like a louse."

"Dakier." Brenna smiled. She could have sworn she saw something pass across his face when she said his name. "You're great. Don't worry. Let's finish the song."

They fell into silence, continuing their circle in time with the music. Brenna glanced up at him, as he was over a foot taller than her. His jawline and cheekbones angled into sharp points, and hours of farm work had given him broad shoulders and a lean, muscular build. She wondered how she hadn't seen before that he was this attractive. Somehow, despite seeing him around for years, she had failed to notice.

He met her gaze, and her eyes darted away, as if that would prevent him from reading her mind. He smiled again, the same smile that lit up his face and everything around him, and slid his hand down from her shoulder to the small of her back.

She met his gaze again. For a second, it was just him and her and the twinkling lights around them. She didn't know which was boring into her more: the hand on her back, or the gleam in his eyes. He was not smiling anymore. At all.

It was like she was gravitating toward him despite herself. This seemed like the perfect moment for her first kiss. It had to be.

She lifted onto her toes and sucked in a breath, debating if she was bold enough to go for it, when the crowd around them came alive with activity. Brenna and Dakier both turned toward the commotion.

"Out of the way! Out of the way!"

The crowd was parting as someone passed through. It was a man no older than thirty, with a thin ponytail at the nape of his neck. Brenna didn't recognize him, which meant he was most likely not from Fir Kelt, since she made it a priority to know everyone. He walked over and stopped by the bandstand. "Excuse me, attention all!"

Someone handed him a milk crate, and he flipped it over and stepped onto it.

Henred and Katiel were both by Brenna's side now, though she hadn't noticed them arrive. Like her and Dakier, they were facing the bandstand.

"Attention all!" the man shouted again, now from his elevated position. "Listen all! There has been horrific news today."

Henred tugged on the back of Brenna's shirtsleeve. "Brenna," he hissed, "let's go. Let's get out of here."

"I want to hear what he's going to say," she hissed back.

"My compatriots," the announcer said, "it is with great sadness that I bear this news to you all today." He took a deep breath. Brenna's wide eyes surely matched those of everyone around her, all of them now huddled around the man with bated breath. "The King of Bar Kur is dead."

Shrieks and gasps went out in the crowd. A woman ahead of them fainted, the surrounding people shuffling to catch her.

"Yes, you heard it right," the announcer continued. "Stefan the Fourteenth, King of Bar Kur, is no longer with us. The authorities have determined that the Tibedese operative Inigo Farro orchestrated the assassination."

Everyone gasped and shrieked even more vehemently. People started yelling various things, but Brenna could not make them out. She could feel the anger rising in the air, mixed with fear.

"We need to go." Henred yanked Brenna's shirtsleeve hard enough that she stumbled back. "We need to go *now.*"

But the man on the crate wasn't done. "Bar Kur has declared war on Tibedo, to defend our great nation against further attack!"

Katiel raised a hand to her gaping mouth as the bellowed words echoed in Brenna's ears. Henred was still pulling on her arm. She wanted to follow, tried to follow, but her feet were not obeying.

"Tibedese scum!"

A swift motion to her right snapped her out of her shock. Dakier reeled back, staggering to a crouch and clutching his cheek. Someone had struck him in the face. Hard.

"Stop!" Brenna shrieked.

A few other young men were gathering near them. Dakier was back on his feet as quickly as he went down. He swiftly dodged another fist, this one aimed straight for his head.

"Aye, aye!" Henred grabbed the shoulders of the man closest to Dakier and flung him away with a rough shove. "Stop." The men who were harassing Dakier turned to Henred, looking like they were about to harass him, too, until they took in his face and hair and saw that he was Barkurian. And likely someone they recognized.

Brenna started to scream at Dakier to run, but he was no longer where he'd been. Looking around her, frantic, she spotted him sprinting down the road, already past the town square.

He glanced over his shoulder, probably checking to make sure she and Katiel were still all right.

Henred mouthed, "Run."

She bolted.

THE FOUR OF THEM raced back to Galvey without stopping, though no one appeared to be on their tails. Brenna panted as she came to a halt next to Henred on the manor lawn, trying to regain her breath after the long near-sprint. Katiel and Dakier stopped next to her, all of them staring at the stone manor.

"Look." Henred gestured to the carriage house, where the horses were being untethered from their brother-in-law's phaeton.

Brenna cursed under her breath. Jay was home early. If he found out about what happened this evening in the town square... "Not a word about tonight, not to any of them," she said, "especially not Jay." She was still facing the house, scanning the windows for any trace of movement, but the warning had obviously been for Henred.

Henred tossed his hands in exasperation. "Come on! You think I am just going to go in there and say, 'Oh, hello, Jay, you'll never believe the night we had—'"

"Swear you won't tell him," Brenna cut him off. "If he brings it up, we say it was someone else. Say there was a different Tibedese person there tonight, and that was who the crowd went for."

Her brother huffed. "Fine."

She stared him dead in the eye. "Swear it."

Katiel and Dakier wore the awkward expressions of people trying not to eavesdrop, despite standing right next to the siblings on the otherwise empty lawn. Henred rolled his eyes, but put his hand across his chest nevertheless. "I swear I will go along with whatever ridiculous story you come up with."

That was good enough for her. She rolled her eyes back for good measure before taking a deep breath and heading inside.

When they entered the foyer, the sight was worse than expected. Everyone was standing up, waiting for them, save for Katiel's father, and that was only because he was ancient. Mam pressed her mouth into a nervous line. Derenta was wiping her hands on her apron over and over again, and Jay, with his sandy hair and long chin, was positively glowering.

He got right to the point, not even bothering to greet their guests.

"He can't stay here." Jay didn't specify Dakier's name, but it was clear who he was referring to. He addressed Brenna alone, as if she was the one who would raise an objection about this.

He wasn't wrong. "You can't be serious!"

"I am serious."

"It's already dark out. Where do you expect them to go? The inns will be full for the holiday."

"That's enough, Brenna," Derenta interjected.

"No, it isn't! They live a whole day's ride away!" She was full-on shrieking now. "You gave permission for the Salzbrucks' stay in advance. They were counting on being able to stay here."

"I would never give permission for a citizen of an enemy nation to stay at Galvey," Jay countered.

"He hasn't even been there for ten years!" Never mind that Tibedo hadn't been declared an enemy nation until earlier today. Brenna turned to her mother. "Can't you do something?"

But Mr. Salzbruck saved her from having to answer by coughing forcefully and standing with his cane. As he strode over, Brenna noticed that he already held his hat and coat in hand. "It is no trouble." Nothing could rile his soft demeanor, and it eased Brenna's worry slightly. "We should get going." He turned to each person individually to thank them for their hospitality, despite Jay turning them out.

Wordlessly, Dakier lent a steady hand to help Mr. Salzbruck put on his coat, since the elderly man struggled to stand with his bad leg.

Brenna wished she could think of something to say to fix this. Instead, she blurted out the first thing that came to her mind.

"Can I at least go with them?" she asked, looking at her mother. Visiting Katiel in A'slenderia was the thing Brenna looked forward to most every summer, and she was afraid with everything going on, Henred wouldn't be able to escort her like he did in years prior.

Mam hesitated, her eyes darting between Brenna and the others. "Would that be all right with you, Feniel?" she asked, using Mr. Salzbruck's first name.

Her mother's hoarseness struck Brenna. Mam hardly talked since Da passed, and it seemed so long ago since Brenna had heard her utter a word.

"Of course," Feniel said with a nod and a stroke of his short white beard. "Brenna is always welcome in the Yule Valley."

Derenta and Jay reeled on her, Derenta objecting with, "Mammy, no! What are you thinking?"

Henred was expressionless, stunned.

But a beat passed, and Mam said nothing.

"It might be helpful to go with Brenna to pack," Mr. Salzbruck told Katiel, who waited for Brenna to start up the stairs before trailing after her.

She was about to ask Katiel if she knew what was going on with their parents, when Henred pushed past them into Brenna's room.

"Katiel, I need to speak to Brenna alone," her brother said, before noticing that Katiel looked stricken by his commanding tone. "Sorry, it'll just be a minute."

Katiel's expression softened, but she remained where she was, lingering in the doorway.

"Brenna, you can't do this." Henred did not seem to mind if Katiel overheard because he didn't close the door. Rather, his hushed tone suggested he was trying to prevent the adults downstairs from hearing. "You can't leave Bar Kur. Not during wartime."

She grabbed her overnight bag and started shoving her clothes into it from the dresser. She was taking almost everything she owned, since she didn't know how long she'd be gone. "Mam said I could. She must have her reasons."

Henred hushed himself further. "You know how she's been...since..."

Brenna's mouth gaped open. They had never talked about this. Never. Until now, neither of them had mentioned how their mother had been since Da died—how distant she was, how she never spoke, or how sometimes it felt like they didn't have any parents left at all. Katiel knew they never talked about it, and her friend peered at her from the doorway with a troubled expression.

"No, how has she been?" Brenna phrased it as a question, but her flat tone suggested a challenge. Or that her voice was breaking.

He must have noticed, because his eyes softened. "You know"—he struggled for the words—"not herself lately. She must not be thinking straight. You can't go."

"Mam spoke for the first time in a week, and you want me to disregard what she said?" Brenna's voice cracked again.

Henred stepped back, the hurt written across his face. "You're my best friend. I'm scared you're going to get hurt leaving the country. I want you to stay home."

Heat rose to her face. He was such a hypocrite. "Who are you to talk about staying home and staying safe? You're going to volunteer for the front lines the first chance you get!"

Henred's face was red now, too. "You bet I am!" he spat. "I'm going to the recruitment office tomorrow, and I bet they'll let me volunteer early. By the time I see combat, I'll be old enough."

Tears blurred her vision. All she could think to say was, "See?"

"Da served his time in the army. Jay's still serving the country." Henred scraped a hand through his cropped hair. "I have to serve, too. For the country's safety."

"No, you don't," Brenna said, though she knew the argument was futile. Henred had always been the king's biggest fan. Since he had already been considering joining the military before, after the news, she feared nothing could change his mind. "They never served during wartime. You have no experience. You'll get yourself killed."

She didn't add the other parts she wanted to say. That she loved him. That he was her best friend. And that he was the only family member left from her blissful childhood who was still himself, who hadn't been lost to sadness or marriage or worse. And now she feared if he saw combat, she might lose him, too.

Henred's jaw tightened, and he said, "I have to."

Brenna shook her head and grabbed her bags, tears streaming down her cheeks. She had finished packing, so she may as well get on before the sky grew even darker. Katiel stepped closer and scanned the room, as if checking that Brenna hadn't forgotten anything she would miss.

Katiel said, "Goodbye, Henred."

Henred said, "Goodbye."

And after she left, Brenna couldn't remember if she said goodbye to him or not.

3

Katiel

Two weeks later, in the Yule Valley, things were almost back to normal.

A soft breeze shook the surrounding wildflowers, and in the distance, a thin waterfall trickled into the stream. Katiel was sitting in the meadow with Brenna, playing with the baby goats born that spring. Katiel's home was nestled at the base of the Great Mountain, its planes of gray stone jutting high above the green gradient of the valley and dwarfing the surrounding mountains. The Yule Valley was home to her family's livestock farm and one well-kept road that led the way for travelers into Bar Kur. Master Larinne's supply outpost stood in the lowest part of the clearing, surrounded by the homes of the few other families who lived there.

It could be mistaken for any other summer day were it not for the gloomy mood that lingered after how horribly the festival had gone. Since the assassination and Bar Kur's declaration of war, Tibedo had retaliated by denying the assassination was their country's doing and mobilizing troops to the Tibedese-Barkurian border, which led Bar Kur to send their own troops to meet them. Mercifully, no other news had yet come, but everyone was on edge, anticipating a horrible update any day—whether it be first shots fired at the border or that Henred had indeed volunteered, a concern had Brenna sprinting to the mailbox every time the post came. Katiel did her best to comfort her, but it was a struggle when her own mind kept going back to the letter.

She had told no one about what she had found. She still hoped it was a coincidence.

But something inside her doubted it.

Five—no, six days ago now, Katiel had been cleaning her room while Brenna chatted with Dakier in the smithy. She was reorganizing her stationery when she noticed Brenna's most recent letter askew above her teal-painted desk. On the wood-paneling, she had hung a corkboard covered in layers of pinned letters, with the surprises that came in them—charcoal drawings and pressed flowers—interspersed overtop.

When she stretched onto her tiptoes and reached out to straighten the letter, the strangest sensation came over her. Her fingertips sizzled with the tiniest of sparks, like the note held a static charge, and the tiny metal pin slid free, falling with a *ping* against the desktop. The letter swirled through the air above her head before landing on the rug behind her.

As Katiel bent to reach for the paper, her mouth went dry. The page had landed with Brenna's words face down. She was already aware of her friend's recent habit of keeping parchment from work, but this note was different. Unlike the others, on this one, Brenna had not crossed out the old text. As she picked up the stray note, Katiel could hardly hold her hands steady enough to read the letters scrawled in ink at the top of the page, as if addressed to the name.

INIGO FARRO

The messy capitals appeared to have been written in haste. Katiel blinked several times and moved the parchment closer to her nose. There was no mistaking it. *I-N-I-G-O F-A-R-R-O.*

She did not have to check the newspapers to know it was the same name as the infamous Tibedese assassin, down to the spelling. The headlines had etched the name in her memory. Hastily, she checked the date Brenna had written atop the other side of the page. The 25th day of Beltaine. Ten days before the assassination took place.

If the letter was intended for the assassin, then that meant it had never reached him, since Katiel already had it in her possession before the assassination. It meant his enemies had not found the letter, either, since they would have destroyed the note. What did that make her, she wondered, since she had not burned it yet?

"Katiel," Brenna said, ripping Katiel's mind from her musings. She spoke with the tone of someone who had already repeated her name six times before this.

"Was I..." Katiel offered a sheepish smile. "Staring into space again?"

Brenna returned the smile with her own. "Yes! For an impressively long time. What were you thinking about?"

"Nothing." It was not a lie, not entirely. It was nothing she knew how to explain, at least.

"Sure," said Brenna. "I bet it starts with A and rhymes with 'Talfien.'"

She knew what Brenna was referring to, of course—Katiel's recent breakup with Alfien, her boyfriend of nearly two years. It was not a bad guess.

Before the events in Fir Kelt, the breakup had been all Katiel wanted to talk about. When her parents refused to let her attend university the previous fall, Alfien had broken up with her abruptly and headed off to attend alone. Other than their general overprotectiveness, Katiel could not understand her parents' refusal to let her go. They had not given her a reason beyond 'concern for her safety.' Before that decision, Katiel had felt close to her parents, but since then, she had struggled to forgive them. Or understand them.

Brenna never forgot to ask after Katiel's feelings, though, and could always say the right thing to make her problems seem manageable. Brenna was everything Katiel was not—outgoing, funny, unafraid of a challenge—but somehow she seemed to understand her better than anyone else in the world.

Katiel crossed her arms. "There is no such thing as 'Talfien.'"

"True, but it does rhyme." The baby goat slammed its apple-sized head into her calf, and Brenna gasped. "I think that little demon goat gave me a bruise."

Katiel laughed. "She probably didn't like your joke."

Brenna rocked to a standing position and pulled up her skirts to examine the back of her leg, while Katiel absentmindedly chewed on a piece of hair that had come loose from her braid. "What's wrong?" Brenna nodded toward the wet strand of hair. "You only do that when you're stressed. Did something new happen with Alfien?"

Katiel debated not telling her. Why bring her friend into this if she did not have to? But, on the off-chance Brenna *did* know something about the letter's contents, could Katiel really resist finding out what she knew? If she did not speak up, she might always worry, so she decided to tell her. Even if she did not know how to broach such a subject.

"Brenna," she said, forcefully steadying her voice. "You remember hearing about that assassin? The one who killed the king?"

Brenna's head shot up as her skirts fluttered back to the grass. "Huh? What do you mean?"

Katiel shrugged a tiny shrug, her face hopefully revealing nothing. "I do not know exactly, but it's about him."

Her face must have revealed something, because Brenna replied with concern. "What is it?"

Katiel did not know how she could explain this. It was just a coincidence. Hopefully. "Just look," she said, pulling the paper from her apron pocket and unfolding it. She knew she should not carry it around, but she did not want her parents to find it until she figured out what to do. Brenna took a seat next to Katiel in the grass, placing her fingertips on the opposite end of the note to hold it steady.

Brenna scanned the lines for a moment before she gasped a huge gasp and covered her mouth with her hand. "I can't believe it. I can't believe it. Inigo Farro. There is no way that is a coincidence. What should we do?" she asked before immediately attempting to answer her own question. "I guess the first step is to figure out what the rest of it says."

Katiel's eyes stretched wide. "Why would we want to know? There is nothing we can do about it, regardless. We have in our possession a letter addressed to the name of a criminal. Perhaps we should just burn it."

Brenna leveled her gaze with her friend's. "Don't you want to know what it says?"

"If an A'slenderian was involved with this plot, they could get into trouble." Katiel hated the thought. But perhaps the individual deserved it if they assisted in an assassination. However, she was *more* concerned that it could get her and Brenna into trouble.

Brenna ignored the logic and asked her question again, this time adding an eyebrow wiggle. "Don't you want to know what it says?"

"Yes, of course." She had to admit it. If she did not find out now, she would always wonder. She knew Brenna felt the same.

"We could go ask Dakier." Katiel had figured she would suggest as much. Brenna and Dakier seemed to grow closer these past weeks, despite the state of their warring home countries.

"I don't know that I want to bring it up to Dakier. If it's nothing, he's going to think we are the strangest people on the Continent."

"If anything," Brenna said, "he will think you are a normal person with a very strange friend. I don't doubt he knows I am odd."

"Actually, I think he might be in love with you," Katiel said. Brenna widened her eyes and then forced them back to normal, a gesture Katiel might have teased her for were it not for the pressing matter of the letter. "But regardless, he might tell Father we have it. And Father will make us get rid of it."

"We could go ask Master Larinne, then." Brenna nodded toward the teacher's home in the center of the valley. "Didn't you say she has an enormous collection of books to lend out? She might have a Tibedese-to-Endran translation dictionary we can use."

"No, not Master Larinne," Katiel said, far more emphatically than necessary. Master Larinne had been Katiel's tutor back when she was a student. Katiel adored her, but the problem was that Master Larinne was also Alfien's grandmother, who he lived with, and Katiel did not want him to think she was making an excuse to see him. Avoiding the embarrassment was also worth never returning the last stack of books she had borrowed.

Brenna noted her friend's reaction and knowingly said, "I see," before clasping her hands together and bouncing to her feet. "Dakier it is, then!"

Before Katiel registered what her friend was planning, Brenna was racing across the meadow toward the house. Katiel's home was a traditional A'slenderian chalet, a three-story wooden structure with staircases wrapping around the outside of the building. The steeply gabled roof allowed snow to slide off in the winter, and in the spring and summer, velvety edelweiss spilled over the balcony railings.

"I do not like this idea," Katiel muttered as she followed Brenna up the stairs and into the kitchen.

Sure enough, Dakier was there, leaning against the counter while Mother warmed a turnover on the stove for him. Probably ham-and-Halstat cheese, the lunch he requested almost every day during his break.

Brenna sidled up next to the apprentice, standing way too close. "Dakier."

He took a half-step away, smirking down at her with a raised brow. "Yes?"

"Would you happen to have a Tibedese-to-Endran dictionary we could borrow?" she asked, propping her elbow on the counter. "Katiel's trying to read a book in Tibedese."

Katiel fought the urge to clap a hand across her forehead at the flimsy excuse. No one would ever read a book that way.

"Oh?" Dakier winced as he bit into the steaming turnover Mother handed him. As predicted, ham and cheese. "What book?"

Brenna locked eyes with Katiel, looking like she had not expected this half-baked plan to be foiled so quickly. The name of one was on the tip of Katiel's tongue—that one where the lone explorer hunted for treasure along the famous Tibedese coastline. But before she could remember it, Brenna said, "She can't pronounce the title, since it's in Tibedese."

Dakier's eyes narrowed as he looked between them and took another evidently scalding bite, based on the steam still wafting off the crust. Katiel had a mind to tell him to just wait a minute for it to cool, but he said, "I don't think I have one. Anyway, don't you think translating every word as you go would be a *very* unpleasant way to read a book?"

As if on a mission to be as conspicuous as possible, Brenna slung her arm around Katiel's shoulders. "You know Katiel, always up for a challenge!"

Now even Mother was eyeing them with suspicion. "Girls, your turnovers are ready. Apple cinnamon for both of you."

Brenna hissed an excited, "Yes," while Katiel asked, "Can you please wrap them up for us?" Right now, she would be happy to eat in her room, outside, or anywhere else but near Dakier, in order to end this embarrassing conversation. It was all she could do to avoid smacking Brenna upside the head.

Back in her room, Katiel slumped against the side of her bed, contemplating if she was in the mood to finish her now-cold turnover. And contemplating if it was for the best that they did not know what the letter said.

"Oh, great," Brenna griped as a dot of apple filling fell on her brown tweed vest. She reached for the top button as a knock sounded at the door.

"Come in." Katiel assumed it was going to be Mother asking about earlier, but when they caught sight of Dakier pushing open the door, Brenna fidgeted with her hair, trying to cover the already-invisible stain.

"Is now a good time?" Dakier asked hesitantly.

"Yes, it's fine," Brenna assured, smoothing her hair in front of her vest again.

Dakier stepped one minuscule step farther into the room and held up a book. "It turns out I do have a Tibedese-to-Endran dictionary," he said. "I went back to double-check in my room. I haven't used it in years." He handed it to Brenna, despite her saying earlier it was Katiel who needed it. "By the way, why did you really want this dictionary?" They must have both looked stunned because he added, "You made me curious earlier. I had to ask."

Katiel said, "I really did want to read that book."

But Brenna surprised her by saying, "Promise you won't tell Katiel's parents, and I'll tell you."

Dakier's mouth fell open as he looked at Katiel and back. "What? I can't do that. I have to tell them if it could be dangerous."

Brenna shrugged. "Okay, then I won't tell you the real reason."

To Katiel's shock, Dakier conceded, "Fine. I won't tell them."

She stared at Dakier like he had grown a third arm.

Brenna prodded, "Even if it's dangerous?"

"Wait, it actually *is* dangerous?" Dakier asked.

They both revealed nothing. At least, Brenna's face revealed nothing, and Katiel hoped her own did not either.

"Never mind. Just tell me. I promise I won't tell them."

Brenna turned to Katiel, who hesitated and then gave her a curt nod, silently agreeing to show him. Brenna said, "We found a message in Tibedese, and we need help to translate it."

"That's all?" Dakier cocked an eyebrow, like he did not believe her. "Sure, give it to me. I'll translate it for you."

Katiel pulled the letter out from its updated hiding place—the back of her desk drawer—and handed it to him. "Here."

Dakier started reading.

As he read, his eyes widened and his brow furrowed in concern. Katiel glanced at Brenna, wondering why he was not saying anything.

Finally, he asked in a quiet, even voice, "Where'd you get this?"

Katiel did not answer, unsure of how to explain it.

"Where did you get this?" Despite his attempt at calm, Dakier's tension was obvious.

Brenna exclaimed, "What does it say?"

"Where did you get this?" he practically shouted.

"She got it from work!" Katiel shouted back, panic rising in her chest. "At the inn, where she works!"

"What does it say?" Brenna asked again.

Katiel wanted to know the same. What could it possibly say that was that bad?

"Wait." Dakier shook his head. "They're paying you in paper? How long have you worked there?"

"No, it was a piece of mail that never got picked up from the inn. I was supposed to burn it." Brenna choked on her words, sounding like she regretted keeping the papers now that she said it aloud. "But I didn't." Dakier was staring at the page solemnly. Brenna asked again, "What does it say?"

"It says..." Dakier took a deep breath. "It says, '*Inigo Far ro.*'—I am guessing you two recognized the name." Brenna and Katiel nodded in affirmation. "'*Inigo Farro, you do not know me, but I know you. Please heed my warning as a fellow keeper.*'"

"One second," Katiel interrupted. She opened the hutch of her desk and withdrew parchment and an inkwell. "Let me write it down as you go."

Brenna added, "Make sure the translation is word-for-word."

Dakier shielded the page from them as if they could read it. "This could be incriminating! It's bad enough you have this. Don't write it down," he said, looking like he was considering not translating any more of it, either. "It'll be hard to forget, anyway."

Katiel wondered if owning it could actually incriminate them as she picked up her quill and jotted down the translation.

Dakier clearly noticed her disregard his warning, but to Katiel's surprise, he cleared his throat and continued to read. "'*Please heed my warning as a fellow keeper. A Barkurian national is planning to frame you for the assassination of King Stefan XIV during the Bar Kur Day festivities in order to incite a war with Tibedo. Leave Ballynach. Leave Bar Kur, but do not return to Tibedo.*'"

Brenna cut in. "What's a keeper?"

Dakier shrugged. "I don't know what it means in this context. The wording might be purposefully vague. Next, it says, '*I write to you at great risk. Burn this note as soon as you receive it. When you are not where you're expected to be at the parade, they will come for you and attempt to kill us both. Meet me in Linden for further instructions. We must stop the growing threat and the true assassin before it's too late.*'"

"Before it's too late," Katiel echoed.

"Linden is close by, isn't it?" Brenna asked before Katiel could muse about all the implications the note contained.

"Yes, it is the closest city in A'slenderia to the valley." Katiel nodded. "Father and I occasionally set up a booth and sell our wool there. It's only about a two days' ride from here."

Dakier's mouth pressed into a tight line. "And then it's signed without a name. It simply says, '*From, a Loyalist.*'"

Katiel reached to take the page back, but Dakier pulled it to his chest. "I'm going to burn it."

Katiel gaped at him. He was going to *what*?

Brenna shrieked, "You can't burn it!"

"It is mine," Katiel said. "Give it back."

As though he thought better than to force anything, Dakier obliged her and handed it off. "You could get in real trouble having this. It would be treason for Brenna to carry. This letter suggests her country's reason for declaring war is a lie."

Katiel repeated, "It is mine. A'slenderia is neutral in this. Please do not tell anyone what it says."

Dakier slid a hand across his brow before he stood. "I won't tell a soul. But if I were you, I would burn that." He looked like he was going to leave before he had a second thought. "When did you find this? Before the assassination?"

Brenna nodded. Dakier shook his head, forlorn, before slipping out the door.

Katiel and Brenna looked at each other, unmoving, as the reality of the note's contents weighed on them. Neither of them said anything for a while. All Katiel could think about were the armies, the people already heading off to fight. Inigo Farro had been framed. Tibedo did not truly attack Bar Kur. There was no actual need for a war.

Thousands of people, soldiers on both sides of the conflict, were risking their lives for a lie.

4

Brenna

Whether they'd been sitting on Katiel's bed in silence for five minutes or five hours, Brenna hadn't a clue. Time no longer passed as she reeled from the news. Bar Kur wasn't actually being threatened. Inigo Farro, the man she had thought to be the epitome of evil since she'd first heard his name, had been framed. And Henred, she was certain, would volunteer to serve in the army. Henred, who she had left after a fight. Who she hoped she would get to see again.

"Here's your letter," Katiel cut into her thoughts. Brenna must have looked as out of it as she felt because Katiel softly added, "The one Mother gave me earlier? Since you didn't have pockets."

"Right." Brenna peeled open the Galvey house seal to retrieve the enclosed parchment and pored over the letter. When she finished reading, she read it again. And again. "It's from Derenta."

Katiel leaned closer, her legs twisted in a pretzel in front of her. "What does she say?"

"She says Jay has gone to the capital to advise in the Secretary of War's office, but she and Ma and the baby are staying in Fir Kelt," Brenna began.

Katiel looked concerned, even before she heard the worst part. "And Henred?"

"Henred." Brenna swallowed as the words refused to come out. Katiel waited with a soft expression, patient as ever. "Henred enlisted in the army. Derenta said he enlisted the day after I left and left for his post in Fort Donough earlier this week, days ago." Brenna looked up at her friend with glassy eyes. "That means there's no talking him out of it now."

Katiel reached over and enveloped her in a hug. She let Katiel pull her close as she lost the will to move, and the will not to cry. Her tears soaked into the shoulder of Katiel's dress, leaving darkened streaks on the lavender gingham.

Katiel patted her head. "It will be okay. He'll come home."

"He's barely an adult." Brenna's words muffled against her friend's shoulder. She didn't say the worst thing she kept thinking—that he would not make it. "They'll put him on the front lines."

"You don't know that for sure," Katiel assured.

Brenna was still crying, but she sat up straighter and wiped her eyes. "Do you know where Fort Donough is? I am pretty sure it's right on the border with Tibedo. That means they sent him to the front lines."

"Let us try to send positive thoughts to Henred," Katiel said. "You can send him a letter there at the fort."

Katiel set out a pot of ink with a quill and parchment so she could write to Henred, but when Brenna took a seat at the desk, her vision blurred on the blank page. No words were coming to mind.

All she could think about was the letter. Her brother had gone to defend a country that was not actually being threatened. He was living out his dream of service, but not for the reason he believed.

Henred was putting his life on the line for a lie.

She looked up at Katiel's pin board, her eyes roaming over the dozens of scattered words she had written over the years. The souvenirs of their lifelong friendship held another memory now—of finding the letter, of learning the secret origin of the war. It could very well be that no one else knew but them.

Brenna longed to tell someone, but the only person she could think of who might know what to do was Jay. Her brother-in-law was some sort of clerk in the Secretary of War's office, so there was at least a chance he could alert the right person to the framing. If she shared the information in time, perhaps they could find the king's true assassin. The Barkurians could broker peace with Tibedo before blood was shed on the battlefield.

There were only two problems with the plan. The first was that the note itself, despite the letter's date being in the past, wasn't enough evidence alone. And the second was that Jay never listened to her.

If she could find the author of the letter and convince him to tell Jay everything he'd seen or heard, though, along with who the actual assassin was, her brother-in-law would have to listen. If only she knew where the letter's author was now.

Thinking back to the letter, it seemed like there had to be something she and Katiel had missed. The author had told Farro to meet him in Linden, but Linden was a sizeable city. How was Farro supposed to know where to meet? Perhaps the letter contained some clue they had overlooked.

Quietly, Brenna pried open Katiel's desk drawer and pulled out the original letter, along with the translation she had written. Katiel was lounging against her headboard with a book in her lap. If she noticed Brenna was rereading the letter, she didn't comment on it.

Inigo Farro,

You do not know me, but I know you. Please heed my warning as a fellow keeper. A Barkurian national is planning to frame you for the assassination of King Stefan XIV during the Bar Kur Day festivities in order to incite a war with Tibedo. Leave Ballynach. Leave Bar Kur, but do not return to Tibedo.

I write to you at great risk. Burn this note as soon as you receive it. When you are not where you are expected to be at the parade, they will come for you and attempt to kill us both. Meet me in Linden for further instructions. We must stop the growing threat and the true assassin before it is too late.

From,
a Loyalist

She scoured the translation first, looking for any turn of phrase that seemed odd. It wasn't so different from the word puzzles in the paper, really, as simple as identifying any subtle word that might be out of place. But when she re-read it, nothing stood out to her. The phrasing was as ordinary as could be expected, given the extraordinary nature of the contents.

In frustration, she turned to the original letter written in Tibedese. Sure, she couldn't read it, but perhaps there was some tiny note written in the margin or some extra fold or tear of significance. Still nothing. The longer she looked at it, the more she felt her hope draining away. Though now that she was looking closer, she was impressed Dakier could even read the note to translate it at all, with the handwriting as sloppy and irregular as it was.

Wait. That might be the clue.

Only certain letters were written sloppily, larger than the others. But it wasn't just messy handwriting. It was a message.

Though she didn't dare write on the original letter for fear of damaging it, Brenna hastily scribbled down each large letter onto the spare ream of parchment Katiel had gotten out for her. When she was done, though, it made no sense. The string of letters didn't appear to be a word, not even in Tibedese.

RTIERBAFELJHAADOTSO

Even when Brenna tried to rearrange the letters, she drew a blank.

Suddenly, a thought occurred to her. The author had sent the letter from Bar Kur and told Farro to meet in A'slenderia. Most of the people in both places spoke Endran, not Tibedese.

Maybe the author intended for Farro to translate the letter before decoding the message.

With a rush of excitement, Brenna traced her index finger from each large letter on the original to the corresponding word in the Endran translation, marking them down as she went. Then, she did the same with the letters that one would normally capitalize but, in this message, were lowercase. In the end, she held a slightly different note in her hands.

inigo farro,

you do not know me, but I know you. please heed my Warning as a fellow keeper. A barkurian national is planning to frame you for the assassination of king stefan Xiv during the bar kur day festivities in order to incite a War with tibedO. leave Ballynach. leave bar kur, but do not Return to tibedo.

i write to you at great risK. burn this note as Soon as you receive it. when you are not where you are expected to be at the parade, they wilL come for you ANd attempt to Kill us both. meet mE iN linden for further instructions. we must stop the Growing threat And the true aSsaSsin before it is too latE.

from,
a loyalist

"What are you doing with that?" Katiel asked, causing Brenna to jump. Solving the riddle had engrossed Brenna too much to notice her friend come up behind her.

"One second," Brenna said. She didn't want to lose her train of thought, not when she was so close to figuring it out.

She scanned the letters that were now capitalized in the Endran translation.

WAXWORKSLANKENGASSE

"Wax Works Lankengasse?" Brenna read aloud, spinning in her chair to face Katiel. "Does that mean anything to you?"

Katiel quirked a brow. "*Lankengasse* is the central avenue in Linden, the place where Father sets up our market stall when we sell there." She bent over the desk, peering closely at the letter and her friend's notes. "Why? Does the letter mention it?"

Brenna nodded vigorously, unable to contain her excitement. That had to be where the letter's author intended for Farro to meet him. Immediately, she explained everything she'd found to Katiel, the words coming out in such a rush that she hoped they made sense. With every sentence, Katiel looked more wary. Finally, she concluded her speech with, "That's why we have to go there, to this meeting point on *Lankengasse* in Linden. We can ask the author who really killed the king. If we can persuade them to come with us to Ballynach to tell Jay, he can tell everyone the truth and end the war peacefully. It's perfect!"

Katiel did not look convinced. "Could you not go to Jay now and show him the letter?"

Brenna shook her head. "I thought about it, but I don't think it'll be enough. The Barkurians might say the letter's false. But if we have the author with us—the person who witnessed these events—and he can tell them who the true assassin was, I think we'd have a realistic chance."

Katiel chewed on a stray strand of hair, and Brenna could feel her own excitement swelling again. She was considering it. They might actually do this. They could end the war.

But then Katiel said, "It would be impossible—first to locate this person, then to convince them to return to Bar Kur. If they wanted to end the war, I think they would have returned on their own." Brenna opened her mouth to object again, but Katiel interrupted, something she never did. That meant she *really* did not want to talk about this further. "Let us go to dinner."

Brenna decided not to press it and followed her friend out the door.

She knew Katiel was right. It would be hard, impossible even. In fact, she didn't know which would be harder—finding the author, convincing him to return to Ballynach, or convincing Jay to report it. But if there was a chance that she could end the war before Henred saw battle, she had to try.

5

Katiel

"Everyone," Father said as the family sat down for dinner, Brenna and Dakier seated along the wooden dining bench on either side of Katiel. "I have some bad news, I'm afraid."

Father, seated at the head of the ashen dining table, stroked his snow-white beard as he said the words, unable to meet his daughter's eyes. Both of her parents were elderly, far too old to have a child her age, and sometimes it explained why they were so strict. But sometimes it did not.

Nervously, Katiel took a bite of her meatloaf. She wondered if the news could be worse than the discoveries they had made this afternoon, with the letter from Derenta and the letter about the framing.

"We received word today from Master Larinne," Mother said, "of a surprising development in the war. The A'slenderian parliament motioned to enter the war as an ally of Tibedo, and the vote unanimously passed."

Katiel knew little about her nation's government, but based on her mother's tone, it sounded like these matters typically took much longer to resolve.

"I am so sorry, Brenna," Mother continued, "but now that A'slenderia is an enemy of Bar Kur, we think it best to send you home."

Father grabbed Mother's hand on the table, as if for stability despite them both sitting down. "I apologize sincerely, Brenna. A'slenderia allied with Tibedo in the Ten Years' War, but I never expected the conflict to escalate so quickly, and with battle not yet commenced."

"Yes, exactly," Mother added with a fervent nod. "I am sure your mother never expected this, either."

Mother continued talking to Brenna, discussing something about her writing to her family to arrange a rendezvous at the border bridge, but Katiel was barely listening. It did not seem possible for her country, the land she had thought would always be safe, to go to war with the home of her closest friend. She had probably chewed the same bite of food three hundred times when Dakier's voice cut into her daze.

"I have bad news, too."

Katiel barely comprehended the words, and yet she already knew what he was going to say.

"I've been drafted into the Tibedese Army."

Mother put a hand over her heart as if the words gave her chest pain. Father slumped his face into his palm.

"They summoned me to leave this week."

"But you live all the way up here," Brenna objected. "If you don't show up, no one would know."

Dakier nodded, like he agreed with her, but then said, "It would be dishonorable to avoid the draft."

"But you are an A'slenderian now, too," Father pointed out. "And A'slenderia has outlawed the draft for our army."

"We will support you whether you decide to go or stay," added Mother.

Dakier nodded. "I have decided. I'm a citizen of Tibedo, and I love the country. So many of the people I know and love still live there. It would be a dishonor to my heritage not to fight for them. I'll leave for Tibedo tomorrow."

That seemed to settle the matter, and everyone went back to eating their dinner. Meanwhile, Katiel's mind was racing more than usual. She expected nothing less from the farmhand, as Dakier was nothing if not honorable. But now Dakier and Henred were both going to fight a war based on a framing. The Tibedese leadership did not attack the king, so there was no threat that Bar Kur needed to defend itself against. It was all a mistake.

It was all a mistake.

That sentence kept repeating itself in her mind. She could not think about anything else, not until the injustice of it all reminded her of Jurgen.

When she was little, Mother used to tell her the tales of the *Geführtchen*, the magicians who had lived in the region before the practice was outlawed. Of all the tales of Kerafin, Katiel's favorite had been the epic of Jurgen. She used to beg Mother to tell her the same tale night after night.

Mother would ask her, "Do you not tire of the same story? You already know how it ends."

But Katiel, very little and very naïve, would say, "I don't know if it will end the same. I think he might win this time," and so Mother would tell it again.

Jurgen was just a boy in the story, a boy who lived farther north than the Northern Mountains and watched over his tiny flock of sheep day in and day out. Katiel loved that part. Since

Father was teaching her how to watch their own sheep at the time, it seemed like a story written especially for her.

Even though he was young, Jurgen was an extraordinarily powerful magician for his age. He could already do everything that was expected of a *Geführtchen*: he would take a small fleck of the *Erz*, multiply the speck until it had achieved any size he needed, and transform it into any material he desired. He did everything that his ancestors had taught him with ease—building bridges, repairing carts, fixing splints for the injured—all in the blink of an eye. Most of the people in his region were very poor, so there was always a use for his magic.

One particularly harsh winter, a blight of mites destroyed all the villagers' blankets and coats. People were losing limbs to frostbite when they had to venture outside, and the babies, too cold to sleep, cried through the night. Jurgen was used to helping the mountain folk, though, so when he saw them suffering, he decided he needed to do something. He went out to the pasture and took his favorite sheep and a bit of the *Erz* he kept in his room. He multiplied the *Erz* and molded it while he studied the animal, and by the end of the day, he had conjured hundreds of new sheep, all of them already adults with a full coat of wool, ready to be sheared. Happily, Jurgen went all around the region, giving a sheep to every family. With this gift, they wouldn't go cold this year or the next or the year after that.

At first, everyone applauded Jurgen and called him a hero. But it wasn't long before things went wrong. The sheep would bleat ceaselessly, day and night, until, one by one, they went mad and attacked the humans. The people could do nothing to stop the mad animals, and when the weakest villagers did not survive the attacks, the people turned on Jurgen and killed him by tossing him to the wolves that prowled the region.

Mother would say to Katiel at the end of the tale, “You see, humans were not meant to create other creatures. Not even the *Geführtchen*.”

“But I wanted this time to be different,” Katiel would reply. “The boy tried to do something good. It has to go right for him in the end.”

When she was little, Mother would never tell her she was wrong about that, but she would never change the ending to the harsh legends, either. Even though she was older now, it was hard to accept the injustice. She did not understand why the *Geführtchen* should be banned from wielding if they were trying to help people, yet it seemed the law had been universally accepted on the Continent.

“Father,” Katiel spoke up at the dinner table, attempting to sound casual. “If you knew something was wrong, for certain, would you try to do something about it? Try to tell everyone about what you know?”

He gave her a knowing look. “It depends, I suppose, on if you were the one who made the error, or if it was someone else. One should own up to their own shortcomings.”

“What if it *was* someone else who did something wrong, but it’s a very grave matter?”

“It is best to mind one’s own business and let others sort out their own problems,” Father answered. “They will discover their mistakes soon enough.”

Mother hummed in agreement.

Katiel sighed inwardly before attempting to take another bite. She tasted nothing. She and Brenna were the ones in possession of the letter. How could they bear to wait out this war, all the while keeping the truth to themselves?

When they finished dinner, it was already dark out, and all Katiel wanted to do was sleep. Sleep and forget about the horrible war, about Dakier getting drafted, and about finding that Creator-forsaken letter.

But as Katiel started heading up to her room, Brenna turned in the opposite direction. "Where are you going?"

"To the outpost," Brenna said, continuing down the steps as if it were not at all unusual to go to an outpost at this hour. Katiel hurried after her.

"What do you need there?" Katiel asked, in a voice even quieter than normal. "We already got the translation, so do not say a Tibedese-to-Endran dictionary."

Brenna turned to face her. "I need supplies for the journey to Linden," she said, exasperating both in definiteness and volume. "I'm going to find the author and convince them to return to Ballynach to reveal the true assassin. And if the author won't reveal the truth, then I'll do it myself. I'm going to stop the war."

"Keep your voice down." They were in the clearing in front of her house, and, thankfully, no one was around, but she was still afraid her parents would hear. "That is absurd. You cannot go. My parents will never allow it."

"I've made up my mind." Brenna was stone-faced, but mercifully, she spoke much more quietly. "I have to do something. I decided during dinner. Henred is going, and now Dakier. Your parents are sending me home first thing in the morning, so I have to leave tonight."

"Leave tonight, in secret?" Katiel asked, which her oldest friend confirmed with a nod. "Please, be reasonable. Think about it longer. Wait a couple of days and then consider."

Brenna looked away, the typical light missing from her eyes. "If I don't leave tonight, I'll lose the chance."

Katiel sighed. "I know you want to help, but there is almost certainly nothing you can do to stop the war. I wish there were, believe me."

"*Almost* certainly," Brenna emphasized. "What if there *is* something we can do? Could you really live the rest of your life always wondering, 'What if we *had* done something? What if we'd gotten the truth out there and ended it?'"

Katiel shuffled the toe of her shoe in the grass. She did not know what to say. There was nothing she wanted to say. Those words Brenna had just spoken—that was the same thing she had been wondering all evening. She did not want to stay safely at home while others were out there fighting. She wanted to get the truth out, to help misunderstood people like Jurgen and Inigo Farro. If Henred or Dakier did not come home, and she stayed here doing nothing, she did not know how she could live with herself. But what were the chances they could make any difference if they tried?

As if reading her thoughts, Brenna asked, "Even if it's a one-in-a-million chance, isn't that still a chance?"

Katiel could not say she disagreed. "It would be dangerous for a girl to travel alone out there, even just to Linden. Father never lets me travel alone, and neither does your family." She hesitated before saying words she did not want to think about, acutely aware that she sounded just like her strict parents. But the Northern Mountains were treacherous, filled with steep sloping passages and vicious wolf packs, not to mention the risks that a young girl on her own might face in the cities from other people. "You are not familiar with navigating the mountains. You would be risking your life."

Brenna got that vacant, forlorn look in her eyes, the look she had when she heard her brother had volunteered. Then she shrugged and turned toward the outpost once more. "If Henred is willing to risk his life, I'm willing to risk mine."

Katiel could not bear to address that kind of statement from her friend, so instead she said, "The outpost will be closed by now, anyway."

6

Brenna

Despite her friend studying under the teacher for years, Brenna had never met Master Larinne. The elderly woman kept to herself in her home, and Katiel had always been on school holiday breaks when Brenna came to visit. Brenna had never been to the outpost before, either, since she never needed anything while in A'slenderia that she couldn't ask the Salzbrucks for. Until now.

The outpost was exactly as Brenna expected. The building was similar to Katiel's house, with a sloped roof and staircases on the outside. It was just off the road in the center of the valley, to make it easy for passing travelers to gather supplies along their way. There was a covered area with hay and water troughs where travelers could rest their horses while the humans rested inside. Predictably, there were no horses at the moment, as war was enough to cancel most people's travel plans.

"If the door's locked," Katiel said as they approached, "do *not* pick it. It's ridiculous that you even learned how to do that."

Brenna chuckled, remembering the recent pranks she had pulled on Henred once his room was no longer safe. "Says the person who doesn't have any siblings."

A sign in the window claimed the store was open, at the sight of which Brenna couldn't resist shooting Katiel a smug grin. Katiel had begrudgingly agreed to come with her on the pretext that she did not want Brenna to come across as suspicious or make it seem like she was trying to spy on Alfien. She would do her best for her friend, but even Brenna herself knew that subtlety had never been her strong suit.

Katiel cracked open the door enough to peer in, and Brenna craned her neck to see past her, a difficult feat considering Katiel was a few inches taller. Inside, goods packed every inch of the outpost. Heaps of sausages and cheeses and blankets and cigars filled every cubby, and snowshoes and canteens hung haphazardly from the wooden ceiling. On the right side, a fireplace with cushioned chairs invited travelers to warm their feet, and to the left, an open passageway promised more wares beyond. Brenna couldn't tell if it led to a storage room or a secondary part of the shop, but either way, there was no one behind the counter to ask.

"Hello, Master Larinne?" Katiel called, her torso still halfway out the door. Brenna had always found it odd to call a teacher 'Master,' since she had never done that with her teachers back in Bar Kur, but she chalked it up to a quirk of the translation from Aslen.

There was no reply. "Hello?" They waited for a beat, but only silence greeted them. Katiel took a step back as if to return home. "I suppose this means they're closed after all."

"No way!" Brenna snaked around Katiel and stepped fully into the space, gesturing to the lit gas lanterns hanging from the ceiling. "Look at that. Master Larinne wouldn't leave the lanterns on all night, so she'll probably be right back. And if she isn't back soon, I can leave the money on the counter with a note listing what I bought." She pointed to the pad of paper and quill sitting next to the cash register. "See, someone even left the stuff out for it. I bet that's what she wanted us to do."

Katiel folded her arms across her chest, but she let the door close behind her.

Brenna set out gathering the things she needed and debated with Katiel as to which type of map would be best before settling on buying all three—a detailed map of A'slenderia, a detailed map of Bar Kur, and a topographical map of the whole Continent of Kerafin. When she finished selecting the maps, a compass, and a bedroll, no one had returned to work the register, so Brenna laid her items on the counter and started jotting down the tab.

Just as she set the note on the wooden countertop, she noticed Katiel reaching for a lantern behind the counter, the luminary placed unlit on one of the many full shelves.

"What are you doing?" Brenna asked, taking a closer look at the object. A black metal frame suspended glass on six equally sized sides, an interesting glass with metallic flecks sprinkled throughout, but other than that the lantern seemed ordinary—no more noteworthy than the hundred other knickknacks adorning the walls.

Katiel cocked her head to the side. "Does the glass look like it's moving to you?"

"Not at all," Brenna answered, cocking her own head to match. But Katiel's fingertips inched closer to it, haltingly and oddly enough that Brenna grabbed her hand and pulled it down on instinct. She didn't have a chance to apologize for the rash action before she realized her mistake. The motion set the bedroll tumbling off the counter, and before she could catch it, the thick palette collided with the lowest shelf. One glass jar clinked into another, and then the whole lot was cascading toward the wooden floor, each piece shattering more loudly than the last upon landing.

Master Larinne lived above the store, that much Brenna knew, and even if she were asleep, there was little chance she'd sleep though such a commotion. When she found them having broken all her things, she would surely go tell Katiel's parents what they'd been up to. If she didn't flee now, Brenna's chance to leave for Linden unnoticed was all but ruined. But she couldn't let Katiel take the fall for the mess, either, seeing as this was her own doing.

Brenna was still debating the matter when Alfien charged into the room, baring a hatchet in front of him like he was about to defend the keep. When he took in the sight of them, and then the colossal mess they'd made, he dropped the hatchet, instead rubbing at his eyes with the back of his hand like he'd turned in for the night early.

"What are you two doing here so late?" Alfien had a round face, deep brown skin, and close-cropped, curly black hair, and he crossed his exceptionally muscular arms as he leveled them with a glare. "I see what's going on here. Katiel, please just go home. I told you I needed space."

Brenna had always liked Alfien, but that sentiment had seriously diminished when he callously broke up with her best friend, and now it vanished completely with his last statement. "Get over yourself, Alfien," she snapped. "I dragged her here to buy stuff from your grandmother, and you never closed up the shop. We didn't know you were in town, and if we had, we wouldn't have come."

He picked up the note off the counter, and Brenna smugly said, "See?" But when he read it aloud, she realized it was pretty embarrassing.

"I.O.U. the following items," he read dubiously. "Blah, blah, blah, heart, smiley face, heart with an arrow through it, Brenna Malley." He paused for emphasis as Brenna stifled her laugh. When he put it like that, it sounded like the worst theft attempt in history, but she did not want to make him think she was amiable toward those who broke her best friend's heart. "Seriously?" He looked back at the note. "Why'd you get so many maps?"

"Brenna's taken an interest in cartography lately," Katiel said.

"Do you seriously expect me to believe she got a hankering for mapmaking at dusk that couldn't wait until tomorrow?" Alfien shook his head, eying the absolute disaster on the floor once again. "Listen, if you expect me to cover for you with my grandmother, you have to tell me what's really going on."

"Fine," Katiel huffed. "But it's not what you think."

It was all Brenna could do not to gape as Katiel relayed every minute detail about the letter and what the translation revealed. It was far more than was necessary to placate him, but Brenna knew her friend. Deep down, Katiel was hoping Alfien would offer to come with them. Instead, he shook his head again and pulled out a price ledger to tally up the items. "That letter's probably a fake."

"How can you say that?" protested Katiel. "Brenna had it before the assassination happened. Someone had to have known beforehand to have written it."

"It comes out to forty-eight marks."

Brenna fumbled around in her coin purse and handed him about a hundred separate coins. He rolled his eyes and started spreading them out on the counter to add up the total.

"Alfien?" Katiel asked. The name came out as a whisper. It seemed she had given up trying to hide how hurt she was, or maybe she simply couldn't anymore. Her reaction was clearly about more than the ledger or the letter, or even about the war. The tears were welling up in her eyes because Alfien made it so apparent that he did not care for her anymore, even as a friend.

"Forget it, Katiel," he maintained in his icy tone. "Even if it were real, the war has already started. There's nothing you can do about it."

Katiel darted out of the shop so fast that Brenna barely registered the motion. She considered leaving Alfien with some choice words before parting, but after deciding he was not worth it, she grabbed her newfound belongings and headed into the night after her friend.

Outside, she glimpsed Katiel slipping into the main house, far away enough to look like a tiny black ant ducking into the dirt. Katiel must have sprinted to get over there so fast, but with how much Alfien got to her, that wasn't exactly surprising. When Brenna arrived at her room, Katiel was slouched against her red-and-white patchwork quilt, her face already puffy and pink.

Brenna opened her borrowed dresser drawer and started folding clothes for the journey. "It's okay," she said. "Don't worry about what Alfien thinks. He used to be nice, but now he's a jerk. So having him break up with you is a good sign. It means he can't date a nice person anymore and has to find a fellow jerk."

Katiel offered the faintest of smiles, dabbing at her eyes with her shirtsleeve until she registered what Brenna was doing. "Wait, are you packing? You are really going to Linden?"

"Yes, I really am." Brenna dragged her carpet bag over to her. She folded a dress as she looked up at Katiel, imploring her with her most desperate expression. "Please, please, *please*. Come with me. I want to find out the truth. But I can't do it without you."

Katiel walked over to the dresser and sat by her on the rug, her folded knee brushing the tip of Brenna's. "You know I can't leave my parents."

Brenna hesitated. "I mean, you could."

"I don't think I can," Katiel said, fidgeting with the tip of her braid. "They would be terrified worrying about me."

She hesitated again. Though she didn't want to be pushy, she didn't know what else to do. She had to fix things to help Henred. "What about the letter? Don't you care about Henred and Dakier going off to fight for a lie?"

"Of course I care," the A'slenderian said with a bite of defensiveness, "but we can't do anything about it, anyway."

Brenna bit her lip. "But what if we can?"

"Why are you asking *me* so much about this?" Katiel asked, her terse tone barely restrained from snapping outright. "You didn't get onto Dakier and Alfien for not volunteering to accompany you."

Brenna could hardly believe that was a question. "Because I can do it without them! But I can't do it without you. *You're* my best friend. You're right that it's dangerous to travel alone. But together, I *know* we can do it. We've always been better together."

Katiel stared at a random loop on the rug like she might not reply at all, so Brenna asked, "Do you remember before you dated Alfien, how you'd always talk about leaving the valley one day? And your da would say, 'The grass is always greener,' and it would annoy you to no end?"

Katiel gave the smallest of smiles. "Yes, 'the grass is always greener on the other side of the pasture.' That phrase irks me just thinking about it."

Brenna smiled back. "Well, I never liked the saying either. Honestly, it made me sad when you stopped talking about leaving the valley. I thought it was great how you had big dreams of seeing the world."

Katiel regarded her thoughtfully. They never talked about stuff like this aloud, only in letters. It was harder to be open when someone was watching and reacting instead of reading the words later.

"Growing up, I never minded Fir Kelt," Brenna continued. "I liked hanging around with Henred and doing nothing. But you were never like that. When we were walking across the meadow earlier, I still wasn't sure if I could leave, or if I wanted to go back to Galvey and forget about it. But then I noticed the grass wasn't as green as usual and thought of that phrase.

"I know the saying means you're taking for granted what you already have. But I still hate it, because what if there really is greener grass somewhere?" As she went on, Brenna became unsure whether she was trying to persuade Katiel to leave or persuade herself that she should do it. "Wouldn't you want to see it for yourself, rather than taking someone else's word for it?"

Tears pooled along Katiel's lashes, but she still shook her head in resignation. "I am truly sorry, but I cannot leave my parents. It would worry them too much."

"I understand," Brenna said, solemnly placing the last few items into her bag and buckling it shut. Something about packing up made it feel more real. She was actually doing this.

Katiel seemed to think the same as she said, "Take good care of Gunnel for me."

It took Brenna a second to comprehend that Katiel meant for her to take her favorite horse. She must really believe Brenna could do it, then, to lend her the mare she loved so much.

"Thank you," she said, squeezing Katiel into a tight hug.

Brenna tried not to make it obvious that she was tearing up now, too, or that she was shaking not just from crying, but from anxiety as well. Try as she might, it proved impossible to shake her fear as the reality set in. She was going to travel across an enemy nation alone—through the mountains, in the dark, riding on horseback, which she was not all that good at, and then confront a stranger about a hidden letter she wasn't meant to have.

All she hoped was that the war would end soon.

Brenna couldn't recall ever walking through the valley alone at night, and as she walked over to the stables, she had to admit it was pretty unnerving. The wind whistled eerily, the lush-smelling air held a tinge of smoke, and she could swear her footsteps were never this loud in the daytime. She wasn't sure what Katiel's parents would do if they discovered her sneaking off in the night, but since her mother had entrusted her to their care, she figured they would try to prevent her from leaving. Send Dakier running after her to tackle her, maybe. But if there was one thing she was certain of, it was that she had to leave tonight.

She reached the stables, the hay crunching under her feet despite her tiptoeing. If anyone was going to hear her, it would be Dakier, whose room wasn't far from the stables. When she slid open the wooden door latch, the horses started snorting and whinnying in a panic. "It's just me," she whispered, though that was likely of little consolation to a bunch of horses she rarely interacted with. She hoped Dakier was a deep sleeper.

Unlike the other horses, Gunnel seemed to recognize her and refrained from going berserk. The mare wore her usual bored expression, like she couldn't be bothered by anything or anyone. It was an odd quality in a horse, like she was an animal version of a moody preteen.

As she saddled Gunnel, the less-apathetic horses were still making a fuss, so Brenna took some carrots from the bin. She had successfully bribed one of them when she heard footsteps outside. In a flash, she ducked into Gunnel's stall. Katiel had already given her a satchel full of food, so either the sound was a trick of the wind, or someone heard her sneaking out. She hoped it was Dakier. At least she could probably convince him not to snitch.

With a creak, the stable door slid open, and she let out an involuntary scream, sending all the horses into a tizzy again. Her stealth abilities were going to need some serious work.

"Brenna, it's me," Katiel whispered, patting the horses to calm them as she shuffled in. As she lifted the carpetbag in her hand, she flashed a rare smile brimming with confidence. "I'm coming with you."

"Why?"

Katiel raised an eyebrow. "I thought you wanted me to come."

"I'm worried I pushed you, is all." Brenna sighed. "You sounded so sure you wouldn't before. I don't understand what changed."

Katiel pressed her lips together. "After you left, I started thinking everything over."

"And?" Brenna prompted when she said nothing else.

"It seemed like this would never work. There was no way we could help anything or anyone. We cannot speak Tibedese. We have almost no money and no survival skills."

"But?" Brenna prompted again, this time feeling slightly concerned for her friend's sanity.

"I am tired of listening. I'm tired of being good and doing what's expected of me, of hearing stories about Alfien's time at university when I had to stay home. Somehow, against the odds, I think you will make a difference. Besides, trying to end the war before people needlessly die is the right thing to do." Katiel huffed and tucked a tendril of hair behind her ear, like she felt bashful after talking so much. "When I was packing meals for you, ready to see you off on your adventure, I realized how much I wanted to be there when you save the day."

"Correction," Brenna said, grabbing Katiel's hand in both of hers and giving it a triumphant little squeeze. "When *we* save the day."

7

Dakier

Dakier Mandia awoke to the sound of Katiel's name being shouted repeatedly. He rubbed the back of his hand across his eyes and sat up in bed. It was barely light out. Where would Katiel have run off to at this hour? He recalled her mentioning something yesterday. If only he could remember—wait.

His eyes shot open. Instantly, he was on his feet and sliding into his shoes. They didn't. They wouldn't. At least, he hoped not.

He pulled on some pants and darted over to the main house, slipping on his tunic as he ran. He raced up to the second floor and knocked on the Salzbrucks's door.

Feniel answered in a second, clearly already waiting there. A crushed expression overcame the joyous look on his face. He was hoping to see someone, and it was not Dakier.

Katya and Feniel both began talking at once as Dakier entered the room.

"She's gone!"

"Katiel is gone."

"Where could she be?"

"My baby is gone—"

"—left this note—"

"I'm sorry, I couldn't quite follow what you were saying," Dakier said. "Katiel is missing?"

Feniel moved to the kitchen table and took a seat next to Katya. "Dakier, my boy, something terrible has happened in the night." He paused as if he could not bear to say it. "Katiel has left us."

Dakier stepped closer to them, propping his arm on the back of an empty chair. Katya's elbow rested on the table, her hand cradling her temples.

"She left last night, and Brenna is gone as well. We're so glad to see you. I thought you might have gone with them. Feniel, read him the note."

The Salzbrucks were not a talkative group, and they were not particular on touch. Dakier had never seen them so much as hug. But they had always been a family who spent every meal together and who worked the farm every day together. Katiel traveled to sell her wool, but never without her father. After only one night, this might have been the longest Katiel had ever been apart from her parents.

Feniel held up a small piece of parchment and read the cryptic message aloud. In the note, Katiel said she loved them, that she and Brenna had left for an important reason, and not to worry because she would be back soon.

Katya's eyes welled with tears. "We have not been involved in a war for a century, and when one happens, my daughter runs away." When she blinked, tears trickled down her cheeks. "Two girls out there, traveling alone. We shielded her far too much from the world. She doesn't realize the dangers she is facing."

Feniel wrapped his arms around her. "Don't fret, dear. We will find her. She's not in danger." The look in his eyes betrayed his words. "She is a kind girl who loves her friend. She must have gone back to Fir Kelt to help Brenna with something."

"No, she didn't," Dakier interjected. "Or at least, I don't think so."

Katya's and Feniel's heads snapped up at him.

Katya said, "You know about this?"

Dakier averted his eyes, heat flushing across his face. "I think I know where they went. They asked me to go with them. I didn't think they would actually leave." He paused, sucking in a breath. He had told himself they wouldn't go, at least, but he knew it was a lie. Now he had lied again, this time aloud. He was responsible for this. "I think they might be heading to Linden."

Katya furrowed her brow. "Linden? What's in Linden?"

Dakier wrestled with how he could explain. "They found this letter that they think is the key to ending the war. It mentioned Linden as a meeting place."

"What?" Feniel started. "Never mind, it does not matter. I have to leave. No time to waste." He stood up quickly, and his weak knee, which had never healed right from a previous injury, buckled under his weight. His stifled grimace revealed the pain he felt.

"Feniel, you can't go like this," said Katya. "You can't ride."

The way the Salzbrucks looked now stood in stark contrast to the people Dakier had worked for over the past four years. Where he normally saw joy and soft smiles stood the hollow shell of two people he hardly recognized. The desperation to have their daughter back was written on their faces—it was the look he had wished he had seen on his own mother's face when he announced he was leaving.

"I will go," Dakier said before he had too much time to think about what he was promising. Before he decided that Katiel and Brenna would be better off without the help of someone who'd already refused to help them. "I'll go after them."

Katya and Feniel turned toward each other and exchanged a long look. Feniel nodded, but it was Katya who spoke. "I think Dakier going after them would be best, dear."

"Fine," Feniel said, his reluctance apparent. "That will be best. We have no time to spare. Gather your things, and I'll meet you at the stables."

Dakier nodded, hurrying down the stairs and across the clearing to his room. It was hard to know what to bring since he did not know how long he would be gone, but he settled on repacking his leather bag with the same items he had brought to Fir Kelt. A vision of dancing with Brenna drifted into his mind, but he stifled the memory, lest he lose focus.

He straightened the quilt on his bed and did a quick scan around the room. The space was already empty, save for his stack of books. It was difficult to forget anything when one had so few possessions—a deliberate choice, since minimalism was a tenet of his religion. He picked up the draft letter from his nightstand and slid it into his book of scripture to keep the letter from bending before rethinking it and sliding both separately into his bag. He did not want to risk the ink from the envelope bleeding onto the pages.

When Dakier arrived at the stables, Feniel was already waiting for him with a bundle of supplies and food strapped to Kranich, a cranky chestnut-brown horse. "Kranich isn't as fast as Gunnel, of course, but Katiel took her." Gunnel was Katiel's favorite horse. Of course she would take her.

Dakier turned to attach his own bag to the saddle when Feniel said, "Dakier, wait. There is more I need to say before you go."

"There is something I should have mentioned as well."

Feniel's white eyebrows lifted in surprise. "Go on."

Dakier sighed, turning the prayer beads on his wrist. "If I can't find them in time, or if they won't return, I'll need to go on to Tibedo to report for the draft. I have to report to Fort Cajetan in less than a week."

"I know," Feniel said. "And I also know Katiel. That is why I believe she will not return for some time. I should have seen the signs when she was asking so many questions earlier. She believes in this."

Dakier cocked his head. "What good is it for me to go after her in that case?"

"I want you to go after them and stay with them while you can. You are like a son to me, and I know I can trust you." Feniel placed his hand on Dakier's shoulder, grasping it. He paused, like he was deliberating with himself still about the next thing he would say. "You know the necklace Katiel wears? The one she wears every day, with the clear gem?"

Dakier nodded, although he was no longer following where this was going.

Feniel continued, "Make sure she never takes it off. She must keep it on her neck constantly. It is powerful, and it can protect her. Make sure she keeps it hidden beneath her clothing."

"The necklace can protect her?" Dakier was familiar with the elderly man's beliefs. Like his mentor, Dakier knew all the scripture and its teachings: the divine Creator formed the first humans from the Ore at the Icemark, the mountain at the top of the world, and left behind the sacred scripture to guide human conduct. But this was an unusual suggestion, even for Feniel. Nothing in the scripture said anything about protective jewelry or gems.

Feniel's expression was deathly serious. "You must tell no one about the necklace, other than Katiel. And take this. Give this to her as soon as you see her. See that she knows its importance and does not lose it."

Dakier outstretched his hands, and Feniel placed a parcel shrouded in cloth into his palms. His arms dipped down before he steadied himself, not expecting the hefty weight of such a small object. With his smallest finger, Dakier pulled up a corner of the cloth to see what was inside, but Feniel swatted his hand away. "No need to look. It's a box. Neither you nor Katiel should open it."

It made little sense to give Katiel a box that she should not open. But Dakier didn't want to question Feniel. As mysterious as it was, he trusted him to have a good reason. Burying his doubts, Dakier tucked the parcel away and mounted Kranich.

Feniel waved him one last goodbye. "There's no way I can repay your kindness."

As he rode away and felt the mountains growing less familiar with each yard, a deep bitterness weighed on Dakier's chest like a stone. He could never repay the kindness he had received, either. But perhaps helping Katiel would be a start.

8

KATIEL

AT THE CREST WHERE the Northern Mountains met the Great Lake stood the city of Linden. Some of the buildings ran up the base of the mountain, while others, supported by iron pillars, veered out over the water. Each of the buildings was two or three stories, with ornate filigree lining the roofs of the dark walnut structures. The town was like a thousand copies of Katiel's house, the lights from each reflecting across the smooth surface of the lake like fireflies blinking in the night sky.

On the third evening since leaving the valley, Katiel and Brenna came into view of their destination, and their supply of food and water had proven wholly inadequate for the journey. The homemade sausages and cheeses ran out after a mere day and a half, and Katiel was certain she had never once gone this long without food. The water had disappeared even sooner, as revealed by a disappointing swig from an empty canteen the afternoon after leaving home. The pursuit of fresh-enough-looking streams along the way added a good five hours to their trek at least. Meanwhile, each night, the howls of wolves seemed to grow ever closer. For extra security on the first night, they had slept with their backs against a large tree trunk, which resulted in being plastered to the bark with sap upon waking, and they both lost a sizeable chunk of hair prying themselves off. Though she was used to being outside for her daily work, Katiel had never slept outdoors without a tent at least, and she was immensely relieved to return to civilization.

The humble town of Linden had no gates or battlements, so it was easy to pass into the throng of the city unnoticed. As she and Brenna walked Gunnel through the city center, Katiel let her gaze roam. The once-familiar town had expanded considerably since the last time she had visited. She and Father had not bothered going to Linden for a couple of years, since their wares fared much better in Bar Kur than they did in their own country. In this area, every other person sold cheese and wool skirts.

When the sun began to set, sweat beaded on Katiel's brow despite the fair weather. Now that A'slenderia had joined the war, she feared traveling openly with a Barkurian would incite jeers from some of the more patriotic A'slenderians. Her anxieties prohibited her from seeking out any unfamiliar establishments, lest they need to make a quick escape out a back exit, but her nerves were wreaking havoc on her usually-reliable sense of direction. Each step could be bringing them closer to or farther from the hostel she had visited before, an unassuming place called Gengerich's. Katiel could only hope she was heading the right way as the golden orb of the sun slowly slipped below Linden's rooflines.

Night had only just fallen when they finally turned a corner to spy their destination. Loosing a sigh of relief, Katiel ventured inside to secure a few nights' lodging while Brenna settled Gunnel in the inn's stables with fresh water and hay. Then it was on to the most important thing to either of them—finding food. While she would prefer to stick with places she knew, the late hour and pain in her stomach forced Katiel to try somewhere new. Unwilling to venture too far after dark, they chose a decent looking tavern called Heidel's, situated on the same block as the inn.

The tavern was a quaint place, all the walls covered in the same worn walnut planks as the exterior. Wooden figurines adorned the shelves above each booth—miniature sheep and goats and tiny little shoes—and ivory curtains embroidered in red and blue encircled the windows and doors.

Upon entering, a hostess greeted them and led them into a second room, decorated the same as the first but filled with rowdy diners who had likely partaken in one too many pints of ale. Katiel wished they had arrived only a bit earlier, in order to go somewhere she was more comfortable with. At least the hostess seated them off to the side, at a small table tucked away beside the fireplace.

As soon as they sat down, Brenna unfolded the red-and-white checked napkin and wiped down her hands. "Thank goodness we get to eat something other than goat cheese and sausage."

But Katiel did not reply. A quiet that had befallen the room, and every eye was turned toward their little corner. "Brenna," she hissed.

Oblivious, Brenna raised her palms in innocence before poring over the menu. "No offense, Katiel, you're terrific at cheese-making. But you can only eat the same thing for so many meals straight."

"Brenna!" Katiel repeated, quieter yet more emphatically.

"I'm sorry. I didn't mean it like that. You know what, I am so grateful you packed all that food for us. It really was good."

Katiel smacked her palm onto her forehead. "No, Brenna, look. Everyone's staring at us."

Brenna lifted her head to be met with the looks of a good twenty people. Instead of turning away like Katiel, or any ordinary person, would do, she opened her eyes even wider and jutted her chin out, meeting the gaze of a few random people among the bunch. The crowd snapped their necks back to their tables, suddenly preoccupied with their menus and food.

Brenna turned back to Katiel and smirked. "Problem solved."

"Not quite," Katiel whispered, leaning closer to her friend. "It's your hair. They know you're Barkurian. We're lucky they even seated us at all."

Brenna squished her hair down with both hands. "Do you have a bandana or something?"

"No." Katiel shook her head. "It's too late now, anyway. You can wear one tomorrow, though."

"Can you give me your hair ribbon?" Brenna asked, continuing her hushed tone.

"What good will that do?"

"I can at least braid it down my back. It will be less noticeable."

It was then that the server came to take their orders for dinner. When she left, Brenna grumbled about the fact that all the selections involved sausage and cheese.

Katiel chuckled, loosening the yarn that held her braided bun in place and handing it to her friend. "That's all we eat here, seriously. It's not just my family." She pulled the braid over her shoulder and began running her fingers through it to even out the waves.

"Well, I figured that out a little too late." Brenna reached her hands behind her head to attempt the braid, her elbows jutting out awkwardly to the side. Her arms were still in that position when her lip curled into a mischievous grin. "Someone is still staring at us."

It was so like Brenna to speak that loudly and think she was being quiet.

"You know what? Forget about it," Katiel said at a much more appropriate volume. "You're allowed to be here even if you are Barkurian."

Brenna shook her head, pulling the finished braid in front of her shoulder to tie a bow at the end. "They're not staring at me." She grinned like her teeth were covered in whitening charcoal, which was never a good sign. "Or, rather, *he*. He is definitely staring at you."

Katiel instinctively looked down. "That can't be right. Where?"

Brenna looked down, too, seemingly mimicking her friend without realizing it. "To your right." She wiggled her eyebrows. "He's handsome and wearing fancy clothes."

"Look away so I can look," Katiel ordered. Brenna rolled her eyes and looked in the other direction conspicuously. Katiel rolled her eyes back and turned her head slightly to the side, peering out of the corner of her eyes so whoever he was would not notice.

He definitely noticed. He was not even trying to hide the fact that he was staring, his upper body turned toward her despite his chair facing the opposite direction. If anything, he appeared to be purposefully making his staring as noticeable as possible. He sat between several other people, one guy and three girls. All of them appeared to be around the same age as Katiel. The one who stared at her had light, olive-toned skin, a sharp jawline, and tousled, ebony-brown hair, with loose curls cut short to expose his neck. He was easily the most handsome boy she had ever seen.

His companions were laughing at him and shaking their heads in what appeared to be amazement. Or maybe it was pride. The other male at the table smacked him on the shoulder, and the handsome one gave her a parting smirk and turned around.

"That was strange," Katiel muttered as the server brought them their orders.

Brenna grimaced at her food for being the thing she was sick of eating. They noticed they had never gotten drinks, and Katiel offered to fetch them some at the bar. Normally, that would be something Brenna would do, on account of Katiel's general anxiety about asking for things, but she did not want Brenna to attract any more attention.

She walked into the other room and went up to the long bar, absentmindedly clasping her hands together and leaning her forearms on the surface. "Two summer ales, please."

"That was thoughtful of you to get me a drink."

Katiel's eyes shot open. She reluctantly turned in the voice's direction.

It was the same boy, propping himself on his forearm. He was slim, about six inches taller than her. Seeing him this close was unnerving. His soft eyes stood in stark contrast to the rest of his chiseled bone structure.

Katiel cleared her throat. "This is obviously not for you," she did her best to snap.

He ignored what she said. "Your friend is certainly the center of attention."

Katiel glanced in Brenna's general direction, unable to see their table from where she stood. She was not at all surprised that he had been staring at Brenna rather than her. "You should talk to her if you like her. Her name is Brenna. She's also a very bold person, like yourself."

The boy smirked, looking down his nose at her. "Considering she's your friend, I would say you seem to like very bold people." The edge of his face curved inward between his square chin and the sharp corner of his jaw. She did not know that was possible. She needed to stop looking at him.

The barkeep spared her another moment of suffering by coming back with the drinks. "You can put those on my tab," he told the worker.

"No, do not do that." Katiel fumbled with the coin purse tied to the waistband of her dress, felt for a two-leaguemark coin, and slammed it against the counter. "Please keep the change."

She turned to the boy curtly. "If you will excuse me."

He smiled, flashing his perfectly straight teeth, while still looking down at her. "It has been a pleasure to meet you, Miss..." he trailed off, clearly expecting her to tell him her name.

"Katiel." She tried to make her impatience as apparent as possible.

Before she recognized what he was doing, he took her fingertips in his palm and pulled her hand to his mouth. He gently pressed his lips to her knuckles, lingering there for a moment before pulling away. "It has been a pleasure to meet you, Miss Katiel."

Katiel blinked at him several times and hurried back to their table.

9

Brenna

"He did *what*?" Brenna's voice rose in excitement as Katiel recounted her experience at the tavern. It was the following morning, as Katiel led the way from the inn to the meeting place mentioned in the letter. Brenna could hardly believe Katiel had kept the details to herself this long. Brenna, for her part, never could've sat through an entire meal and slept through an entire night without relaying the exciting boy-related events that had transpired.

"He was so impertinent." Katiel studied the back of her hand. "He just went ahead and kissed my hand. Right there." She pointed to a precise point on her knuckles. Brenna refrained from quipping about how he must have had awfully small lips then. "It was quite strange."

This reminded Brenna of when Dakier had done the same thing before they danced. It hadn't seemed strange to her, so much as unexpected and magical and likely the best night of her life. Or, rather, it would have been, had they not later received horrid news and effectively been chased away by an angry mob.

"What did you do then?" Brenna asked.

"I just went back to the table."

"And you didn't get his name?"

"No, I didn't ask." Katiel had her arms crossed and shook her head, but there was a smile tugging at the corner of her mouth. "I don't care what his name is."

"Good for you, then," Brenna said, though she wasn't sure if she believed it that her friend didn't care. Actually, Brenna thought Katiel seemed to like him. "Do you think he was A'slenderian? I thought—"

Brenna lost her train of thought when Katiel said, "This is *Lankengasse.*"

The street was bustling with activity. Pedestrians in fine suits and dirt-smudged aprons alike shared both sides of the lane, keeping near the buildings to leave room for the steady stream of carriages and carts that occupied the center.

"It means 'broad street' in Aslen," Katiel added, and it was no wonder why the street got its name. The space in the center was wide enough for two carriages to pass one another side by side. To Brenna's surprise, there were no people trying to sell their wares like there always were on the streets in Bar Kur, save for a young boy trying to entice people to buy a newspaper by waving one wildly above his head.

Brenna went over to him and traded him a copper coin for the day's paper. She had a mind to tell him to save his arms because there was no point in waving the paper so violently, but on second thought, she couldn't be sure that his technique hadn't worked, since she was buying one.

"This is so we can sit and inconspicuously read it if we need a cover," she whispered as she returned to Katiel's side.

"Great," Katiel remarked flatly, making that face she made when Brenna talked too loudly. She peered down the street in both directions before pointing to the left. Brenna's stomach knotted as they stepped into the bustling throng of people. This was the actual street from the letter. They were so close. "It looks like there are a lot of shops in this direction," Katiel said. "Let us try this way."

Brenna nodded, then gulped as she inspected the buildings. Most were two stories, with what appeared to be apartments on the floors above the storefronts. The nameplates were hard to see amid the elaborate floral arrangements along every balcony. If the place they were looking for was up there, they might never find it.

Then Katiel halted so abruptly that Brenna kept going for a second and had to double back to her. "This is it."

The building stood in stark contrast to the lively street surrounding them. The whole façade was of worn gray wood. Shabby, withering planks boarded the windows and front door, attached by nails driven in at odd angles. Whoever had left this place had done so in a hurry. Above the door, faded blue paint marked the shop's name: Linden Wax Works.

The people making their way down the street grunted and grumbled as they hustled by the two of them, now standing still on the sidewalk. Someone slammed into Brenna's shoulder, and she winced, but the person kept going without so much as a glance in her direction.

To get out of the way, she and Katiel took a seat on a bench across the street with a view of the shop. But Brenna did not think any patrons had visited this shop for a while. "Do you think this is really the place from the letter?"

"I would say so." Katiel nodded. "I doubt there are any other stores called 'Wax Works' along this street." After a second, she observed, "You don't seem happy to have found it."

Brenna hung her head, rested it on her palms, and released an involuntary grunting noise. "I'm annoyed that we found the meeting place, but it turns out to be an actual store that's all boarded up." She shook her head in frustration. "What kind of shop do you think it is, anyway? A store that sells wax for envelope seals?"

"I would suppose so, but it *is* an odd name," said Katiel. "What were you expecting to find?" She asked the question in her nice way, not sarcastic like other people. Whenever Katiel asked questions, it was obvious she genuinely wanted to know what the other person thought.

In this case, Brenna didn't know what she'd thought. "Honestly, I guess I was imagining we'd walk into a bustling store, show the clerk the letter to prove our trustworthiness, and then meet the author, who would tell us everything. I thought the struggle would be convincing them to agree to come with us."

Katiel let out a giggle. "Me too, actually."

For a moment, everything was back to normal—just two girls sitting on a bench and laughing about something silly as the busy people went by. But then the heaviness set in again. Brenna wondered if things would be the same as before once the war was over.

"What should we do now?" Katiel asked. It sounded like the melancholy had come over Katiel at the same time as it had Brenna.

But there was no room for melancholy on their adventure, so Brenna crossed her legs and opened the newspaper with a crack. "Now we wait."

10

KATIEL

"DID YOU SEE THAT?"

Katiel jolted awake as Brenna tapped her on the shoulder, realizing she must have dozed off. Katiel glanced at the word puzzle Brenna had been working on. Naturally, she had already finished it. They had been watching this building for hours, until the sun blazed above them, but there had been no sign of activity.

"What did you see?" Katiel asked. The door to the wax shop was still shut. She surveyed both of the lower-level windows. Nothing.

"A movement in that window, there." Brenna jerked her head toward the left window. "The curtain rustled."

Katiel's breath hitched in her throat. "Are you sure?"

"I'm sure. Someone's in there." Brenna stood from the bench and brushed her skirt flat.

Panic surged into Katiel as realization dawned on her. "What're you doing?" She was suddenly feeling much less brave than when she left home.

Brenna took a step toward what was now the last place Katiel wanted to go. "I'm going in." Brenna seemed to take in Katiel's terror at the prospect. "Why don't you wait and keep watch?"

"No." Katiel released her white-knuckled grip on the bench. She would go in, even if every instinct in her was telling her not to. "I'm coming with you."

They crossed the street and approached the shop. Brenna reached between the boards stretched across the doorway and rapped several times on the door, earning quizzical looks and raised brows from a group of elderly people passing by. Brenna shot them an awkward smile that was not at all reassuring. They shook their heads before, mercifully, walking away.

As predicted, no one answered the knock. Brenna yanked on one of the boards, but it held firm.

"Perhaps we should leave," suggested Katiel. "There's no way in."

Katiel followed Brenna's gaze as she looked up and down the street. Other than the elderly group, who now had their backs turned to them as they walked away, the crowds from the morning rush had disappeared.

Turning away from the nearly empty street, Brenna grabbed the doorknob between the loose planks. Before Katiel could object, the door clicked open.

"What are you doing?" Katiel hissed.

In the blink of an eye, Brenna pushed the door open, ducked between a gap in the planks, and stepped into the shop. "Come on, before anyone sees."

Katiel went wide-eyed. If someone had told her two days ago that she would be breaking into an abandoned store in Linden, she would not have believed them. But now, there was nothing to be done. She hurried in after Brenna and closed the door, praying no one had spotted them.

"You know, a door that opens inward like that is a fire hazard," Brenna mused as soon as the door clicked shut behind them.

"Hush," Katiel snapped. Only Brenna would say whatever was on her mind even as they chased down a potential war criminal. But as their eyes adjusted to the dim light that streamed past the curtains, she saw how much of a fire hazard it actually was. Stacks of candles in all different colors filled the room, some piled as high as her shoulders.

"What on Endra?" Katiel mumbled despite herself before scanning the room. There was nothing and no one else there other than a wooden register-stand near the back and a glass-front cabinet spanning the back wall filled with, naturally, more candles.

Ahead, Brenna gingerly wedged herself between a gap in the candle stacks. A narrow path between the stacks wound aimlessly through the space, not appearing to lead anywhere in particular.

"I guess this is what they meant by 'wax works,'" Brenna muttered. "You would think they'd have stopped making so many until they could sell the others."

Katiel was about to say she thought the shop was vacant and that the rustling curtain had been a trick of the wind, when Brenna cupped her hands around her mouth and announced, "Attention to anyone here: Please reveal yourself. We are here to help."

As if in response, a distinct *thunk* sounded in the front corner of the room.

"What was that?" Brenna said at a normal volume before adding loudly, "We just want to help. We know about the—"

Abruptly, Brenna let out a sharp wheeze, like something had knocked the breath out of her. The next second, Katiel screeched as something struck her own back, and she tumbled to the floor. She collided with a candle stack and collapsed to the ground, wax cylinders falling in every direction. Brenna stretched a hand and Katiel took it without thinking, leaping back to her feet in time to see someone dart out a back exit behind the register.

Katiel knew it had to be the person who wrote the letter. Something in her could feel it.

Taking no time to consider, Katiel dashed after the shadow, zigzagging through the stacks and out the back door. She stepped out into an ordinary alley, Brenna fast on her heels.

Despite the alley continuing straight in both directions with no discernible nooks or offshoots to hide in, there was no one there. The figure had vanished.

11

Brenna

THE MOOD WAS SULLEN as Brenna and Katiel walked back to the inn after the run-in at the candle shop.

Brenna had never felt more defeated. One blow each took them out of commission. They had found the meeting place indicated in the letter, yet they had made no progress toward anything. They'd waited on the bench until dusk, just in case the cloaked person came back to the shop, but of course, they hadn't returned. Though she dreaded the thought, Brenna couldn't help but wonder if Dakier and Alfien had been right. Perhaps there was nothing they could do. Now she had no information to help end this war, plus a painful bruise forming in the middle of her back.

"I can't wait to lie down," Brenna said when she glimpsed Gengerich's around the corner. "I don't think I'll ever be able to feel my back again." She craned her arm around to massage the place that hurt the most—directly between her shoulder blades and, irritatingly, just beyond her reach.

From her twisted position, all she could see were the pedestrians rushing by when she heard a scream—unmistakably Katiel's.

Brenna watched helplessly as Katiel crumpled onto the pavement in front of the hostel, flat onto her back with a painful-sounding thud. She hadn't so much as flinched to catch herself.

Brenna dropped to her knees on the pavers, hooking her arms under Katiel's and pulling her onto her lap. "Katiel," she said, expecting the name alone to wake her. "Katiel." She patted Katiel's cheek frantically. "Katiel!" Her skin was cold to the touch. It had a grayish tint that Brenna had never seen before, not even when she visited the valley during Yuletide and they stayed out too long in the snow.

Brenna racked her brain, trying to comprehend what had occurred. One minute they were walking back to the inn. The next, Katiel was lying in the street, barely conscious. It could have something to do with the person from the wax shop, but she didn't see how someone could have attacked Katiel without being seen and without leaving a mark.

Leaning in, she put her ear near Katiel's mouth. The feel of breath wasn't hitting Brenna's skin like it should have up this close. Her chest did not rise and fall. Brenna desperately wished she knew what was happening. "Help," she tried to cry out, but it came out softly, barely above a whisper, like the words got caught in her throat.

And then Dakier was in front of her, crouching over Katiel and putting a hand on Brenna's shoulder. "Brenna! Brenna," he said in a rush, huffing hard. "Brenna, it's me."

"Help," she tried again. It came out quiet again. She didn't even consider why Dakier was here, with them, in Linden. "Help her. I don't know what happened. She isn't breathing."

Dakier's face was registering Katiel's gray skin, his mouth hanging open in shock. "What happened?" He put one hand over the other and started thrusting the heel of his hand into Katiel's chest. "Did someone strike her?"

"I didn't see anyone." Brenna frantically tried to recall anything she might have missed. "We were about to go into our hostel when she dropped out of nowhere. It was like she fainted."

Abruptly, he stopped the compressions, as if something had occurred to him. He reached out a hand to Katiel's throat, grabbing at her neck and slipping his fingers under the high neckline of her blouse, feeling around the collar.

"What are you doing?" Brenna cried, hearing the desperation in her own voice.

"Where's her necklace?"

"What?" She had no idea what he was getting at. They needed to revive Katiel, though the chest compressions weren't helping.

Dakier's gaze met hers, his charcoal eyes ripe with panic. "The necklace she always wears. Where is it?"

"Who cares?" Brenna screamed. "She isn't breathing!"

She clasped her hands in front of her to press on Katiel's chest herself. With no idea what she was doing, she lined the heel of her palm up with the approximate area of Katiel's lungs and thrust all of her weight onto her friend's abdomen. She pressed once, twice, three times, but nothing appeared to happen. Brenna had the frightful thought that she might be touching a corpse, but she didn't see how it could be possible, when her friend had been alive and well only a moment before.

Katiel let out a gasp so tiny Brenna worried she'd imagined it. But it was enough to spur her onward. Dakier was crouched next to her, muttering words of encouragement, but she barely heard what he was saying. Time seemed to slow as she repeated the motion, but she couldn't have been trying for more than a minute or two when someone behind her shouted, "Here, I have it!"

It was then that Brenna noticed a crowd had gathered around them.

A young man pushed through the throng of people, panting like he'd been running. He shoved the necklace toward them, and quick as a whip, Dakier took it from him and clasped it around Katiel's neck. He took the crystal pendant at the end and pressed it firmly against the bare skin above her clavicle.

Instantly, Katiel sucked in a tremendous gust of air and sat up, Brenna's arms still wrapped around her shoulders. Katiel registered the dozens of eyes looking down at her and seemed to shrink into herself. She asked, "What happened?" quietly enough for only Brenna to hear.

Brenna shook her head, unable to gather any words. She could be of no help. She had no worldly idea what had just happened, either.

Gently, Dakier asked, "Can you stand?"

"Yes, I think so," Katiel replied before doubling back to look at him again. "Dakier?"

Dakier and Brenna helped her to her feet, though Dakier lifted her weight easily on his own. Regardless of why he was in Linden, Brenna was immensely relieved that he was.

Dakier held on to Katiel, though she seemed to stand fine on her own now. "Where are you staying? I think we should take you inside to lie down."

Brenna gave an emphatic nod in agreement. Thankfully, the crowd was dispersing now, turning away with mumbles and shrugs. Apparently, an unexplainable street fainting was not enough to hold their interest.

"What are you doing here?" Katiel asked, but before Dakier could explain, someone else rushed toward them, pushing through the now-dwindling crowd.

"Can someone please explain to me what is going on?" the woman shouted as she approached. Brenna recognized her as the manager of Gengerich's, who Katiel had spoken to the day before. When she registered Katiel and Brenna as the objects of the crowd's interest, she ground out, "You two. I should have known."

"Us two?" Brenna had no idea what the woman was referring to. The interaction of the day before had gone smoothly, in her reckoning. "What do you mean?"

"I think you know what I mean," the lady said.

"How long was I out?" Katiel asked. Her face looked fresh and healthy. The color had completely returned to her cheeks, as if she hadn't just turned gray. However, her expression was that of complete and utter mortification. If there was any snow around, Brenna was sure Katiel would have burrowed down in it until none of these people could see her.

"I have absolutely no idea what you mean," Brenna answered the woman honestly, electing to explain to Katiel once they were no longer a spectacle in the street.

"I received a bit of a warning earlier about you two. One of my fine associates saw you breaking into a shop down on *Lankengasse* and recognized you from breakfast. And now here you are, drawing negative attention right outside my inn."
She was shaking her head like Jay did sometimes, right before he would say that Brenna and Henred should have known

better than to do whatever they'd been doing. "I don't allow criminals to stay here—not in the fine establishment that has been in my family for four generations."

Brenna cursed herself. She knew they shouldn't have had breakfast in the inn's tavern. It was probably that group of elderly people who spotted them, and it was just her luck that they would know the innkeeper. "It isn't what it seems like," Brenna protested. "We are trying to help with the war effort. We think we know a way to restore peace."

"Well, if that isn't a convenient cover story," drawled the innkeeper. She looked from Brenna and Katiel to Dakier and the man who had found the necklace, who Brenna now noticed was still with them, like he was waiting for a reward.

Katiel shrugged away from Dakier, who had continued supporting her with an arm around her shoulders, and added shakily, "It isn't a story."

But the woman was not having any of it. "I hereby ban you from staying here. Your things are already packed and waiting in the lobby."

"Then give us our money back! We already paid for the entire weekend!" Brenna was shouting now, not caring about all the people around. The crowd from the fall seemed to have decided that this development was interesting enough to stay and gawk some more. "And you people, get out of here! Don't you all have jobs?"

The people in the crowd craned their necks, suddenly engrossed in random parts of the pavement, the sky, and the buildings behind them, and then promptly backed away to leave. It was like the morons hadn't realized she could see them until she revealed herself.

The innkeeper shook her head, like she would expect nothing less than a rude display from the likes of her. "Certainly not. I'm not returning your ill-gotten gains. Get out of here before I call the watch on you," she said before turning back to the inn.

"Ill-gotten gains?" Brenna muttered to herself. She was seriously considering giving the innkeeper a swift kick in the back when she heard a throat clear from behind her. The necklace-finder was still standing there when everyone else had left. She wheeled around to him. "Look, thank you for returning that, but we don't have any money—"

She stopped her sentence short when she registered the face. It was not just a random bystander, like she had assumed, but the boy who had been staring at Katiel at Heidel's the night before. He wore a black, tailored three-piece suit with an intricately patterned silk vest, quite possibly the most expensive clothing Brenna had ever seen. "It's you," Brenna blurted.

His arrogant facial expression made Brenna regret her merriment at hearing he'd flirted with Katiel the night before. "It's me."

Dakier looked bewildered. He squinted and jutted his neck forward with the development. "Do you know him?"

"Not really. We ran into him yesterday," Brenna said. "Wait a second. Have you been following us?"

The boy's unusually chiseled face looked completely unfazed by the accusation. "No, I was heading to meet a friend at Gengerich's tavern. Forgive me for not introducing myself yesterday. Anton Dvorsky." He didn't blink as often as he should, which Brenna found unnerving. "I heard you are in need of a place to stay. I may be able to help with that."

The boy—Anton—flashed a dazzling smile that seemed to be for Katiel alone. His teeth were the whitest Brenna had ever seen. She snuck a glance at her friend. Brenna had been about to tell him to get lost, but upon seeing Katiel's face, she decided against it. Katiel bore her tight-lipped smile with one corner turned down—her most genuine smile—and she was swallowing for no reason.

Brenna settled for ongoing questioning instead. "Where did you get the necklace, anyway? Did you swipe it?" She stuck out an accusatory finger for good measure. Maybe if she caught him off guard, he would admit what he was up to.

"I found it lying on the pavement there." He gestured to the street in the direction from which they'd come.

Before Brenna could think of anything else to throw him off, Katiel asked him in her quiet way, "How might you be able to help us?"

That settled it. Katiel definitely liked him. She would never willingly consider help from a complete stranger for any other reason. Normally, Katiel would think a situation like that had a painfully high potential for awkwardness.

"Katiel, don't you think you had better lie down and rest?" Dakier talked in a hushed tone, but they could all hear him. "You took a pretty hard fall." It seemed he found Katiel's behavior just as strange as Brenna did. Perhaps he assumed she'd hit her head.

"Yes, absolutely," Anton agreed. "Exactly what I was going to suggest. My lodging is just down there at The Imperial." He pointed behind them, but Brenna didn't bother to look. "I would be happy to lend one of our rooms, at least for a few hours of rest, while you recover. My traveling companion is waiting for me at Gengerich's, but I am sure he wouldn't mind if you all go ahead of us. My companion and I can share a room for the night, too, if you need longer." He held out a key that had a bit of leather dangling from it, marked with the number 502. "I insist. It would be no trouble at all."

Brenna barely heard his words as her ears rang, disappointment swelling within her. Going to Linden had been a terrible idea. And going to A'slenderia when the war started had been an even worse idea. She was hiding out in an enemy country, and she had already spent most of her money on the hostel and supplies.

She looked down at her hands, raw and cracking from the laundry. All her hard work had been for nothing. Henred had been right when he said she shouldn't leave, and now she hadn't been able to give him a proper send-off to the war. She figured it was time to cut their losses, apologize to Katiel's parents for leaving, and head home to Fir Kelt.

"No, thank—" Brenna meant to tell Anton that they would be on their way, sure her companions would agree with the decision, but she was cut off by Katiel, who shocked her, first by taking the keys from him and then with her reply.

"That would be lovely, thank you."

12

Katiel

"Are you out of your mind?" Brenna demanded as she, Katiel, and Dakier headed to the Imperial. Anton had gone on to Gengerich's tavern to meet with his friend and had insisted they go on ahead of him. Katiel had to admit that it *did* ease her suspicions that he wanted them to go ahead, but she wasn't doing this because she thought he seemed trustworthy.

"No, Brenna," she explained. "It's because of where he's staying." The Imperial was a landmark of Linden, a beautiful building right off of *Lankengasse*. Katiel remembered first passing it as a little girl and fantasizing about what the inside might look like. "The Imperial is the tallest building in the city, so it likely has a view of the candle shop. Maybe even the back alley, too." Katiel grinned as she took in Brenna's surprised but impressed expression. An expression that quickly sank back into the worried one she'd had before. Katiel jingled the key in front of her face. "And seeing as how he's in room 502, I bet that puts him on the top floor."

"Katiel, I can't say I'm not impressed with your hidden talent for sleuthing, but we need to go back," Brenna said. "I know this was my idea in the first place, but after seeing you take that fall, I think coming here was a mistake. Maybe you should go back to the farm, and I'll go back to Derenta's house. Cut our losses."

"I agree," Dakier said immediately. He walked so quietly that Katiel had nearly forgotten he was there. "That's why I came here. Your father sent me to come get you and bring you home before you get hurt."

"I don't think I should travel today, after my fall," Katiel said with a helpless shrug. Truthfully, she felt fine to travel. Physically, she felt like nothing at all had happened. But she knew it would convince Dakier to stay in Linden another night, and she couldn't give up now. She couldn't face her parents and Alfien, with nothing to show for leaving. When she had seen the person in the candle shop, she knew they were onto something. The letter was important, much more than a fluke. She couldn't go back to the Yule Valley and stay there in her infinite loneliness without even Dakier to keep her company. She couldn't go back and worry about what might have happened if they had been brave enough to do something.

Day after day, sitting on her perch in the mountain grass, watching the sheep, she knew the war would be all she could think about, and sometimes wars could last for years. She had finally mustered the courage to go off on her own, and she couldn't turn back. Not yet.

"Who are you?" Brenna asked, a grin spreading across her face. Katiel could practically see the wheels turning in her friend's mind. It was like she wanted to talk Katiel out of staying and ended up talking herself out of leaving. "What have you done with Katiel?"

"Well, it would be beneficial for you to get some rest," Dakier conceded. "If the place is suitable, we can stay one night if you would prefer it." He sounded like he was trying his hand at a firm tone but finding it uncomfortable. "But tomorrow morning, we're going home."

Katiel smirked to herself. Father had once told her that the Prime Minister of A'slenderia stayed at the Imperial when she visited the northwest region. "The hotel should be suitable." As if on cue, they rounded the corner to see a building ahead decked in the finest splendor. "There it is."

The Imperial was on the corner—a wide, opulent building. Its crisp, white-painted façade stood in contrast to the darker wood tones of the surrounding establishments, and each level had an intricate wrought-iron railing topped with planter boxes, spilling over with flowers in every shade of purple and red. Balconies wrapped around the entire structure and, as predicted, would give an excellent view of the surrounding streets. "Wow," Brenna breathed. "I can see why you wanted to stay here."

Katiel had to admit that the prospect of finally seeing the inside excited her. She and Father would never have been able to afford a stay at the Imperial, not to mention the fact that Father would think it a frivolous waste of money.

"Let's go see the rest," she said, giddy from all the adventure one day could bring. Brenna clasped her hand, mirroring Katiel's own excitement, and they hurried inside.

The lobby was every bit as opulent as the exterior, with a wide iron stairwell twisting up the center of the room, and a massive grandfather clock that reminded Katiel of one of her favorite fairy stories.

As she had guessed, Anton's room was on the top floor. When she unlocked the door and stepped in, she realized that a single suite took up the entire floor.

In front of them was a large living space, with several chaises and couches arranged in the center. The decor was a classic example of A'slenderian finery. While other nations decorated with gold leaf and silver trimmings and jewels, A'slenderia was known for its signature look—black ironwork woven into meticulous, complex patterns. Even though the trimmings were crafted of metal, they looked like black lace laid across the white walls. The living space had double doors open to bedrooms on both sides and a large glass door that led onto the balcony. Katiel wondered if the parliamentary *schloss* in Klostern looked anything like this.

"Holy Halstat cheese," breathed Brenna. "This inn might as well be a palace."

Katiel peered into each of the bedrooms. It was unclear which one Anton intended for them to take because both rooms were a colossal mess. The sheets were unkempt, clothes were thrown thoughtlessly onto the floor, and crumpled papers were tossed aside. There was a pillow on a desk, textbooks on the bed, and a stack of blueprints on the dining table.

"Slobs," Dakier muttered, earning a laugh from Brenna.

"Looks like your boyfriend is rich, Katiel," Brenna said.

"Rich slobs, then," Dakier amended, and Brenna laughed again.

Katiel said, "You two, stop. We are here for surveillance."

"And rest." Dakier pushed his hair back from his face. "You need to rest. And I need to get my horse from where I tied him up back there. But before I go, Katiel, your father asked me to give this to you."

From the pocket of his tawny overcoat, Dakier pulled out a cheese cloth and unwrapped it to reveal a tiny wooden box. It was teal, the same shade as the furniture in Katiel's room, and accented with simple tulip silhouettes painted in dark red.

"Your father said not to open it for any reason," Dakier said.

That had to be the strangest thing she had ever heard, and Brenna echoed the sentiment. "Why would he give it to her, then?"

Dakier shrugged. "I asked the same thing. But that's all he said."

Katiel had always been obedient, perhaps even to a fault. Strangely, the older she became, the stricter her Father seemed to get. He had kept her from university, and the sacrifice had cost her Alfien. Surely, even Dakier could see that Father's overprotectiveness had gone too far. But once she left that night with Brenna, something in her changed. She would do what she felt was right, rather than blindly obeying her parents.

"I am done listening to Father," she said, more to herself than anyone. Dakier raised his eyebrows but refrained from saying anything against it.

With a steadying breath, Katiel clicked open the latch that held the box together and lifted the lid to reveal a mouse-gray velvet pouch with a drawstring—the type that Mother's earrings came in. Katiel did not hesitate to pull open the fabric and look inside.

She did not know what she had been expecting, but whatever she expected, it was not what she found. All the pouch contained was some gray dust—sparkling, like finely ground metal. "What on Endra could this be?" she asked, holding the pouch open for Brenna and Dakier to have a look.

Brenna raised a brow comically high on her forehead, the face of pure confusion, and Dakier cradled his chin. "It might be worth money, like silver dust," he suggested. "Perhaps he gave it to you in case you needed extra money on the trip."

Katiel doubted it. Father would have sent a bag of league-marks in that case. As far as what it was, though, she had no idea. She noticed it looked like the filling of the charm on her necklace, which seemed significant after what had happened earlier.

But she did not want to discuss it now. She needed to think about the matter privately to sort out what it could be. Despite her hatred of being alone on the farm, it seemed she had grown accustomed to the comfort of solitude during her long hours watching her sheep, and being with Brenna constantly for the past few days was irrationally grating on her nerves. It took a while to convince Dakier and Brenna to fetch their horses from Gengerich's stable without her, but their obvious interest in being alone together won out. After a bit of back-and-forth, Dakier insisted on taking the key, "as a precaution," and assured they would be back quickly.

As soon as they left, Katiel dutifully went out to the balcony and peered over the rail. As predicted, the fifth-floor perch gave a view of the entire street, and if she leaned over the edge, she could see the alley and the shops behind.

Leaning her hips against the metal railing, Katiel tried to steady her feet as well as her mind, thinking back to everything she had yet to process. No matter how she considered it, her fainting had been so strange. Brenna had said she had seen no one there, but Katiel could have sworn she felt someone yank off her necklace before she fell unconscious. Strangely, she believed it was not Anton who did it. But what would a necklace have to do with reviving her, regardless?

Dakier seemed to relate the necklace to her recovery, but Dakier always had believed in fairy tales and improbable stories. After all, he read from the scripture every morning like her parents did. At first, she had been sure the timing of her necklace being replaced and her resuscitation must have been coincidental, but after receiving the pouch of dust as well, it seemed obvious it was more than happenstance. Still, she did not know what the connection could be.

She turned the pendant over in her hands. It was glass, shaped like a long crystal and hollowed out to hold the decorative, dark metal dust. She had worn this necklace every day since she could remember, every day since her parents had given it to her. They had called it good luck, and she had grown used to it. But it was not even a gem. It was just a worthless piece of costume jewelry. She tucked it back down into her blouse, like she usually wore it. Father said that the best luck came not from what others could see but from deep in the heart.

She did not know how long she had been out there waiting when she heard the door click behind her. Before she had time to turn, Anton was standing next to her, leaning his elbows on the wrought iron rail.

"Where's your friend?" Katiel asked.

"Back there." Anton nodded toward the suite. Through the glass, Katiel could see a boy about their age tidying up the area, the same one who had been with Anton the other day in Heidel's tavern. He had a bronze skin tone and short black hair, wore glasses low on his nose, and bore the faintest hint of facial hair. "His name is Simeon."

It was a name she had never heard before, and it did not sound A'slenderian. Neither of the young men looked it, either, though Anton had no accent she could discern. "What are you doing in Linden?"

"We're students at university together," he said. "We're here to study A'slenderian culture." That would explain all the textbooks and notes, at least. "From New Drezchy."

Katiel tried not to look too surprised. New Drezchy was a country known for its ruthless culture and even more ruthless, inhospitable climate. The current king was infamous across the world as one of the cruelest rulers in history, and the Crown Prince, rumored to be almost as bad, held the ominous nickname of the Ghost. Katiel had met no one from the nation before, due to New Drezchy being a two-week voyage from the Continent, but she had expected its citizens to be scarier. "You've come all that way just to study this place?"

"Ja, ilt nodebinchen eich?"

Katiel blinked. *Yes, and should I not?* Anton spoke Aslen perfectly. She had met no one outside of her valley who still spoke it. She had not even overheard it so far during her stay in Linden.

He did not have an accent in Aslen, not exactly, but the way he pronounced the words made it sound like she was hearing the language for the first time. It was very distracting.

She turned to look him in the eye, which was a mistake. His umber-brown eyes had a way of making her lose track of her thoughts.

"How do you know our language?" she asked in Endran. It felt wrong to speak Aslen with a foreigner she had just met. In her mind, it was for her family. And the fact that she did not want to lose her thoughts again had nothing to do with it.

"I study Aslen at university, of course," he answered with a smirk. Katiel realized that should have been obvious. "Where have your friends gone?"

"They went to fetch something. They'll be back soon." A'slenderia had strict laws and was typically a safe place, but it could not hurt to emphasize that she was not alone here.

"So I take it you are not really a lady of," he asked, "shall we say, of an unscrupulous profession?"

It took Katiel a moment to grasp his meaning, but then she remembered the words of that horrible innkeeper earlier. The heat rushed to her cheeks as the humiliation of the events in the street rushed back to her. "No, certainly not."

"Don't worry, it was clearly a misunderstanding," he said. For the first time since she had met him, he sounded genuine and, dare she admit it, kind. "What are you three doing in Linden? If the man who came to your aid is with you, that is."

The edge to his tone was not lost on her. Could it be possible that the most gorgeous boy she had ever laid eyes on was checking to see if she was with someone else? Surely not. That might suggest he was interested in her, of all people.

"That's Dakier. He works for my father. We're in town looking for someone." After she said it, she realized how oddly vague that sounded. She wished she had thought of a cover story in case she needed it. But she stupidly had not anticipated having to speak to anyone but Brenna during their travels.

"Someone we know." That sounded little better. "It's a long story, really. Too long to explain."

"Of course." It was clear he was clever enough to know she was hiding something, but he did not press the issue. "So—I'm guessing from appearances here—Brenna is Barkurian, Dakier is Tibedese, and you are A'slenderian?"

She was surprised he remembered Brenna's name from the other night. But she said, "Yes, that is right."

"And you all realize your countries are at war, yes?" He looked down at her over his shoulder, his elbow rested on the rail. Humor twinkled in his eyes.

Without thinking about it enough, she said the first thing that came to mind. "I suppose some things are more important than one's country."

After she said it, she made the mistake of meeting his gaze again. Anton was studying her face like she was a particularly interesting book. His eyes invited her in, and the bizarre thought passed through her mind that she wanted to stay.

In response to the look that was probably, unfortunately, written on her face, he adjusted his hand such that his fingers were now resting on the rail, a pin's width from hers. She forced a cough so she could cover her mouth with her hand. "Thank you—for returning my necklace, that is. And thank you for allowing us to stay here."

"It's my pleasure." He drew out the sentence in the most flirtatious way possible. Surely he knew what he was doing when he said things like that. Or perhaps she had knocked her head when she fell.

She coughed again, this time involuntarily. "If you would excuse me, I feel I could benefit from some time alone. What with my fall."

"As you wish," he said, with a last glance down before she disappeared into the suite.

He had a way of looking at her that made her feel tiny and powerful at the same time.

13

Brenna

A FIERCE STOMACH GROWL awoke Brenna the next morning, so she didn't bother to change out of her nightdress before heading out to hunt for some breakfast.

In the common area of the suite, Dakier sat alone reading a newspaper, though his fast-tapping foot gave away his continued anxiety about being there at all. He'd made it clear the night prior that he did not trust Anton and Simeon in the slightest, and Brenna knew him remaining with them had much more to do with wanting to protect them than having any faith in their plan.

"Katiel's out there," he said upon seeing Brenna, with a gesture toward the balcony. Katiel was where she'd been yesterday, leaning against the rail and surveying the street. Unlike Brenna, she had already gotten herself ready for the day. Even if she was still playing at feeling ill, Katiel would rather die than have Dakier or one of the others see her in her nightclothes. "She said she needed a bit more rest this morning. I don't know where anyone else is."

It was the mildest of remarks, one that hardly required a reply at all, but when she looked at him, Brenna could barely muster a nod. Dakier's hair was still unkempt from sleeping on the sofa, and his outer garments had been stripped down to reveal an unbuttoned linen shirt, the thin material stretched even thinner across his broad shoulders. Light brown, leather suspenders cut his shape into a stark triangle, appending flax work pants stretched tight over his strong thighs. Somehow his typical work overcoat had been hiding a *lot*, and she was still trying desperately to think of some clever quip or conversation starter when a hiss of, "Brenna," sounded over her shoulder.

She gave a little jolt, realizing with a second's delay that Katiel had come up behind her. Brenna whispered back, "Why are you whispering?"

Katiel craned her neck toward the room Anton and Simeon now shared.

"They aren't here," Brenna supplied. "No idea where they went."

"Oh, they were up when I went outside," Katiel mused before reprising the urgency she'd had a moment before. "Regardless, hurry and get dressed. I saw another movement."

Brenna leaped to her feet. "Time for the plan."

"What movement?" Dakier asked, no longer attempting to hide his frantic toe-tapping. "What plan?"

Brenna didn't take the time to answer, and she also didn't take the time to dress properly, instead throwing on the complimentary housecoat and slippers that nice hotels evidently provided. "Do you have the letter?"

Katiel nodded and patted the chest area of her high-collared dress.

The letter seemed to click something together for Dakier. He showed them his palms like he was a traffic officer trying to halt a carriage. "Wait, wait, wait. I thought we were abandoning this effort, waiting for you to feel well enough to travel, and going home."

Brenna noticed he'd said we, as if he were a part of their quest, instead of here only on assignment from Mr. Salzbruck. Brenna thought Katiel might have picked up on that, too, because she merely said, "Let's not abandon it yet," and headed out the door.

Dakier sighed, though he didn't hesitate to follow Katiel out the door and down the stairs, and Brenna was right on their heels. As they stepped onto the street, Dakier asked them, "What do you want me to do?"

"I don't know." Brenna considered. "Just stay with Katiel."

"Your plan involves splitting up?" Dakier looked mildly panicked.

Come to think of it, so did Katiel. "Brenna, I cannot do it," she said, even though they were still approaching Linden Wax Works in the distance.

They had formed the plan last night in their fancy room before either went to sleep. They needed to be better prepared if they found the person from the candle shop again to avoid getting whacked in the back—the person who Brenna was pretty sure, despite having no evidence, was in fact the author of the letter. Katiel had surprised Brenna by offering to take the speaking role while Brenna guarded the other door, so it was no surprise she wanted to back out at the last minute.

"Okay, let's switch roles, then. I'll talk."

"Okay," Katiel said, slipping Brenna the letter so swiftly that it was almost imperceptible.

"Change of plans. Stay with me, instead." Brenna took Dakier's hand and yanked him along with her, heading down an alley while Katiel kept going along the street. She turned the corner and led him down a narrow stretch until she reached the back door of the dilapidated building.

She tried to step back to get a good look at the exterior, just to be sure it was the right place, when she noticed she was still clasping Dakier's hand in hers. He seemed to notice at the same moment, and she hastily shook him off.

The shop before them looked like it was one story, but it might have an attic under the steeply gabled roof. If it *did* have an attic, that might be where the author was hiding out. Brenna was fairly certain that, whoever the author was, he wasn't staying there for the merchandise, and a hidden second floor above an abandoned storefront could provide an ideal hideout.

"Where are we?" Dakier asked.

"Linden Wax Works."

He furrowed his brow, like he was trying to remember if that name meant anything to him. "And what are we doing here?"

Brenna took a deep breath and, mustering all her boldness, stepped up to the door. "Probably something stupid."

14

Dakier

"That is not reassuring," Dakier grumbled.

Brenna had said they were about to do something stupid when he'd asked why they were lingering in an alley behind some beaten-down store. He wished she were only joking, but he had a feeling it was not a hyperbole.

Brenna was pressing her ear against the door of the ramshackle establishment, which looked completely out of place in the nicest part of Linden. Dakier was essentially regretting all his life choices up until now, on account of them landing him in this situation.

Brenna's eyes widened, but Dakier didn't have to press his own ear against the wood to hear the commotion coming from within. First, there was a faraway knock, then the creak of footsteps against the floorboards, and then several clunks, as if a stack of weighty items had tumbled to the ground. Whatever they were doing here, he knew this must have to do with the letter the girls had found.

He felt guilty that he was effectively aiding them in this endeavor, when he was supposed to convince them to return home. Until an hour ago, he'd thought he'd succeeded in the goal. But he should have known better. Feniel had known, at least. He had said Katiel wouldn't return.

Dakier snapped out of his thoughts as the door swung away from them, and Brenna stepped back to avoid losing her footing.

Standing in the doorway was a woman wearing a cloak, clearly trying to flee the building. It must have been Katiel who had knocked on the front door, then, forcing this woman to duck out the only other exit. He didn't know whether to be impressed or concerned. Brenna and Katiel had laid a trap to force this person to talk to them. That meant they must've already come here before he made it to Linden. Brenna and Katiel wasted no time.

Brenna had said she thought the letter's author still occupied the shop, but the woman in front of them wasn't as old as Dakier assumed the author would be. Really, he hadn't imagined the author was a woman at all. The person in front of them appeared to be in her mid-twenties, with deep brown skin, a smattering of freckles, and a hood pulled over her braided black hair. Rather than any sort of political operative, she appeared to be an ordinary woman, with an expression more frightened than anything. Quickly, she reached into her cape and brandished a knife.

Before he had time to register his own action, Dakier shot his arm out to the side, positioning himself between Brenna and the knife.

"I don't want to hurt you," the woman said slowly, deliberately. "Let me pass and do not follow."

"No, wait, please," Brenna said, stepping around Dakier. She was edging her way into the doorframe as she spoke, and Dakier wondered if it was purposeful as he stepped forward to match her. "We need to talk to you. We want to help."

The woman appeared to analyze them—how young they both were, and the fact that neither had pulled out a weapon in return.

"Trapping someone by blocking all exits does not seem very helpful to me," she retorted icily. "Does it to you?"

"Have you ever gone by the pen name 'Loyalist'?"

Brenna's question sent recognition flashing across the woman's face. She tried to blink it away as she steeled her expression into that of indifference once more, but it was too late. They'd both seen it.

"Let me be," the woman snarled. "Now." She jutted the blade out for emphasis. "I don't know who you are or what you think you know, but you children need to leave. This is your last warning."

"Wait," Brenna said as she reached her fingers into her neckline, to where she had tucked away the letter. The cloaked woman must have thought she was reaching for a weapon because she slashed her blade in Brenna's direction.

Dakier lunged in front of her, pushing Brenna back into the alley. He felt a sting across the back of his forearm as the sharp metal broke the skin. The cloaked woman gasped in horror and stepped back, like her swing was a bluff that she hadn't intended to act on.

"We have—" Brenna began when she registered what had occurred, blinking at the red drops prickling Dakier's shirtsleeve. "We have your letter," she finished weakly. The letter was still unfolded and displayed in front of her chest as her attention turned to him. She looked like she might be sick at the sight of his blood, though it wasn't much. "Dakier..."

"It's fine, really," he reassured. Some irrational part of him hated the thought of worrying Brenna. Even though, if it weren't for her, he wouldn't be standing in a back alley with a bleeding arm. He pushed up his sleeve to confirm his suspicions. The cut was long but shallow. He turned it toward her. "See, no deeper than a cat scratch."

The woman opposite them now held impossibly still, but she didn't seem concerned with his bleeding. She was staring at the letter in Brenna's hands. "Where did you get that?"

"Royal Kelt hostel," said Brenna, "but please, please, hear us out. We want to talk to you."

"We can speak at a location of your choosing, if you would be more comfortable," Dakier added. If he were in her place, he would want to meet on his own terms, if at all.

Her expression softened, but she took a long moment before saying anything. It seemed his words had made the intended difference. He cursed himself for helping them. He was supposed to convince Katiel and Brenna to return home, not advance their quest. Then again, he didn't favor getting cut again.

"The Royal Kelt hostel," she repeated when she spoke again. "In Fir Kelt?"

"Yes." Brenna nodded. "I'm Brenna Malley. I work at the Royal Kelt. Or, well, I did until a couple of days ago."

The woman leaned into the alley, craning her head to the left and right. "No more talking here. I'll meet with you and answer your questions, but only if you agree to leave me alone afterward."

"Fine, we will never contact you again"—Brenna took a dramatic pause—"*if* you decide not to join us in our efforts during our meeting. I have a feeling we can convince you before it's over."

Dakier had to give it to her. She *was* pretty convincing when she wanted to be.

The woman looked like it was taking her a great effort not to roll her eyes. "Unlikely. I can meet you at noon at The Cooked Goose. And don't be late. Noon on the dot, or else I'll leave."

Noon was in less than an hour. It surprised Dakier she would want to meet so soon. He supposed she wanted to be rid of them as soon as possible, if she even planned to show up at the meeting at all. The offer of a meeting could be a ploy to get them to leave.

"Where—" Brenna started to ask when the door slammed in her face. A clattering sounded from inside, like someone was climbing a wooden ladder.

"I knew it," said Brenna. "Attic."

15

Katiel

While Brenna distracted the Loyalist out behind Linden Wax Works, Katiel sucked in a breath and slipped in the front door. Though she crept as quietly as she could, every tiny sound seemed to be magnified. The hinges certainly had not creaked that loudly the day before. This was exactly why she had volunteered to talk to the Loyalist while Brenna searched the shop—before she recalled that speaking to a stranger was no less terrifying and chickened out of that plan, as well.

The night prior, between bouts of fretful sleep in their gifted hotel room, Brenna made an idle quip that changed everything. Hung up on the asinine amount of inventory the abandoned candle shop kept stocked, Brenna said, "With that many extra candles, they might as well sell them to the military and recoup some of the money."

Katiel eyed her blurry form in the darkened room. "What do you mean?"

Brenna shrugged, an awkward feat with her arm scrunched under her pillow. "In history class, I remember learning about spies hiding messages in wax during the Ten Years' War. With that many, it'd be impossible to find if you didn't know what you were looking for."

Mulling over the odd fact, a tingle rose up to Katiel's cheeks. The secret note had led Inigo Farro to this very place, so it was not that much of a stretch to think its author may have left a message, lest Inigo arrive first. It was a fool's hope, but that was all they had gone by so far. With the place mere yards away, her heart soared with the infectious possibility that they may have found a clue.

But the next day as she entered the shop, Katiel realized they were more than fools. Only a true muttonhead would expect to find anything in this mess.

The lighting was dim, just a few streaks of sunlight streaming in past the curtains, and each candle looked the same, all ivory pillars with short white wicks. There was certainly no time to inspect every candle or even every stack. The cloaked figure Brenna was distracting could turn about and see her at any moment. She could not make out every word of the conversation, but from the irritated tone, it did not sound like the woman would tolerate Brenna for long.

Katiel had a mind to retreat when she noticed something. The slightest shape curved within a candle at the top of a stack, backlit from the open door to the alleyway.

The wax was barely translucent, but she was sure she had seen something. It might be nothing more than a bad mold clumped in the center, but it was her only chance. The woman would be heading back into the shop at any moment. Without another thought, Katiel snatched the candle from the pile, stuffed it into her apron pocket, and snuck back out the front door. As she listened to the sound of footsteps retreating to the second floor of the shop, she realized it had not been a moment too soon.

Now she just hoped it actually had something of value inside.

"DID YOU GET IT?" Brenna asked as Katiel stepped into the suite and the door clicked shut behind them.

"Get what?" Dakier started. "Shouldn't you be looking for the meeting place the woman mentioned?"

Katiel could not fight the grin that spread across her face as she reached into her apron pocket and pulled out the treasure she had collected. With a *thunk*, she set it down on the delicate entryway table, locking eyes with Brenna in triumph. To the untrained eye, it looked like an ordinary white candle, but when held up to the light, a faint silhouette shone of something inside.

"A candle?" Dakier furrowed his brows.

Quickly, Brenna recounted the plan they had concocted. It was clear that Dakier seconded the muttonhead notion but was attempting to hide his doubts. Crouching down, he stuck his face close to the wax, like there might be fine writing on the surface if he looked close enough. "And you think this one in particular has a message?"

Katiel nodded. "When the sunlight lit the stacks from behind, this was the one that appeared to be filled."

Truthfully, her statement implied much more certainty than she felt, and Dakier did not seem convinced, either. "What about getting to the Cooked Goose?" he asked. "There's less than half an hour left before noon, and the woman said she wouldn't wait."

"The Cooked Goose?" Anton chimed in. "That sounds like a false name if I ever heard one."

Katiel's face fell. In her excitement at having even possibly found the right candle, she had somehow failed to notice Anton and Simeon in the suite but a few feet away from them. "Pardon," she said hurriedly. "I did not see you there."

Anton sat with his back to them at an ornate dining table at the far end of the room. He was looking over his shoulder at them, though Katiel had the odd feeling that he was looking at her alone. He wore a brown velvet three-piece suit with a silky, white cravat folded neatly into the vest, and some strange orange fruits were stacked in a footed dish in front of him. The food looked untouched, but the papers scattered around the table were a jumbled mess—blueprints, from the look of them. Meanwhile, Simeon didn't so much as glance up from the textbook he was poring over.

Katiel wished she had been more careful and not let them overhear about the candle, but Brenna seemed unfazed by their presence as she cursed and muttered, "It does sound like a false name. But let's worry about the candle first. Should we burn it down or cut it?"

Katiel gulped, not particularly eager to see what was inside. "Cut it, I would think."

"Here," Anton said, clearing his papers from the table and waving them over.

When she got close enough, Katiel could make out the sketches he had drawn—an array of objects varying from large machinery to eyeglasses. Freshly done, too, judging from the ink smudges down the side of his left hand.

"This should be enough space," he said.

It certainly was enough space, though Katiel hesitated to reveal the clue in front of the two scholars. Anton had helped them so far, but she knew virtually nothing about him. Yet, here they were, mere feet apart, and he already knew it contained a message of some sort. Warily, she set the candle down. Judging from the look on his face, Dakier shared her misgivings as he pulled out his pocketknife and began cutting into the wax.

16

Brenna

Brenna watched with bated breath as Dakier sawed away at the candle in painfully small slivers—to avoid damaging whatever lay inside, no doubt.

Finally, a scrap of parchment peeked through the surface, confirming her wildest hopes. It was another letter.

Dakier carved the rest of the note free and handed it to her. It was a letter folded into thirds, secured with an unbroken, bronze wax seal, which she immediately peeled open with her fingernail. The fancy-pants gentlemen in company might think it uncivilized that she didn't use a letter opener, but she was too eager to wait.

"Curious that the seal's still intact," Anton commented. "Perhaps it's of a clay compound." But Brenna was far too engrossed in the note's contents—and the good fortune that they'd found it at all—to pay attention to the details.

Plain Endran stretched down the page, in a similar—albeit neater—scrawl than the first letter. Not knowing what she might discover, Brenna angled it back such that only she and Katiel could read it, but it didn't take long for her disappointment to sink in. It was merely a list of names, not a letter with a distinct message like the first had been.

Netheniel
Wendelle
Eris
Silka
Eoghan
Narilla

No one had addressed or signed it, like one normally would a letter. And yet, the author had sealed it and concealed it in a candle, which showed it held something of importance.

"Do you see anything hidden, like a coded message?" Katiel whispered.

Brenna shook her head. "No, not yet. And I don't recognize any of these names." There was no special capitalization, no words written in a different script than others, and no misspellings. "Could this be a list of safe contacts that the letter's author left for Farro?" she asked, halfway to Katiel and halfway to herself. "But if that were the case, why would it list only first names?"

Dakier leaned over her shoulder to have a look, which threatened to make her blush, until Anton leaned toward her as well. On reflex, she folded the note closed so he couldn't read it. Brenna would've expected him to take offense, but strangely, he didn't seem to mind. Instead, he reached out a long, slender finger to point to the seal. An uneven, six-sided shape indented the wax, not unlike the crude outline of a gemstone. "That symbol—I've seen it before, on a building in the southeast district. We were in the area just—when was it, again? Yes, three days ago." He said it like someone had answered his question, even though no one had.

Simeon seemed mildly interested at best, cradling his chin in his hand as he watched them. "You mean the—" he started to ask, but Anton cut him off.

"Perhaps that would lead to the meeting place you were looking for."

Brenna thought he had to be hiding something, and she had a mind to say so, when Katiel cut in. "That's such good luck," her friend said with little, nervous cough. "Would you mind writing the directions for us?"

"I'll do you one better." Anton stood, neglecting to push his chair under the table. "I'll walk you there myself. I could use a break from my studies."

Dakier and Katiel both looked at Brenna and then at one another, panic lining their features. Katiel gave another forced cough, like she was stalling. "That is so kind of you to offer, but we will be fine on our own. It may take quite some time, you know, our dealings there."

"Surely you wouldn't deny me the pleasure of accompanying you and your friends on such a lovely day. I've tried to be most hospitable," he said, his tone almost menacing. "Truly, I insist."

Dakier's words rang back through Brenna's mind. There was definitely something off about this boy. But what choice did they have but to let him lead the way? Scarcely any time remained to find the meeting place—if the woman actually intended to meet with them at all—and they had no other leads.

Katiel must have thought the same, because she said, "Very well, let us leave at once, if it would please you. Your hospitality is much appreciated."

Katiel had such a natural way of sounding formal. She never talked like that with Brenna, but Brenna heard it when Katiel tended to customers. Brenna herself couldn't manage to speak that way. "I knew I couldn't have done this without you," she whispered to her friend as they followed Anton out the door. Katiel sent her a sheepish smile in return.

The group stepped back out onto the street, the summer sun warm on their backs. "How far is it?" Brenna asked their temporary guide.

"Quite far." Anton glanced over his shoulder and raised his eyebrows before setting off at one of the swiftest walking speeds Brenna had ever witnessed. "We had better hurry if we mean to be there in half an hour." They all did as they were told, keeping up with the brutal pace Anton set as they traversed the walkways of the city.

No one talked for a while. On Brenna's part, it was to avoid revealing how deeply she had to breathe in order to walk this fast. Though he kept silent to her right, Dakier was being pretty expressive as he shot daggers into the back of Anton's head. He may as well hang a sign around his neck reading: *I don't trust the guy in front of me.*

As they made their way through town, the buildings grew less like The Imperial and more like the current state of Linden Wax Works. "What sort of establishment are we heading to, exactly?" Katiel asked.

"Disreputable," Anton said matter-of-factly.

Katiel shot Brenna a worried glance. "Why have you been there, then?"

"Cultural research," Anton answered smoothly, "but I'd be careful asking too many questions, lest you want the same asked of you."

It hadn't occurred to Brenna until then that they were being just as dodgy about their dealings in Linden as he was. They hadn't explained their true motives for staying in the suite, and it seemed Anton wasn't one to pry. But Dakier's jaw clenched at his words nevertheless.

They came upon a section of buildings that looked as run-down as the rest when Anton stopped walking. "This is it."

"This is it?" Brenna repeated, incredulous.

No nameplate or door marked the part of the block they were standing in front of. The section Anton indicated appeared to be a part of the establishments on either side. A little wooden plaque jutting out from the roofline was the only thing that might suggest otherwise.

The plaque bore the same oblong hexagon as the seal, a faint indentation carved into the wood. Now that she looked again, Brenna found the shape familiar, but she couldn't recall where she recognized it from.

"See there?" Anton nodded toward the plaque. "It's the same as the seal."

Dakier shook his head. "But there's no door."

"No, look," Brenna said, stepping closer to the wall in a rush of excitement. "If you look closely, there's a tiny seam." She trailed her fingers across the wood. Though it was barely visible to the naked eye, there was a six-sided ridge carved into the surface. It was a hidden doorway.

"Should we knock?" Katiel whispered.

Anton shook his head. "I tried it when I saw this place before. Nothing happened."

Without hesitation, Brenna rapped on the surface as loudly as she could, earning concerned expressions from her companions and scowls from the few other people walking along the street. "What? I had to at least try again. Maybe Anton isn't very good at knocking."

Dakier smirked, likely appreciating her poking fun at Anton. But they waited a few minutes, and still no one answered the door. Brenna knocked again, even more raucously than the first time, but still, nothing.

After a few more minutes of suspense, Katiel's braid found its way into her mouth. She stopped chewing on it momentarily to say, "Perhaps we should turn back. We could see if the Loyalist is still hiding out in the wax shop and question her more."

"Let's not go back yet," Brenna said. She had just pulled the second letter out when a carriage driving entirely too fast peeled past them down the narrow lane. Katiel jumped back to avoid getting her toes pummeled, causing her to lose her balance and fall back against the building.

"Careful," Dakier said as he steadied Katiel's shoulders. But when she pushed off the wall to right herself, Brenna noticed something peculiar. Where Katiel's hand had touched the wood, the surface gave way an almost imperceptible amount, and Brenna could have sworn she heard a click. Peering closer, she realized there were four small squares cut into the surface of the door, arranged like the points of a compass rose.

She couldn't help but let out a tiny squeal as she unfolded the second letter to read it again. She was so close to cracking something, she could almost taste it.

Netheniel, Wendelle, Eris, Silka, Eoghan, Narilla.

The names held no significance to her, but it seemed odd that they all began with a N, S, E, or W, only letters used to abbreviate the cardinal directions. "This might be a stretch," she said to the group, "but I wonder if this isn't a manifest at all, but a code to open the door."

Anton surprised her by saying, "That's what I was hoping for."

Dakier added, "It's worth a try."

Katiel nodded her agreement.

Picturing the squares on the concealed door as a compass, Brenna pressed on the top center. That time she heard the click. She was sure of it.

In a rush, she pressed the rest of the sequence. Left, right, bottom, right, top.

For a fraction of a second, nothing happened, and Brenna thought the clicks she heard were nothing more than a fool's hope.

That was, until the section of the loose planks caved inward and slid to the side to reveal an open pathway.

17

Brenna

ANTON PROCEEDED CASUALLY THROUGH the doorway, as if hidden pathways in the sides of buildings were of no consequence to him.

Brenna wanted to stand there and gawk at what had just happened. Instead, she followed him through the passage, any hesitation she had overcome by her determination not to let this overly bold stranger ruin their chance to find the Loyalist.

When she entered, Brenna found herself in a small tavern with a large, elk-antler chandelier in the center and curtained-off booths all around the edges. Smoke billowed from behind some of the velvety, maroon curtains.

"Are they lighting fires indoors?" Katiel whispered to her, wide-eyed with concern, and Brenna shrugged. After the hidden doorway business, nothing would surprise her.

Anton waltzed through the open space like he knew where he was going, but Brenna didn't have time to ask where he was headed before a man in a black cloak approached them and said, "State your business."

Brenna stepped around Anton and said, "We're here to meet someone."

The man's brows lifted the slightest bit, which Brenna took to mean she should go on. "A Barkurian woman with black braids, staying at the wax shop. Do you know her?"

Without uttering a word, the man turned on his heels and left the room.

Brenna glanced back at Katiel, who gave the tiniest shrug in response. She had no ideas either, then, and there were no other people in sight. Brenna tapped her toe on the hardwood floor, drawing a blank as she tried to think of how to proceed. She was nearing the point of opening a smoky curtain to ask someone else when the man returned.

He didn't say to follow him, but they did regardless as he wound his way to the back of the tavern and stopped at a corner booth. Wordlessly, he pulled the curtain aside.

Behind it was the same woman they'd encountered earlier, seated at the far end of a booth against the wall with her brow fixed in an icy stare. She showed no emotion as she said, "Hello."

"Hello, the Loyalist," Brenna drawled as she slid into the booth opposite her, trying to be as smooth as possible. The way the woman was sitting, her cloak had rolled back to the elbows and a delicate bracelet was on full display. On a thin chain was a tiny glass charm cut into the shape of a long crystal, a near replica of the pendant on Katiel's necklace. The pendant was where she recognized the shape on the sign from, Brenna realized. "Nice bracelet, by the way."

The woman's eyes flashed as she darted her hand under the table. "Don't call me that."

Brenna glanced at her companions. They all stood within the tight space of the curtained section, but none of them moved to sit down. "Then what should I call you?"

"Mara Quigley." Her eyes flickered, like she regretted saying it. It was likely her real name, then. "You shouldn't have brought others. Who are these people?"

"This is Dakier, the one you sliced through earlier. He thinks he's here to protect us." Brenna patted Dakier on the shoulder before pointing to Katiel and then Anton. "Katiel, Anton. Her—closest friend, trust her with my life. Him—don't know him from Queen Sylka, don't trust him as far as I can throw him, but he knew the way here, and we were pressed for time."

"Is that a joke?"

Brenna shook her head. "No, not at all."

Mara looked like she was considering strangling her.

"We met yesterday," Anton added unhelpfully.

Dakier tossed his hands up in exasperation.

Mara jutted out her chin toward Anton. "In that case, leave."

He seemed to take the direct request to leave as an invitation to stay because he slid into the opposite side of the booth as Brenna. "Not a chance."

As he pulled in beside her, Mara slid closer to the wall. "I'll kill you on sight if you cross me," she said to him before adding, "or any of us."

"Fair," he said casually, like his life was threatened on a daily basis. For all Brenna knew, perhaps it was.

Dakier said, "Unbelievable." He was still standing up, and he didn't seem to have any plans to change that. Katiel's mouth pressed into a worried line, but she took a seat beside Brenna.

Brenna turned to level with the Loyalist—er, Mara. "Let's get back to why we're here. How do you know Tibedese?"

Mara shrugged. "Never said I did."

Brenna refrained from tossing her hands up like Dakier had. "But you wrote the letter, so you must. How did you learn about the plot? The framing, I mean?" She was careful to avoid saying the name Inigo Farro in front of their unwelcome guest, but she knew Mara would know who she meant.

"None of your concern."

Brenna looked at Katiel for help. Katiel stared back at her with wide eyes, frozen in place. Seemed she was on her own, then. "Isn't that what we're here to discuss?"

"Hardly."

Brenna looked at Katiel again, silently pleading with her to say something. She was out of ideas. The plan had seemed so simple: find out who framed Inigo Farro and then convince the Loyalist to come back to Bar Kur to tell Jay who it was. She hadn't considered that the person who knew might not want to tell anyone at all. If Brenna had been the one to uncover the plot, she would've told everybody.

Katiel kept silent as Brenna drew in a breath. "Why did you agree to meet with us, then?"

"Simple." Mara leaned back and crossed her arms. "I didn't. There is no such place as the Cooked Goose. In fact, I'm impressed you found this place at all."

Brenna tried to hide her surprise, but she was guessing it did not work.

"You lot are going to blow my cover and get me killed if you keep following me around."

"But we want to help you," Brenna said. "We're on your side. All we want is to stop the war. We aren't a threat."

"Incorrect." Mara shook her head. "When you first came to the shop, I thought you were a threat. Then I realized you are just a band of idiot kids who have no idea what they're doing, which makes you *more* of a threat."

Brenna reeled back at the affront. "How?"

But Mara retorted, "What do you need to hear to leave me alone?"

Brenna crossed her arms, trying to mimic Mara's collected posture. "Who framed him and who was the actual killer?" she asked, careful again not to mention any names.

Mara scoffed. "And what would you do with that information if you had it?"

"Tell my brother-in-law," she said. "He works for the Barkurian government."

Mara's eyes flickered with interest that she appeared to be trying to hide. "And who would that be?"

"Jacoby Donnell."

As the name left Brenna's lips, Mara launched herself across the table, hauling Anton up with her. She wrapped an arm around him from behind and pressed a knife to his throat.

Katiel shrieked, while an unexpected realization dawned on Brenna. Mara knew Jay.

"Now let's see if you are willing to lose someone you supposedly don't know." Mara was trying to call their perceived bluff, jutting the blade dangerously close to Anton's artery. Something in her eyes betrayed her, though—like it was the first time she'd ever threatened someone's life, and she was wildly uncomfortable doing so. "Someone is going to start talking. Who do you work for?"

Katiel screeched, "Let him go!"

"Honestly, we do not know him!" Brenna added.

Meanwhile, Anton still managed to look unfazed as he said, "We really did meet yesterday."

Mara whistled a single, shrill note, and several men dressed in ordinary clothes rushed into the curtained-off space, along with one young, black-haired woman wearing a cloak. The woman wrapped her hand around Brenna's upper arm with an iron grip. Before Brenna could react, the woman hauled her up and pinned her elbows together behind her back. Brenna thrust her shoulders backward, trying to wrench her way out of the woman's grip, but it was of no use. In seconds, the woman pulled her to the center of the room and pushed down onto her knees. Brenna cried out in pain as her kneecaps slammed into the hardwood.

Next to her, Katiel yelped as her captor forced her down as well. Then, Dakier cried out, out of her view, and Brenna struggled against her captor's grip enough to glance him over her shoulder. He appeared to have made it to the far end of the room, and now three men were circling him. He had a clear opportunity to take out one of them, but for some reason, he didn't, and his hesitation cost him. Another man wrapped an arm around his neck, and the third lunged out to restrain his legs. Then they dragged him over with the rest of them and pushed him onto his knees next to her.

Katiel's eyes steeled on Mara, who was still holding the knife to Anton's neck. She dragged him over and forced him down to face them. He hit the ground without uttering a sound.

"Let us go!" Brenna demanded. She knew it sounded stupid, but nothing else came to mind.

Mara clenched her jaw. "Not until someone tells me the truth about who you work for."

"We don't work for anyone," Dakier said.

"Then you won't mind losing him." Mara still held Anton and pressed the knife deeper still. It was a wonder he hadn't started bleeding yet.

Truth be told, Brenna didn't know how to prove she didn't know someone. But she didn't want to watch a person die in front of them just because he showed them to this location.

"We honestly do not work for anyone," Brenna insisted. "We aren't trying to trick you."

Dakier added, "It's the truth."

Mara clearly did not believe them. Wordlessly, she drew the knife across Anton's skin, drawing the slightest line of blood.

Anton sucked a sharp breath in through his nose. "Would it make a difference if I told you she wields the ore?"

The knife slipped from Mara's hand and clattered onto the floor in front of Katiel.

Clearly, it made a difference.

18

Katiel

Katiel tried to steady her breath as the knife fell from Anton's neck, reeling at the thought of witnessing a death before her very eyes.

"Who, the Barkurian?" Mara demanded, looking at Brenna.

Anton was calm as ever, despite the bright red line trickling down the side of his throat. The image of him losing his life was still flashing across Katiel's vision.

"No, her." He pointed to Katiel. "She wields the ore."

"What?" Katiel shrieked. She did not know what Anton was talking about, but whatever trick he was trying to pull, it surely would not work out in Katiel's favor when the woman discovered the truth. "I don't know what he is speaking of."

Mara reeled on Anton, but before she had time to say anything, he said, "She doesn't know. But she does wield it."

"She doesn't know?" Mara repeated. "Unheard of."

"What is 'wielding the ore'?" Katiel cut in.

Anton ignored her. "It might be unheard of, but it is true. It's strong in her. When she loses contact with it, she goes down instantly. I saw it for myself."

Katiel had tried to forget about the event yesterday, since it terrified her that she did not understand what had happened.

It had not occurred to her that this stranger might know exactly what had caused her episode.

Mara pushed up her sleeve and lifted her arm to reveal a mark inked onto her inner arm, just above the elbow. It looked like an outline of Katiel's necklace, the same symbol on the seal and the plaque outside. "Are you in the business?"

Anton shook his head. "No."

She looked at Katiel. "Are you?"

"In the business?" Katiel repeated. She assumed they did not mean the wool business.

Mara scoffed impatiently, gesturing to the tattoo again. "Are you marked?"

"No," said Katiel, though she could not believe she was being asked the question. She had already said she did not know what they were talking about. Having a tattoo of some mysterious symbol would surely negate that.

"Then why should I believe you?"

She would have expected Mara to have reeled back on Anton the second Katiel said he was lying, her knife once again pressed against his throat. By this point, his far-fetched, fabricated story should have gotten him stabbed. Instead, Mara was studying him calmly. Despite having no reason to trust him, it was like some deep part of Mara thought he was telling the truth about this.

Katiel hated to admit that a deep part of herself felt the same.

"She keeps it in a necklace."

At Anton's words, Katiel's chin tucked reflexively toward her chest, where her charm was tucked safely down the front of her dress. It was starting to click. She always wore the necklace—always. Father said to never take it off because it was good luck.

It was more than good luck.

To her shock, Mara said, "Release her." The man holding Katiel lifted her to her feet and let go. He backed away quickly, hanging his head in a sheepish apology. Whatever it meant to wield the ore, it was enough to earn their respect. Or lying about it was enough, at least.

"Show me," Mara said. She was looking at Katiel's hand, now spread across her chest.

"I honestly do not know what he is talking about," Katiel said, so quietly that she was not sure if anyone could hear her. But she walked over to Mara, anyway.

"Show me."

Though Katiel had never heard of ore and did not know what it could mean to wield it, Mara obviously took this seriously. And Katiel *did* want to persuade Mara to tell them who had killed King Stefan. She pulled on the chain until the glass pendant was in her palm and held it open for Mara. Brenna and Dakier were still being held down behind her, while Anton stood free. All of them watched with bated breath.

Mara stroked the charm once—slowly, reverently. "Release the others." On command, the man and woman holding Dakier and Brenna let them go, though they did not help them to their feet as the man had with Katiel. "Forgive me," Mara said, looking only at Katiel. "You must understand, I cannot be too cautious these days."

The man who had held Dakier retreated out of sight, but the woman who had held Brenna lingered. Mara gestured for the group to retake their places at the table. They complied, everyone taking a seat except for the hooded woman, who introduced herself as Sera. Now that Katiel looked at her closely, she did not look to be much older than them, maybe nineteen or twenty. She had fair skin and gray, almond-shaped eyes, and her hood covered straight, black hair that blended in seamlessly with her cloak.

This time, Mara did not bother to draw the curtains. Besides them, the place seemed to be deserted. Smoke no longer puffed around the curtains of any of the other booths. Where the few patrons from earlier had vanished to, Katiel did not know, but there had been no crowd to watch the spectacle.

"What does it mean," Katiel asked, "to wield ore?" She met Mara's eyes across the table once they were all back in place. It was an awkward arrangement given what had just happened, but Katiel would ignore it for the sake of the knowledge.

Mara declined to answer her question, instead asking, "What are your parents' names?"

"Katya and Feniel. That is why I'm called Katiel."

"Impossible," Mara scoffed. "Katya and Feniel were legendary wielders. They'd have to be hundreds of years old."

"Your parents are pretty old," Brenna remarked, "but they couldn't be *that* old, could they?"

"What is wielding the ore?" Katiel repeated, frustrated that she seemed to be the only one now who was not following.

Mara opened her mouth to explain, but Anton whispered in Aslen, "*Geführt das Erz.*"

Katiel sucked in a breath through her nose as the realization struck her. Mother had always told her stories in Aslen, and at first, the translation had not resonated. All the magicians in those tales *geführt das Erz*. Wielded the ore.

But the *Geführtchen* had been outlawed from having children for two hundred years. If what they were insinuating was true and she was a seventeen-year-old with the ability to wield the ore, her very existence was illegal on the Continent.

Until about two minutes ago, Katiel would have insisted it was all a mere coincidence. But now she was second-guessing everything she had ever known. She wanted to deny it, but thinking of everything—her necklace, the fainting, all the stories her mother would tell—she could not bring herself to.

Instead, she said, "Perhaps my parents were both merely named after the wielders."

"Wielding is hereditary," Mara argued. "If you can wield, at least one of your parents can, as well."

Katiel considered the information. She could not picture her parents partaking in hobbies more interesting than knitting, much less practicing magic. And she certainly could not imagine them breaking the Kerafin Pact to have a child illegally. She had to change the subject. She could think of her parents more later, if any of this somehow turned out to be true. "Then does that mean you also wield it?"

"No." Mara shook her head. "I am a keeper, loyal to the old ways of the wielders and sworn to protect the ore from falling into the wrong hands. Inigo Farro is one as well. That is why I signed that letter as 'A Loyalist,' as further proof to him."

Katiel reeled at hearing his name spoken aloud, lest anyone hear and accuse them of treason. Then again, discussing her potential ability to wield was treasonous enough. She had assumed the pseudonym 'Loyalist' referred to loyalty to Stefan XIV, but this made more sense, considering Farro would have no fealty to the king of a foreign country.

"As keepers, we campaign for the Kerafin Pact to be lifted," Mara continued. "In the meantime, we ensure the ore never finds itself in the wrong hands." She lifted her arm again, showing the ink etched into her flesh. "That's what this means. I have sworn my life to protect the ore and serve the wielders should they ever return."

Brenna drew her fingertips to her chin. "Then that means, since Katiel wields it, you have to help us?"

Mara looked like she was about to object when someone spoke behind them.

"Precisely."

Katiel whipped around at the sound of the familiar voice, only to see someone she knew well descending the steps in the far corner. "Master Larinne?"

The old woman approached their table slowly. Alfien's grandmother looked like a much older, female version of him, with deep brown skin, widely spaced eyes, and gray hair flecked with black.

"I see you've met my pupil," Master Larinne said, looking directly at Katiel.

"You know these people?" Mara turned from the teacher to Katiel and back. "Does she wield?"

"Yes," Master Larinne answered, "though she does not know."

Anton looked incredibly smug at the phrasing.

Mara stared in disbelief at the teacher. "Why didn't you tell us a wielder lived in the region?"

"To protect her from the law." Master Larinne clasped her hands in front of her. "If too many people know, even among the keepers, the information could slip out. Why didn't you tell me you were meeting with non-keepers in our safe house to discuss some sort of plot?"

Katiel tucked away the information. This was a safe house for people in "the business," as they had called it. Katiel wondered how many people were lurking in the shadows, waiting for someone to snap their fingers or mention something intriguing. Or how many people heard the supposed revelation that she could wield.

"I didn't arrange it," Mara argued. "I thought I had gotten them off my trail. Also, the damage was already done by the time I found you. I couldn't get word in time to stop them."

Master Larinne only scoffed. "I should've known there was a reason you turned up here so abruptly."

Mara hung her head. "I apologize."

Katiel shifted a bit in her seat, having the uncomfortable feeling of eavesdropping, and Dakier let out a forced cough.

"It is no matter," said Master Larinne. She turned to Katiel, who did her best to look self-assured. "Where are you headed?"

"Ballynach," Katiel squeaked out, her attempted confidence failing miserably.

Master Larinne's face flashed with surprise. Clearly, she had not expected Katiel to head into the capital of an enemy nation during wartime, but she declined to say anything against it. "Very well. Mara will accompany you."

Mara looked like she wanted to object, but Larinne's stern expression silenced her. "You should keep her safe on her journey to Ballynach and explain to her what you know of wielding."

"But I know nothing of wielding," Mara said. "I have never seen it done."

"Then Sera can accompany you as well." Master Larinne nodded toward the girl, who stood so still that Katiel had forgotten she was there. "She grew up outside of the Continent and has seen it practiced."

Sera dipped her head. "It would be my honor."

"Very good," Master Larinne responded, curtly implying they should leave at once. "Perhaps she can master it herself by the time she arrives there."

Brenna whooped, triumphant about getting Mara to join them.

Meanwhile, Katiel swallowed hard at the mention of mastering the ore. She was not Jurgen. She was not even Brenna Malley. She was Katiel. And she doubted she would master anything anytime soon.

19

Katiel

As Gunnel carried her away, Katiel soaked in the beauty of Linden's Great Lake one last time. She, Brenna, and Dakier were leaving the town as quickly as they had come, Sera, Simeon, and Anton along with them.

Back at the safehouse, Mara had instructed them to meet her at a fork in the road outside of Linden, one that Katiel and Brenna had already passed on their journey in. From there, they would ride on horseback to Halstat, home to the only rail station in the western region, and take the direct train to Ballynach. The plan suited Dakier as well, since he could take the train from Halstat to Jinensin and then ride to Fort Cajetan to report for the draft. He had not mentioned it to them, but Katiel was fairly certain he was already past his deadline to report.

Despite it being the fastest route for all of them, the journey to Halstat would still take a week, which Katiel worried would be far too long. Though she knew little about warfare, she reasoned that the longer the war went on, the less people would care if the catalyst for the fighting was a hoax. Each side would have a new reason to hate the other once the first battle commenced and they lost their loved ones to the cause. Time was of the essence.

"We make for Halstat within the hour," Anton had said to Simeon when they returned to the suite before the door even shut.

Simeon sat at the same table as before, writing something with a quill while simultaneously reading from the book open next to him. Katiel wondered if he had been doing this the entire time they were at the safehouse.

He looked up when he noticed them come in. His forehead crinkled in surprise as he said, "Hello, Sera."

Brenna's mouth fell open. "You know each other?" She looked at Katiel and Dakier as if to confirm they were equally caught off-guard, which Katiel definitely was.

"Yes," Simeon said, drawing out the word like he found her slow on the uptake.

Brenna reeled on Anton, looking from him to Sera and back. "Then that means *you* two know each other."

Anton stepped away, toward the room he and Simeon were now sharing. "Nothing gets by you, does it?"

"All right," Dakier snapped, whipping around to block Anton's path. "Start talking. I've had enough of your secrecy. Why do you want to come with us?"

"Halstat is our next stop, so it seems advantageous to travel with a group," Anton replied smoothly. Dakier loomed over him, but he did not so much as flinch. "And I would hardly call it 'secrecy.' I was as surprised to see her as anyone. She hasn't informed me of her whereabouts for over a year."

"How do you know each other, then?" Katiel asked him.

Anton looked at Sera, who scoffed. "I dated his sister."

"She left New Drezchy last year when they broke up," added Anton.

"We must leave this town at once," said Sera, while striking Anton with a glare that could slice a man in two. "And for the record, I do not care who any of you other people are or how any of you know each other."

Katiel felt an odd twinge at the implication: since she was the only wielder, she was the one person here who Sera *did* care about. She wondered why Master Larinne had kept her a secret from the keepers, the people sworn to protect wielders. And why Father and Mother had not told her she carried a rare, valuable mineral with her constantly.

She shook the thoughts from her head and focused on packing alongside Brenna and Dakier. Anton ordered a week's worth of food from the hotel restaurant and insisted Katiel pack as much as she wished for her group. She felt like a thief, but she did not have time for a market run, given the time constraints, so she took a sizable amount for the three of them.

In short time, the six of them had regrouped outside the hotel. Anton had offered Mara his horse before she departed for her mysterious errand, guaranteeing his group would have to accompany them as far as the rendezvous point for her to return it. It was a flimsy excuse for joining them, but truthfully, Katiel had no interest in objecting. Anton was clearly more than an ordinary scholar, but he had helped them so far, and Katiel thought his knowledge might come in handy again before the journey was over. Judging by Dakier's forcibly relaxed expression when Katiel agreed that the Drezchy could join them, the farmhand did not share the sentiment.

When they headed into the Imperial's stables, they were met with Kranich, Gunnel, the fine brown stallion Sera had walked over from the safe house, and another ragged horse that could have passed for a mule. It seemed Anton was strangely selective in his expenditures.

Simeon looked at the already tired-looking beast and said, "I am not sharing." Apparently, riding tandem was where Anton's companion drew the line with his fealty.

"Well, I'm not sharing either," Sera retorted.

"You have to," Simeon said. "Ride with Anton. You're both light. It makes no sense for me to share. I'm the heaviest. And just look at what he rented for me."

Though she had not noticed before, Katiel now saw that Simeon had the opposite build to Anton, though they were both Drezchy. Where Anton was slight, Simeon had a thick build down to the ankles, not unlike a tree trunk.

"Brenna can ride with me," Dakier said before immediately amending, "I mean, you can ride with me, Brenna, if you would like." Dakier knew better than to suggest Katiel join him. Gunnel would refuse to move if she saw Katiel riding a different horse right next to her. Plus, there was the matter of him obviously wanting to be alone with Brenna.

Brenna lifted a hand to her cheek in a feeble attempt to hide her blush. "Okay, that would make sense."

"Then that leaves Miss Katiel available." Anton smirked. "Would you allow me the honor of sharing a steed with our resident *Geführtchen*?"

Katiel blinked furiously, flummoxed by his perfect accent coming out of nowhere again. She suddenly wished it were illegal for foreigners to speak Aslen. Or for handsome foreign boys, at least. She tried to look as disinterested as Gunnel when she said, "Fine."

It took them hours to reach the designated fork. Anton seemed to have good balance, because he rested his hands on his own knees throughout the ride, rather than wrapping them around Katiel's waist. It was a good choice on his part. Gunnel could nearly read her mind, and if he made her uncomfortable at all, Katiel fully expected the horse to buck him off. Besides, she had to steer, and his chest grazing against her back was distracting enough.

"Aren't you going to ask me anything?" Anton asked after they had traversed for hours. Silence seemed to unnerve him. Actually, his going this long without speaking surprised her. It was like he had an impulse to fill the space with sound, something Katiel never felt herself but noticed in others.

"What about?" Katiel replied primly.

"Why I'm really heading to Halstat. How I know about the ore. How tall I am. Take your pick."

Katiel glanced back, satisfied that Gunnel had taken enough of a lead to prevent the others from hearing them. She did not know why it would make a difference, but something in her would be mortified by anyone overhearing them, especially in this awkward position. "You find yourself quite interesting."

Anton leaned closer, the warmth of his breath brushing against her hair. "Are you really that uninterested?"

Katiel sucked in a breath through her nose and said, "Yes." She was not one of those people who had a witty response to everything, but in this moment, she desperately would have liked to be. "You are insufferably full of yourself to think otherwise."

"I've been called insufferable often enough that it must be true," he said, "but I hardly think it a crime to be aware of a lady's interests." He let the words sink in before adding, "I tend to be particularly aware."

She let his flirtatious words hang in the air. "Like those girls you were with at Heidel's?"

"You could say that."

Dakier was right. This guy was unbelievable. "Gunnel is going to throw you off if you do not shut up."

"Wie du möchtest." As you wish.

He leaned back again, and after that, they did not speak for ages. She may have wanted to know the truth about his motivations, but asking him was useless. She would have no way of knowing if his answers were genuine. Besides, his smugness was simply too much for her to justify asking him anything.

In the distance, Katiel noticed a familiar boulder by the side of the road. That meant they were approaching the designated meeting place. She gave an inner sigh of relief at the thought of dismounting and being free of her insufferable passenger. There was no way she would share with him the rest of the way to Halstat. She would force him to share with Simeon or talk Dakier into switching passengers if she had to. Unintentionally, she released a tiny giggle at the idea of Dakier's face when he had to ride double with Anton.

"Is something humorous?" Anton asked.

Whatever brief merriment she had was extinguished. "Hardly."

He took a huge breath in, though he managed to avoid touching his chest to her back while he did so. "Katiel, I apologize." He spoke softly, so only she could hear. "Truly, I know how I can be. I was trying to joke, but I didn't mean to make you uncomfortable."

Whatever she had been expecting him to say, that was not it. Hearing him speak in that earnest tone, it was hard to hate him. Still, she knew not what to say.

As if he could read her mind, he added, "I don't want you to hate me."

That was not something she expected him to say, either. Before she could think better of it, she asked what she honestly wanted to know. "Why would you care what I think?"

"We have quite a long way to travel together." The answer was immediate, but Katiel could tell there was more behind it. More he wanted to say. "And honestly, there is something about you. You remind me of someone."

"Someone you know?" Katiel clarified. She did not know what else to say to that.

Katiel could feel him nod behind her, but she kept her eyes steady on the road ahead. It was easier to talk to him like this when she could only hear his voice, though she still could see his hands on his knees in her peripheral. "I will take your bait, then. Why did you want to come with us?"

"The answer to that is simple. Knowledge."

"Knowledge?"

"About the ore, about how to wield it," he said. "I find it fascinating."

Katiel glanced back at him. "Even though you cannot wield it?"

He shrugged. "I crave knowledge. The ore is a substance that can form into anything. I need to learn more about it."

"That's why you followed us once you saw my necklace?" Katiel pressed. She knew it had not been a mere coincidence he was walking outside their hostel.

"Initially, yes," he admitted, "but once I realized you didn't know you wielded it, I wanted you to." As if anticipating her next question, he went on. "I don't know why. I guess it just pains me to think you didn't know it. After all, what could be worse than not knowing the truth about oneself?"

Katiel initially assumed she could think of many worse things, but as she considered it, she found she was coming up short. He seemed to have a convenient answer for everything, and Katiel was unsure if she believed him. Still, she felt she had made the right decision to let him come along. If anyone was going to help her discover the truth about the ore and her parents, it would be him.

A long silence passed between them, though not uncomfortable like it had been for most of the ride. Katiel thought they may not speak again, but when she caught sight of Mara waiting at the fork, she realized she did have something to say.

"By the way, you shouldn't worry about earlier," she said. "I do not hate you, Anton."

He mimicked her again in a most serious tone. "I do not hate you, either, Katiel."

That time, she laughed, and she could not resist sneaking a glance back to see him laughing with her.

It was just before nightfall when they reached the fork, at which time Mara suggested they make camp in the dense woodlands along the road to Halstat. She said if they continued on the well-traversed route, they would come upon an established campsite, and sure enough, they were not far past the fork when Sera spotted one in the distance. It was nothing more than a long-extinguished campfire surrounded by three logs, but it was more than Katiel had hoped for. Within minutes, Sera started a fire with the leftover kindling, before anyone had time to help her. Dakier volunteered to gather wood to keep it going, and Brenna offered to go with him.

Meanwhile, Katiel felt too light-headed to be much help. She was unsure whether it was from the long ride, or from the revelation about the ore and her connection to it, though logic would suggest it was the latter. She took a seat on a log, thinking she would take a moment to gather herself before aiding her friends, but they returned in no time with plenty of tinder for the night.

Reaching into her satchel, she pulled out a loaf of bread from the Imperial, along with some Halstat cheese for Dakier, since it was his favorite. The others were all sitting around the fire, now blazing bright. Brenna and Dakier, naturally, sat next to Katiel, and Anton was opposite her, the firelight flickering across his face and highlighting the sharp cut of his jaw and cheekbones. Simeon was the last to sit down, but instead of sitting next to Anton, as one might expect, he sidled up next to Mara with a goofy grin plastered on his face.

Despite her glare, he awkwardly asked, "So how did you get into this line of work?"

She made a quizzical expression at the others across the fire. "What line of work do you think I'm in?"

Simeon said, "I don't know, a paladin or something?"

Brenna guffawed and, hearing her, Dakier burst out laughing as well. Katiel tried to contain her giggles, but there was never a time that Katiel could hear Brenna squawk like that and not laugh.

Then Anton said, in his stately tone, "To be fair, I was getting a paladin vibe as well," and Katiel was done for. She met his eyes and burst out laughing, and he looked right back at her and laughed as well. Now everyone was at it, and no one seemed to able to stop.

Something about the way Anton's smile spread tight across his face was infectious, and even though he seemed to notice her looking, she did not look away.

The firelight reflected in his deep brown eyes, and for a second, there was no assassination. No letter. No war. She was just a girl on a camping trip, laughing with her friends and noticing a boy who noticed her.

20

Brenna

As the famished group ate around the campfire, Brenna deliberated how to broach the subject of the assassination. She didn't know what might happen to Mara that would render her unable to tell them, but she figured it would be better to get the information as soon as possible. Perhaps a freak campfire accident would somehow affect Mara's memory. One never knew for sure.

"Could you pass me that, please?" Dakier asked, pointing to the stick they had been using to roast sausages over the fire. She passed it to him wordlessly, letting her fingers brush his as she handed it off. His eyebrows rose at the contact, but he fixed his eyes firmly on the fire. It was odd, since she was starting to think he liked her. They'd had a pleasant time chatting throughout the ride and while collecting tinder. Or at least, she thought they had.

"Mara," Katiel said then, "could you please tell us what you know about Inigo Farro and the letter now? We have come all this way to know."

Mara looked like a mouse caught in a trap. Even after traveling together this far, she seemed to consider not telling them. Brenna's breath hitched in her throat, willing Mara to go on.

The keeper started with, "Where to begin?"

Everyone's eyes fixed on her in anticipation, waiting for her to continue.

"How did you discover the assassination was a framing?" Katiel asked gently.

"And how do you know it actually was?" Anton added, less gently.

Mara looked at the group solemnly. "I was working in the office of the Secretary of War in Ballynach. I was a maid—dusting, cleaning dishes, things like that. One night I was working late after the statesmen had gone home, cleaning some of the back rooms that rarely got seen to. I was hoping to get a raise by going above my normal duties." She took a deep breath. "It was a last-minute decision to stay later that day, but a costly one. A couple of people came into the back room, next to where I was cleaning, and I didn't know how to get away without being spotted, because they started talking right away. So I stayed still, waiting for them to leave and trying not to listen. But then, one of them said he planned to assassinate the king."

It seemed even the crickets had quieted as Mara spoke. She was just an ordinary woman who learned of the conspiracy by circumstance. Brenna felt it was eerily similar to her and Katiel's own experiences so far, catching the name in the letter and then getting trapped by the knowledge.

"First, the man I heard said the king would do anything to maintain peace across the Continent, so the monarchy had to be eliminated." The firelight flickered off of Mara's bright eyes as she spoke. She stared at the fire like she might get lost in it. "Then he said the plan was to frame a Tibedese man for the assassination, in order to start a war between Tibedo and Bar

Kur. To my surprise, his was a name I recognized: Inigo Farro. Farro was a lead keeper in Tibedo who spoke at the ward once."

"Forgive me, I am not following," Anton chimed in. "You were a spy for the keepers, but you supposedly hung around and cleaned a political office late at night, just for the sake of hard work?"

"No, I was not a keeper yet," Mara snapped, her eyes shooting daggers at him. "At least, not really. And I was definitely not a spy. A few years ago, when I was nineteen, I started dating someone who worked for the government, and my parents didn't approve of the match. But I was in love, so we dated in secret. When my parents found out, they kicked me out of the house. They said I was a bad influence on my younger siblings."

"Your parents turned you away simply because of who you were dating?" Katiel asked, shocked.

Mara's answer was flat. "Yes."

Katiel appeared flummoxed by the idea, though she said nothing further, and Brenna felt the same. She couldn't imagine parents turning their own daughter away.

"When I got kicked out, I had no money and nowhere to go. I roamed the streets looking for somewhere to stay, and I ended up finding a ward for the needy in Ballynach. The keepers ran it as part of their charitable mission. At first, I wanted nothing to do with the old religion. It seemed mad to believe the wielders still might be out there. But over time, it grew on me. They asked me to take the oath as a keeper, but I found a regular job instead—so I could save up for a place of my own and leave the ward." Mara paused and sucked in a breath, as if she had already said more than she planned to. "Forgive me. I'm getting off track."

Brenna hoped she might tell them something more useful, something that would persuade Jay and the other Barkurian statesmen to end the war. "What happened after you overheard the plot?"

"Right." Mara gulped. "For a day or so, I tried to forget about what I had heard, go on about my work. But of course, I couldn't put it out of my mind. I worried for the king's safety. So the next day I tried to find out more."

Brenna raised her eyebrows. Maybe Anton was right, that her involvement was more than mere coincidence.

"The other man in the conversation, the one who didn't speak—I knew where his desk was. I waited until the next night, after the statesmen had all left, to search the drawers. Sure enough, there was a letter inside, detailing some vague instructions on how to lure Farro into position in order to frame him.

"I had only just opened the letter when I heard footsteps in the hall. I tucked the letter into my apron and tried to make my leave, but it was too late. A figure cloaked in black came into the room. I couldn't see their face, but I just knew, if I didn't act, they were going to kill me. Without thinking twice, I grabbed a pitcher of water and smashed it over their head before I ran. Somehow that bought me enough time to jump out the window. I ran down the fire escape and didn't stop running.

"I fled the room, the building, my home country, everything. Then, I fell back on the only thing I knew could keep me safe: the old religion. That's when I came to A'slenderia, found Master Larinne's safe house in the first town I landed in, and took the oath as a keeper. I went through Fir Kelt on my way, where I mailed off my letter to warn Farro. But it seems it never made it to him."

Brenna had chills as she listened to Mara's tale. The guilt that surged over her was overwhelming—Mara had gone through so much and then nearly died after hearing about the plot to kill the king. When she finally got to safety, there Brenna had come, blowing Mara's cover and thrusting her right back into the throng of danger. She looked at Katiel and saw the guilt mirrored in her friend's eyes. She must have been thinking the same.

"What did they say," Dakier began before clearing his throat and starting again. "What did they say, exactly, about Inigo Farro?" He sounded like it had taken all his nerve to ask.

"They said they had found the perfect person to take the fall for the assassination they were plotting. They said he was perfect—Farro, I mean—because he was Tibedese and well-known in his community, so it would achieve their goal of starting the war. The plan was to plant Farro in a particular location during the Bar Kur Day parade in Ballynach to make it look like he shot the king, while planting their own assassin nearby to take the shot. Since it would remove the king from power and incense the public against Tibedo, this solution would, as they said, 'kill two pigeons with a single stone.'"

"Who is 'they'?" asked Anton. "Who was speaking?"

Katiel added, "If you recognized them."

Brenna wondered if Katiel felt responsible for Mara—responsible for what had happened, somehow—with the way she was speaking. Or perhaps she didn't want to intimidate her too much, lest she not finish the story.

"I only heard one person speaking. I knew his voice." Mara looked from Katiel to Brenna and held her eyes. "General Taregh."

Brenna let out a gasp and turned to Katiel. "That is Jay's boss."

"He is the Secretary of War," Mara said, seeming to find that the more important detail.

To Brenna, it wasn't. It was the fact that Jay reported to him directly. Jay could be awful to live with, but she couldn't believe he would conspire to kill their king or risk lives in war under false pretenses. She couldn't believe he would risk Henred's life.

"And there was another man there whose shoes I recognized, though I didn't hear him say anything," Mara said. "Ellis Fallon."

No, no, no.

Brenna had known Ellis all her life, since he was a childhood friend of Derenta's and Jay's. Even today, Jay and Ellis were as close as brothers, close enough to want to work together in the Secretary of War's office. If Ellis was involved in this plot, then Jay might be as well.

Brenna asked in a rush, "Was Jacoby Donnell there?"

"I didn't hear him, and I would know that nasally voice anywhere."

In any other circumstance, Brenna would have cheered to hear that someone else found Jay's voice annoying. But at the moment, all she cared about was his potential involvement. "When was this?"

"Six weeks ago, now," Mara answered.

Brenna breathed, "Jay was away in the capital then."

Katiel placed a hand on Brenna's shoulder, looking concerned as she asked her, "Do you think he would have stayed silent for such a meeting?"

Honestly, she didn't. Jay could never shut up for any reason, and the more nervous he was, the more he found a reason to chime in. Brenna had gone with him to a state meeting in Fir Kelt once, when he was trying to convince her to go to university in Ballynach and apprentice with General Taregh. She had seen him enter heated discussions with the other statesmen. He wasn't one to stand quietly in the background.

Still, she didn't know if that was enough proof of his innocence to risk taking this information to him. Her heart cracked at the thought that he could be involved. From the way Katiel started rubbing her shoulder, it was almost as if she'd heard the crack.

"Do you still have the letter?" Brenna inquired. To her surprise, Mara pulled it from her apron and passed it over before Brenna had even asked to see it.

The small scrap of parchment was wrinkled, like it had been fashioned into a paper boat or a crane before being used, with all the folds leading to the upper left-hand corner. That struck Brenna as odd, but she shook away the thought. What the page had been used for didn't matter so much as what it said, and she was clearly procrastinating reading it. With a deep breath, she forced herself to focus, even if what she found would incriminate Jay.

E –

You'll be at the clock tower for the parade. Ask for him by name—Inigo Farro. You'll find him at the west gate corner. The others will be at the mill.

P.S. A word of this to anyone, and you'll only wish you were dead with what we'll do to her.

"The others will be at the mill," Brenna read aloud, locking eyes with Katiel. So there were other statesmen involved in this plot, willing to help Taregh with his treasonous plans. "What do we do now?" Brenna asked. She didn't even have to say again that Jay might be one of them. She knew Katiel could tell what she was thinking. "Who can we tell?"

Katiel's face was inches from hers. She grabbed her hand and squeezed. "I say we continue our mission and tell Jay." Anticipating Brenna's question, she said, "I trust it was not him. I have a feeling. Not to mention, it's our only chance."

"Is that really a good enough reason to go on?" Mara argued.

Sera shot her a sharp look. "We continue for Ballynach as the wielder commands."

Katiel's hand shook at the uncomfortable idea of commanding anyone, while Brenna loosed a breath of relief. If Katiel believed Jay was innocent, then she could too.

Brenna wanted to ask Mara why she hadn't told all of this to Larinne, or Sera, or anyone else. But honestly, she felt like she already knew the reason. Mara had already tried to warn Farro, and it had done no good. The king was already dead. The war was already happening. Anyone Mara told could be targeted for the knowledge they possessed. It made sense that she would give up and lie low. Brenna had a mind to do the same, but if Katiel was still in, then she was, too.

So Brenna asked instead, "Is there anything you haven't yet told us? Anything we should know?"

Mara gazed toward the forest as she considered. "There is one thing, something I couldn't place. When he was speaking to Ellis, the general kept referring to 'the boss.' I heard him say that the boss wanted the king dead by a certain date, and that the boss had selected Farro. But the Secretary of War reports directly to the king." She paused as everyone took in the development. "The general follows orders from someone, but I haven't a clue who it could be."

A moment of quiet passed over the group, each person deep in thought. Then Katiel said, "Thank you for telling us all of this, Mara," before standing up and turning toward the makeshift tents—horse blankets that Simeon and Anton had slung over some tree branches. "I am afraid I must retire for the night early. I'm not feeling well."

"Wait," Brenna said, standing as well. "Aren't you at least going to try today? To wield, I mean?"

A look that could only be described as panic passed over Katiel's face. "Tomorrow."

The way she said it, it occurred to Brenna that she may not believe she really could wield. Like maybe she had only gone along with the idea long enough to secure the information they needed.

"I'll try tomorrow."

21

Katiel

"I THINK WE'RE READY to leave," Katiel called to Dakier. He had gotten up early to do a scripture reading, like he did every morning. At home, he often came up the mountain and sat by Katiel while he read. But this morning, he had packed up the tent he, Anton, and Simeon were sharing even though the other two were still sleeping beneath it, which entertained her and Brenna to no end.

Dakier closed his book and pushed away from the tree he had been leaning against.

"Anton told me to tell you that you are a 'wanker,'" Katiel informed him. "Whatever that means."

A flicker of surprise passed across Dakier's features. He did not bother explaining the term, though he did mutter, "What a class act," as he started following her back to the campsite.

Dakier's reaction piqued her curiosity, but she was not about to embarrass them both by asking him the definition. She had a mind to ask Anton, but that might start a mortifyingly awkward conversation depending on what it meant. No, she definitely would not do that.

Shrugging off the thought, she mounted Gunnel—whose saddlebags she'd already filled with supplies—and squeezed her sides to get her moving.

The swift action earned a look from Brenna, who was obviously onto her. It was not like her to be in such a hurry, and it was not only because repeating an evidently foul term embarrassed her. She wanted to get onto the road to have an excuse not to wield. Part of her still believed it was all a misunderstanding, and she did not possess the ability. Now that she had heard she could do it, though, she was itching to try. Her hands started tingling just thinking about it.

The problem with trying, though, was that she might fail. If the mere thought of wielding could excite her like this, she could imagine the disappointment when she inevitably could not.

The ride was an irritating one, although she was spared from the emotional windstorm that was sharing with Anton. Simeon had flirtatiously suggested that Mara share with him for the day's ride, but one look at that poor mule had Katiel hastily inviting her to share Gunnel, which Mara accepted with obvious gratitude. Katiel led the group, since she knew the way, while Dakier and Brenna rode directly behind her. Anton and Sera each rode solo on their fine stallions in the middle, and Simeon trudged along on the sad donkey in the back.

Everyone was feeling chatty, and the constant conversation grated on Katiel's nerves, though she knew she should be grateful. It was a pleasant reprieve from thinking about the ore—about if she could wield it, about if such a thing were physically possible, and about why her own parents would have kept it from her.

The annoying conversation began with Brenna, though it just as easily could have been Anton. Katiel did not know who was worse about talking right when she was at her wit's end.

"Anton," Brenna asked, "how do you rent a horse and then take it all over the country? How will you return it?"

"He doesn't rent them, per se," Simeon said from the back. "He buys them in Afdot Harbor when he arrives on the Continent and sells them when he leaves."

Katiel shot a glance back at her traveling companions. Simeon's words implied they had been to the Continent multiple times, despite the long ocean voyage that came at considerable cost. What teenage boys could afford it? Besides, would they truly risk the treacherous seas multiple times simply for their studies?

"You just keep the money on hand to afford that?" Brenna asked incredulously.

Her friend's candor was refreshing, and Katiel regretted getting impatient with the chattiness. If the group had to talk, at least Brenna would be genuine about it.

Anton smirked. "Yes. Do you plan to rob me?"

Brenna made a face at him. "I have more questions, don't worry. Here's another. This one's for Mara."

Katiel could not see Mara's face behind her, but she guessed the keeper looked less than thrilled.

"Here's what I was pondering," Brenna began. "This supposedly secret society of the keepers etches their mark on buildings and has the members all get matching tattoos. So how exactly are you trying to keep yourselves a secret?"

"Did you ever figure out the truth?" Mara retorted. Without waiting for Brenna's reply, she went on. "We seem to do well enough at keeping to the shadows. Besides, technically, it's illegal to *wield* the ore, but *we* campaign for the wielders to be allowed to return."

Brenna absorbed the answer before firing back with another question. "But what's the point of campaigning for that, if the wielder lines all died off after the Ten Years' War?"

"There are many still out there, who have fled to other lands and other Continents," Mara explained. "They should be able to practice here as well, and build the structures and tools and machinery that people need on this Continent. Some of it can be life-saving."

"I never thought of that," Brenna said, seeming to voice her thoughts aloud. "Some people in Bar Kur believe it's wrong and unnatural to wield it. And others don't believe it is possible at all. They think it's a fairy story."

"Well, the disbelief isn't exactly surprising," Anton chimed in. "Those ore-worshipping Tibedese people are whack jobs."

"Watch it," Dakier said.

Anton rolled his eyes. "Right. I forgot I was traveling with someone who worships the magic book."

"The Scripture." Dakier looked like he might strangle Anton if he were not a pacifist. And if he were not on a different horse.

"Wait, you knew." Realization dawned on Katiel. She slowed Gunnel to come to the farmhand's side. "You knew," she repeated, unable to form a coherent sentence now that she was facing him. "You follow the old religion, and you replaced the necklace when I fell. You knew about my abilities and did not tell me."

Dakier shook his head. "Please believe me, I honestly didn't. Your father told me to never let you take off the necklace, but when I asked why, he said he couldn't explain. I didn't know it was filled with ore, but I acted on a hunch when I saw you go down. Honest."

"But you read the scripture all the time," Katiel pointed out.

"Scripture doesn't say anything about storing ore in glass necklaces," Dakier insisted. "The stories are all parables about greed and power and whatnot. It helps one learn from example to lead a good life. It doesn't go into any detail about wielding the ore."

"He's telling the truth," Mara said. "The scripture does not directly discuss how to wield or needing to remain in contact with it, though it is implied."

Relief swept over Katiel. At least Dakier was not keeping things from her. She was considering how to apologize for accusing him without furthering the awkwardness, when Brenna obliviously interjected in her cheery tone. Katiel settled for meeting Dakier's gaze with a kind expression, and he returned the gesture.

"Okay, last question, I promise," Brenna said while looking at Mara. "Since you're a student of Master Larinne's, then does that mean you know Alfien?"

Mara asked, "Who?"

"Katiel's ex-boyfriend." Clearly, that did not help Mara's memory, so Brenna went on. "Master Larinne's grandson, who lives with her. University student, muscular for no reason, possibly the most arrogant person you could ever meet."

"Oh, right," Mara said with a snap of the fingers. "Yes, I met him once." As if to explain her memory lapse, she added, "I don't think he knows anything about the ore or the business."

A beat passed in silence before Anton asked, "You did say *ex*-boyfriend, correct?"

No one answered him, but Dakier muttered quietly to Brenna, "I hate this guy."

Katiel was glad she was in the front where no one could see her face, because she was grinning like an idiot. If anyone noticed, she hoped it could pass as a reaction to Dakier's joke.

THE FIRST HALF OF the day passed uneventfully. By the time they took a break to eat lunch, Katiel's legs were aching. She took a seat in the grassy clearing that Sera had chosen, and she was about to pass their food sack to Brenna when Mara's abrupt words caught her off guard.

"It's time for you to wield."

Katiel sputtered, "What?"

Mara held absolutely no expression as she repeated, "It's time for you to wield." She was standing above where Katiel sat in the grass, and Katiel looked up at her blankly. "To learn may take time. You are now in possession of dangerous information, and your very existence as a wielder puts you in danger on this Continent. You should begin immediately."

Katiel stole a glance at Brenna, who raised her eyebrows comically and held her palms up to the side.

Katiel stood to face the keeper. Despite riding all morning after skipping breakfast, she suddenly lost her appetite. With a gulp, she asked Sera, "How do I begin?"

But before Sera could reply, Anton asked incredulously, "When was the last time you saw someone wield?"

Sera declined to answer him, but based on the way her eyes flickered, Katiel assumed it had been ages. "You must inhale the ore, breathe it back out, and imagine the substance you want it to become as you mold what you desire with your hands."

"Mold what she desires with her hands?" Brenna asked. "How is that even magic? That's just sculpting."

"You will see," Sera said. "It is not like sculpting. It's an instantaneous process. She can create anything. She can create life."

If Katiel had learned anything from the tale of Jurgen, it was that she would not be attempting to create life anytime soon. Or ever.

Katiel pulled out the pouch Dakier had brought her and opened it for the second time. This time, she understood the fine metallic powder to be the ore, and holding it in her hands felt much more ominous.

"Breathe it in," she whispered to herself, wondering how she could safely breathe in metal powder, and if it could truly form anything. She squeezed a chunk of the ore between her middle finger and her thumb, pressing it tight to lift it out of the bag.

"Careful!" Mara scolded. "Do you know how much that's worth?"

"No," Katiel said. Honestly, she had no idea. "How much should I take then?"

"Take in only a single grain," Sera instructed. "That's all it should take. Breathe it in, then breathe it out. If you are indeed a wielder, it will multiply. It will become something new."

Katiel pressed her finger into the ore gently to pick up the smallest amount she could, and brushed off the excess until she had only one grain left resting on her index finger. She stared at it, nothing but a tiny gray dot against her skin, until the grass beyond her hand blurred. All she was thinking was the same thing over again: Could she truly wield the ore?

Slowly, she brought the finger up to her mouth and inhaled. She waited a second, then exhaled.

Nothing happened.

She looked at Sera, panicked. She should have known. It was not really the ore.

And even if it were, she of all people would not be one to possess the ability to wield it.

"Place your palm out, in front of your mouth," Sera said. "It will guide the ore. Also, you must have in mind what you are making."

"Try something that's already made of metal," Brenna suggested. "Like a horseshoe or something. I bet that would be the easiest."

Sera eyed her over her shoulder. "How did you know that?"

Brenna shrugged. "Because the ore is already metal."

Katiel nodded. If they all believed her capable of this, even Brenna, she could at least try once more. She would make a horseshoe.

She took another gray grain on her finger and placed her hand as Sera instructed, her horizontal palm facing the sky and the heel of her hand just in front of her chin. Hitching a sharp breath in, she waited a moment to steady herself and slowly exhaled.

A glittering cloud of silver dust formed in front of her, angled as if it had come from her own mouth. The shape danced like a windswept ribbon as it grew in size. She moved her hand outward, and the shape followed her hand, hovering above her fingertips and growing continuously. It was already as large as Katiel.

It was pure starlight before her eyes, twinkling and glowing even against the noonday sun. For a second, it was just her and the ore. Like it was calling to her.

Like it was alive.

Then, all at once, it began to fall, but nothing hit the ground. Instead, it vanished.

Before she even had time to turn to them, everyone broke into thunderous applause. It was only then that Katiel realized how quiet they had all been while watching her. She was unsure what the display had looked like to them, but if the clapping was any indication, it probably had looked the same as it had to her.

Brenna rushed up and enveloped her in a hug, squeezing hard and swaying back and forth. Katiel felt something wet hit her shoulder, and it took her a moment to realize that Brenna was crying.

"It's okay," Katiel said, giving her a pat on the back. "It didn't hurt."

Brenna broke away from her and pushed back, before drying her eyes with an unladylike swipe of the sleeve. "I just can't believe it's true." She wiped at her eye again. "I can't believe it's you."

"Neither can I." Katiel forced a small smile before she suggested the group get going. Everyone agreed and headed back to the horses, while Katiel stayed in place. Each person clapped her on the back and said various words of encouragement as they passed, but Katiel barely heard them. The desire to try it again—to feel it again—burned against her palms, distracting her from anything else. The longing was almost as strong as the fear the longing brought her.

"Katiel," Anton said, standing close in front of her and looking down at her. She noticed then that he had hung back after the others had gone. "Since you have to be in contact with the *Erz* constantly, if I were you, I would take some of it before you put it away and hide it with you. In case someone steals the necklace from you again." She forced herself to meet his eyes, smoldering dark enough to see her own blurred reflection in them. "Wedge it high under your fingernails, jam it into your gums, between your teeth, whatever you have to do. Make sure no one can take it from you again."

She peered down at the stores in her hands, briefly considering. When her eyes met his again, her breath hitched in her throat. There was something ablaze in his expression that she could not place.

Katiel did not know why he would help her, but the second he walked away, she did exactly as he had said.

22

Dakier

It was the fourth day on the way to Halstat when Brenna declared the group needed a break, and everyone readily agreed. It was to be a time for Katiel to practice wielding and for Dakier to prepare for combat. As luck would have it, Sera was a skilled markswoman, and she had been giving Dakier pointers to improve his aim during the brief breaks they'd taken so far. Since it helped ease his nerves about what was to come, Dakier was immensely grateful for her instruction.

Today, though, he was even more grateful for everyone to regain their normal hygiene routines. Since they had been traveling for four days straight without bathing, the group smelled terrible. And they still had two more full days of riding ahead of them.

They had found a deep, clear stream to make camp near the night before, so it made for a perfect place to wash themselves and their clothes for the travels ahead. Dakier had brought a spare set of his usual clothes—brown flax trousers with suspenders and a linen shirt. Other than that, he had the pair of boots on his feet and his typical flax summer overcoat. The others in their group seemed to have packed similarly lightly, except for Anton.

The Drezchy had been wearing a different three-piece suit each day so far, some days with a cravat as well. Dakier noticed he had a spare pair of black boots and matching belt with him, too. "In case of formalities," Anton had said. He even donned cufflinks each day, of which he seemed to have a separate pair to match each suit.

"Where do you keep all those clothes?" Dakier asked the question sarcastically, but in response, Anton pulled out a strange contraption from his seemingly bottomless travel bag.

The object looked like some type of fireplace bellows, but when he attached it to the small bag he had just stuffed his nightclothes into and pressed down on the handles, the bag flattened to the thinness of parchment.

"It's a device of my own invention," Anton declared, though he was not looking at Dakier, who had asked, but at Katiel, who did not appear to be paying attention.

Everyone had just taken turns bathing and changing into their spare clothes, and now Brenna was scooping all the discarded articles into a fluffy pile to wash. At Brenna's insistence, Anton was unsealing all of his—as she so delicately put it—"disgusting, freaky shrinking bags,“ so that she could wash his army of suits "before they grew something."

She had just secured the last garment and headed to the stream when Dakier realized his opportunity. "Wait!" he called after her, at a volume that was far too loud for their proximity. More quietly, he said, "I can come with you and help."

Brenna squeaked out a reply he couldn't make out, but she seemed to want him to come from her tone, so he followed her to the water and wordlessly began scrubbing the first garment she handed him. Her eyes widened when he rolled up his sleeves and pant legs to avoid getting them wet, and he wondered if he had done something wrong.

"I'm glad you came with me," she said with a forced-sounding cough. "Anyone else would have slowed me down, I think." He smiled at her in reply, but he knew all the complaining was just an excuse to help people in her subtle way. A way that made people overlook how much she was doing it.

Dakier remembered one time when she visited the valley two or three years ago. She was visiting with Henred that summer, and they were in their own world as usual. They would speak in half-sentences and then abruptly break out into laughter from some joke no one else understood.

Brenna and Henred had been goofing around trying cartwheels on the hill to keep Katiel company with her shepherding, while Dakier watched from a distance as he cleaned the stables. Suddenly, he heard Brenna scream and saw Henred tumble down a steep part of the hill before slamming hard into a rock. Even from fifty yards away, the cracking sound of the impact was loud enough to make Dakier flinch. Henred stood up and said he was fine, but Brenna panicked at the small dot of blood staining the shoulder of his shirt. She yelled to Dakier to ask if he had any bandages. He yelled back that he did, and then she ran to his room to get them.

She got there first and opened the door before he could, tears pooling along her long brown lashes.

"Don't worry, Henred is fine," he said. He hated to see a girl so worried, though he found her concern extremely sweet.

He walked over to his narrow dresser and pulled out a roll of gauze when she made him very aware that he had literally two pieces of furniture and no decorations. "Where are your things?"

"This is it." Dakier gestured to the entire room with a sweep of his arm. "I don't have many possessions."

Brenna looked a bit concerned. He could not blame her. He didn't even have a nightstand, so he'd unceremoniously placed the bedside candlestick on the floor. "Didn't the Salzbrucks supply you with more furnishings than this?"

"No. Well, I mean, they offered," he hastily explained. He would hate to imply anything negative about the Salzbrucks. Her concern was touching to him, though, like she might actually have a word with them on his behalf if she determined a need. "Don't worry. Feniel is the best boss I've ever had, by a long shot."

She quirked a brow like she wasn't convinced before a realization appeared to dawn on her. "Oh, yeah, Katiel said you follow the old religion, right? Minimal living and all that?"

"Yes, I do." Dakier beamed, pleasantly surprised that she remembered. "But I also don't buy much because I'm saving up. I thought maybe if I saved long enough, I could buy the farm one day. Assuming Katiel doesn't want it by then."

Brenna chuckled. "That's a good assumption. I think Katiel might rather live anywhere else. She thinks it's boring."

"I mean, she isn't wrong." He rubbed a hand on the back of his neck. "But even if she changes her mind one day, I could buy a different farm."

Brenna raised one of her red eyebrows. "You really love farming that much?"

He was about to answer when Henred called her name. Remembering what she had come there for, Brenna took the gauze and ran back to Henred, who jokingly remarked, "Let me bleed out, why don't you?"

Dakier had thought that would be the end of it. But later, when he was done with his work and trying to fashion a new belt buckle in the blacksmith shop, Brenna casually leaned her elbows on the half-door, like they talked all the time. "So, before we got interrupted, I was asking why you love farming so much."

"I don't love farming as much as I love being in the mountains," he explained. "It's like there's something soothing in the air. From the second I arrived here, I felt different." Earlier, he thought she was just being polite, but now it seemed like she actually wanted to talk to him, so he went on. "It's a great place for blacksmithing, too. I love creating things in the shop."

"I feel the same," Brenna said, "about the mountains, I mean—not the blacksmithing."

He laughed, but he could tell from her face that she truly understood what he meant. It was like the crisp mountain air made her skin glow. Or maybe she looked like that all the time.

She kept talking and asking about him and Tibedo and his family. To his surprise, he found himself opening up to her, telling her about everything she asked about, even his former life and the sea and all the good and bad things he had collectively tried to forget. He thought it might be because he was nervous talking to a pretty girl, but, really, something about her made him feel comfortable in a way other people didn't. At one point, she mentioned her father's death and the tension it was causing at home. She had seemed embarrassed, like she had forgotten herself and didn't mean to say it, which he understood more than she knew, given the violent stepfather he had gladly left behind in Tibedo. Once it started getting dark, she left the conversation as unceremoniously as she had started it, but Dakier kept thinking about her for a long time afterward.

That was the day he started liking her, now that he thought about it.

Finally, seeing her standing alone at the Bar Kur Day Festival, he had worked up the courage to make a move. To say that had gone horribly wrong was the understatement of the year. Before they got the news about the war, he had thought she actually might try to kiss him.

"So these people are pretty shifty, right?" Brenna said, snapping Dakier back to the present.

"Yes, they seem to be," he agreed.

"Are you worried about Katiel?"

"I'm worried about both of you." At her widened eyes, he went on. "I wish I could stay and travel on with you after Halstat."

"Are you scared?" She didn't have to add the rest of what she meant. *Are you scared to go to war? Are you scared to die?*

"Yes," he confided, hoping she would not think him a coward. "I believe in pacifism. It's taught throughout the scriptures, and I truly believe in it." Not to mention, physically harming someone else might make him more like his stepfather than he could handle. But he didn't say that to her, not now, when she had so much else to worry about. "I don't know that it is moral for me to take another person's life, even to serve my country."

He expected her to say that he wasn't being fair to himself, or that it wasn't the same thing. Instead, she said, "You might not have to."

"What do you mean?"

She shrugged. "You're skilled at smithing and carpentry. Not to mention you're fluent in Endran and good with horses. If you tell them all the things you can do, they might assign you to a specialized role instead of the infantry. Then you could avoid having to make the choice about whether to kill someone or not."

Dakier had never pictured the draft with this type of complexity, but she said it all like it was common knowledge. "How do you know so much about the army?"

"I don't know." She shrugged again, reaching for the last unwashed garment in the pile. "Seems obvious, I guess."

Of course an army on horseback would need a farrier. It amazed him that he hadn't thought of it. "I'm grateful that you're willing to help me, even though I'm Tibedese."

She locked eyes with him, the freckles on her cheeks dancing in the midday sun. "It's because of who you are, Dakier. I will always help you."

For the first time since he had gotten the draft notice, Dakier did not fear what came next.

23

Katiel

After the promising start with her newfound magic, Katiel discovered that wielding the ore into malleable dust, and actually making something out of said malleable dust, were two entirely different matters.

Despite her best efforts, her practice sessions during their stops and after nightfall yielded no results. Each time, the sparkling mist hung in the air before swiftly fading to nothingness. She watched in dread as the cloud shrank with each attempt, knowing the others had likely noticed. Since she was only using a speck each time, her stores appeared untouched, but she could not shake the feeling that she was wasting it.

The dust never felt alive in the same way it had the first time, either. After a few unsuccessful attempts had passed, she wondered if she had imagined it.

She was practicing late in the evening as the others were preparing to rest, and after failing yet again, she swore silently to herself. It was the same story. Breathe in. Breathe out. Become surrounded by beautiful starlight. Starlight falls to the ground with nothing to show for it.

Brenna and Dakier exchanged a worried look as she walked off into the woods with a brief explanation about catching some air, but they needed not worry. While setting up camp earlier, she had noticed a bubbling stream farther into the forest, and it looked like a serene spot to dip her feet in the water and clear her head.

In the twilight, the brook felt even more peaceful as the calming scent of wet leaves filled the air. Katiel perched on a flat rock at the stream's edge, and she had just gotten used to the chill water on her bare feet when she heard a rustling in the distant brush. Someone was speaking in a muffled tone. In a flash, she withdrew her feet from the water and hugged her knees to her chest. Luckily, there was a boulder behind her back blocking her from view, though it also prevented her from slipping away unnoticed.

"No way we should go into Bar Kur now," she heard someone say. It took her a second to register the voice as Simeon's. "They're at war, and I'm sure they won't take kindly to a band of foreigners waltzing through. I say we head home and forget all this."

"We won't be waltzing through," retorted another male voice. Anton's. "We'll be sneaking. There is a difference. But do what you want. Stay or go. I can travel alone."

Silence passed before Simeon questioned Anton with an accusatory tone in his voice. "Why are you bothering with this?"

Katiel wondered what Simeon was implying, but she honestly did not have a guess.

"Don't start with me," Anton said sharply. It sounded like this might be a recurring argument with them. "Sera is going. We should go."

"Why is Sera going?" Simeon asked. "Why is anyone going, for that matter? Ballynach is heavily fortified. It's wartime. Only a band of idiots would try it. Or zealots, in Sera's case."

"Sera is not a zealot," Anton said in an even more hushed tone. "You know that. She didn't take the oath as a keeper."

Katiel furrowed her brow at that bit. What was Sera doing with them, then, and how could she have tricked Master Larinne?

"She's a good actress," Simeon quipped. "She's starting to convince me."

"Un-convince yourself. It's an act."

"But why?"

Katiel could not make out the reply. Anton's voice grew muffled, like he was speaking into his hand, and then he said, more clearly, "That's what I intend to find out."

Katiel turned her head away from them to face out over the water once more. Some foolish part of her had hoped Anton was coming along simply because he liked her and wanted to help. She hoped that, like her and Brenna, he cared that a war started for no good reason and that people would die for nothing. She knew that was naïve, though. He was not some altruistic student out doing charity work.

Guilt flooded over her as she recognized how selfish she was to even care what he thought about her. Soon people would lose their lives in battle, if they had not already. She should focus on their goal, on the mission. Focus on ending the war.

"Spying, Miss Katiel?"

The words jerked her out of her guilt and out of her thoughts completely. Anton was stepping across the smaller rocks at the edge of the water, balancing easily even in his fine shoes. He wore a navy, leaf-patterned double-breasted waistcoat over a white shirt and black trousers.

She stretched her legs out straight and flattened her skirts. "Please do not call me that."

"Apologies, my lady." He sat next to her, cross-legged on the large rock, and unbuckled his boots, presumably so he could soak his feet in the stream with her.

She looked pointedly at the water and not at him removing his garments. "Do not call me that either."

"A lady?" He smirked. "All right. What would you have me call you?"

"Geführtchen."

She said it without thinking, trying to keep up with his razor wit, but the second she said it, she recoiled with embarrassment. She dared a glance at Anton, whose mouth was curled up in a devious smile.

"Spying, *Geführtchen*?" He was obviously messing with her, but she felt awkward. She should have just coughed to announce her presence when she heard them talking. "Don't worry. Simeon is an oaf. Only I noticed you lurking around."

"If you noticed me there, why did you keep talking?"

Anton shrugged. He had removed his shoes and socks and rolled his trousers up to the knee, with his far leg dangling over the water and the other bent in front of him. "I thought you should know that Sera is not who she claims."

"Why do you care?" asked Katiel. "Why would you care about me?"

He shrugged again. "For whatever reason, I'm drawn to you."

Katiel sighed. "It's likely the ore you are drawn to."

His eyes flashed, and she realized he had picked up on the truth she had not intended to imply: that the ore constantly called to her, ever since the first time she expanded it.

"No," he said, his voice gentle yet firm as he inched closer, "it's you. How do you think I noticed you wore the necklace?" His shoulder brushed against hers. "It's not beneficial for someone with your ability to be so beautiful. It'll lead everyone to discover your secret."

Her heart thrummed rapidly in her chest at him saying she was beautiful. She wanted to know if he really thought it or was only saying words. Instead, she whispered, "It is not a secret."

As quietly as she had, he whispered back, "It should be." Her pulse thrummed madly at his hushed tone. The intensity in his gaze made her think he might try to kiss her. "Katiel, the day after tomorrow, when we go into Bar Kur, we may not get out. Foreigners heading into a hostile nation in wartime—it's dangerous. Especially for an A'slenderian. And especially for a wielder who cannot yet wield. Things could go wrong."

Katiel watched the surface of the stream as it rippled over a jagged rock. She did not know what to say. She knew traveling to Bar Kur would be dangerous, and part of her wanted to turn back. But most of her wanted to keep going.

It was similar to the way she felt about Anton. Even though he was obviously concealing something, she felt an undeniable comfort in his presence. Still, she was curious about the conversation she had overheard between him and Simeon. "You said before that Sera is your sister's girlfriend?"

"Ex-girlfriend," he clarified with a slight edge. Things must not have ended so nicely between them, then.

"Are you and your sister close?"

"Yes," he said, "we're almost the same age, but she is one year older, and she never lets me forget it. Simeon is my closest friend, but my sister and I used to be even closer. People used to joke about us being conjoined—we were that inseparable."

That sounded a lot like Henred and Brenna. "And she didn't want to come with you to the Continent?"

Anton shook his head. "She can't travel far—at least, not easily." When Katiel furrowed her brow, he went on. "She was born with a condition that makes her unable to walk." Katiel let out an inaudible gasp. That sounded terrible to endure. "At home, I try to look after her. I worry about her when I'm away."

Hearing him talk about his sister so fondly, like Brenna talked about Henred, made her heart swell. Since Katiel never had a sibling to keep her company, it made her happy to hear other people appreciate theirs. Every day she was near him, Anton seemed less like a smarmy scoundrel and more like an ordinary boy. Worrying about his sister made him seem more ordinary than ever.

As he watched the water, his lips curled up at the edges, and the bright moonlight caught on his cheekbones and on the hollow of his neck. The light danced over his stately profile, highlighting the way his skin pulled taut over the razor-sharp edge of his jaw.

He cut his eyes down at her sideways.

"What are you looking at, *Geführtchen*?"

An unfamiliar boldness came over her when she answered. "I think you know."

That was when he kissed her. He wrapped his hand around the back of her neck and gently drew her toward him. And when their lips met, everything else disappeared. All the emotion and guilt and pain evaporated. It was just her and him, spinning around in the blackness.

Katiel wrapped her arms around his neck, and his hands pressed into her back, pulling her closer. She might be losing track of time and space and how many times she had tilted her head to the other side, but she loved it. She might not trust him, but it was like they were made to be in contact with each other. She had secretly kissed Henred once, years ago, and kissed Alfien a hundred times, but she had never known it to be so natural. Or so encapsulating.

She moved downward, letting her lips graze the concave part of his sharp jaw, before she kissed the part of his throat she had been watching. He let out a ragged breath and pressed his fingertips into her waist at the contact, so she kept on until he tilted his head down to meet her lips once more.

After what felt like forever, Anton pulled away slightly, keeping his face close. He was looking at her with his wide, dazzling smile, and for a second, she had the strange urge to kiss him again. That was until she noticed how she was sitting. She was in his lap, with her knees apart on either side of his torso. Hastily, she leaped to her feet and smoothed out her skirts in one swift motion.

With a huge smirk plastered on his face, Anton picked up his boots and began putting them back on, and she followed suit. She did not know exactly how long they had been gone, but she suspected it was long enough for Brenna to pick up on things and hound her for details.

They had finished righting themselves and were about to head back when a thought occurred to Katiel.

"Could you taste the ore?"

"No, I couldn't." He beamed like he found the question particularly amusing. Or maybe he was amused that she took his advice to hide the ore between her teeth. "What does it taste like?"

She shrugged.

"Metal."

But her answer was not true. It tasted like everything.

24

Brenna

The days wore on, and as quickly as she had left Linden, Brenna found herself around another campfire with the group, high on a hill overlooking the city of Halstat. From the road next to their campsite, the sparkling lights of the city twinkled against the night sky. Sparks crackled from the fire, and fireflies whizzed through the clearing. Even the smoky taste of roasted sausage had grown on her during their week of travel.

In any other circumstance, Brenna would have found it to be a magical setting. But being their last night in A'slenderia before heading into Bar Kur, nerves wracked the traveling party. The tension in the air burned hotter than the fire before them. Tomorrow, Dakier was heading off to the front, and Katiel, Anton, Sera, and Simeon were heading into foreign territory during wartime. Despite returning to their home country, the Barkurians fared little better. Mara had fled with her life for the information she possessed, and Brenna could be charged with treason for her continuous association with Katiel and Dakier, along with now possessing the same damning information.

Brenna couldn't let the glum mood remain, though, not on Dakier's last night with the group and Katiel's last night in her homeland. Thankfully, she had a fool-proof plan to brighten everyone's spirits.

"Let's tell stories."

Someone groaned.

Sera said, "Absolutely not."

That was not the reaction Brenna was hoping for. She, for one, loved telling stories around a campfire. Or she figured she would, if she'd ever had the chance to before now.

"Ghost stories?" she ventured.

"Ooh, I've got one," Anton said, rubbing his hands together maniacally.

Mara rolled her eyes. "Of course the Drezchy would have a ghost story at the ready."

He turned to Brenna with one of his thick eyebrows raised. "Do you want to hear it?"

"Absolutely." Brenna did not know a single story from New Drezchy, and she would love to change that. It was rumored to be a particularly eerie place.

"This is the true story of the Ghost of Vincencim Bridge," he began, leaning forward so the firelight cast harsh shadows upon his face. "Our tale starts, as tragedies often do, with a young man. He was handsome, had a rapier wit—"

"Do not tell me you are speaking of yourself," Sera interjected.

"—and was very poor."

"Never mind."

"The young man tended the clocktower next to Vincencim Bridge—"

"So far, the only scary thing is how bad this story is," Simeon said, which got everyone laughing.

Anton snatched Simeon's spectacles off his face. "If you don't shut up, I am going to tell everyone you don't actually need spectacles."

"But I do!" Simeon protested as he squinted hard, which made everyone laugh again.

"What happened next?" Katiel asked, biting her lip as she leaned toward the fire. At least one person other than Brenna was interested in the story. Then again, Katiel might be more interested in the boy telling it.

Anton proceeded with a rather long-winded tale about a man called Lubomir being tricked by the Ghost of Vincencim Bridge, which resulted in his entire family's death. "In despair," he concluded, "Lubomir flung himself over the side of the bridge and drowned, taking the place of the previous ghost. In fact, his ghost still haunts Vincencim Bridge to this day." He took a dramatic pause. "And I know, because I've seen him."

"That is the stupidest story I have ever heard," Sera said. "The water beneath that bridge is three feet deep. He wouldn't have drowned."

Anton pulled a face at her.

Brenna chirped, "Anyone else?"

"I have one," Katiel said in her shyest whisper. "A story, that is. It's not particularly scary."

Dakier leaned toward her with his forearm against his knee. "Let's hear it."

"There was once a mountain guide named Oskar Spyri," she began. "He was a young man, and inexperienced, so he was terrified when his unit assigned him to guide Queen Sylka through the Northern Mountains. It was early spring, and he had heard rumors that the *Schattenwulf* would be hungry from the long winter. The other guides laughed at him, saying that the *Schattenwulf* was only a legend, but he couldn't shake the fear."

Katiel's breathy voice had a haunting quality to it that Brenna had never noticed before. Even Sera and Mara now listened intently.

"At night while the others slept, Oskar kept watch, listening for the *Schattenwulf's* howl. And on the third night of their journey, he heard it. The piercing cry echoing through the mountains was nothing like an ordinary wolf's, for the *Schattenwulf* was three times the size of one, impossibly fast, and could kill ten men with a single swipe of its paw. Oskar called out to warn the others, but the *Schattenwulf* was upon their camp in a second. It moved so swiftly that it disappeared as it ran, only to reappear again.

"When Queen Sylka stepped out of her tent to see the cause of the commotion, the beast ran toward her. Her guards fired their arrows, but it was of no use. The creature was too fast. But Oskar was not willing to give up, for he was a *Geführtchen*. His instincts had told him something was wrong, and he would be wrong to deny his instincts now. So with a great cry, he called the *Erz* to him from within the mountains themselves, and *geführt das Erz* from the soul, forming an arrow that would always land true to his aim. So that when he struck, he shot the *Schattenwulf* in the heart." Katiel looked up and smiled at everyone enraptured by the tale.

"So what happened then?" Mara asked.

"They say the *Schattenwulf* crawled away, never to bother humans again," Katiel said. "But others say he's still out there, deep in the mountains, waiting to strike again."

"That was a great one, Katiel," Brenna praised. "I have chills."

"So which one of them turns into a ghost?" Simeon asked.

"That was a decent story," said Mara. "Let's end on a good one."

"Agreed." Sera nodded. "No more stories."

"Wait!" Brenna interjected. "One more. It'll be quick."

Mara rolled her eyes again. "Fine. It's not like anyone here should practice wielding for the day ahead."

Katiel looked sheepish at that, but Brenna was unfazed. "It's quick. Once upon a time, a young man was drafted into a war." Brenna avoided looking at Dakier. She truly had heard this story before, but there was an obvious reason she wanted to tell it. "He was frightened, but a girl from his village gave him a lock of her hair for good luck, and when he went to battle, no bullet could touch him. The end."

Simeon tossed his hands in exasperation. "That wasn't even remotely scary!"

Anton shrugged. "I guess Drezchy are the only ones who can tell ghost stories."

"True, but that does not include you," Simeon told his friend matter-of-factly. "Allow me to demonstrate how a truly terrifying ghost story is told."

Anton grinned, and Sera looked like she might smack both of them, but Brenna was hardly paying attention. She was watching Dakier, who leaned forward to make eye contact with her past Katiel. He stood up slowly and gave a small jerk of the head to suggest he wanted her to follow. She waited a second before heading after him, but it seemed Simeon's story really was good, because no one paid attention to her.

She followed Dakier back to the tents, which the group had set up deep in the woods to give cover away from the clearing. "Brenna, I—" Dakier started, turning to her.

"Wait," she said, "come in here." She walked into the tent she and Katiel were sharing, slung over a particularly high tree branch, and he followed, ducking low to clear the opening in the canvas. After lighting a candle, she reached into Katiel's bag and pulled out the spool of cornflower-blue yarn Katiel kept for hair ribbons. "Do you have a knife?"

Dakier reached into his pocket and produced one of those A'slenderian contraptions that served not only as a knife but also as twenty other tools. He flicked out the blade before handing it to her. She cut off a piece of yarn before pulling her hair over her shoulder and chopping off a three-inch-long chunk. Dakier's brow lifted in shock, and she shrugged. "It really is a superstition for good luck in Bar Kur."

Brenna took the yarn and tied it around the lock of hair, securing it with a fancy four-looped bow she had learned as a kid. It was supposed to resemble a four-leaf clover, for luck. She'd left a lock for Henred tied the same way on her nightstand before she'd left for A'slenderia, in case he went off to the war. She wondered if he'd taken it with him, considering how things left off between them.

"I wanted you to have it," Brenna said as she held the bundle out to Dakier, "in case it helps you come back safe."

Instead of taking the lock from her like she expected him to, Dakier took her hands in his. "Brenna." She looked up at him, her eyes scanning his face. Standing this close, she had to tilt her head all the way back to make eye contact. He took a steadying breath, like he wasn't sure what to say, before his words came out in a rush. "Brenna, I have been in love with you for years now, and I know I waited until the last possible day to tell you, but I want you to know it now. I want you to know, in case"—he took another deep breath and squeezed her hands, still gazing down at her intently—"in case I don't make it back."

Before she could think better of it, Brenna lifted her face to his and kissed him, rising to the tips of her toes and pressing her hands into his for support. She let her lips linger against his for a moment, before she lowered back down and looked at him with a huge, involuntary smile. Dakier briefly smiled his wide smile back at her, before it vanished into something else. It was the same look he had at the festival under the twinkling lights. Before the world interrupted everything she and Dakier were supposed to be.

Suddenly, Dakier lifted her by her thighs, and she wrapped her legs around his waist and kissed him again, deeper this time. Her mouth opened against his, and she tangled her hands in his hair. He gripped her thighs tighter.

After a while, he pulled back and nodded toward her sleeping pallet, already spread out on the grass. "May I?"

"Yes," she said once it registered that he meant to lay her down there, unable to contain her smile. "Definitely."

He started kissing her again, and lowered her onto her back like she weighed nothing. Propped on his elbow above her, he took off his coat and laid it aside, but he didn't try to take off any of her clothes or mess with her skirts, which she was grateful for. He switched between pressing his lips against hers and against her neck, while her hands explored the taut muscles of his back, writhing under her touch. His smile tugged at the edge of his lips between kisses, sexy and warm and longing, and she had no clue how long it had been when he moved back onto his elbow, hovering over her while his face remained close.

"I had better go," he whispered. "Early train and all."

"Of course," she said, nodding emphatically to hide how much she did not want him to.

They both stood up, and Dakier replaced his coat and slipped the lock of hair into the inner chest pocket. But instead of leaving, he lingered by the flaps of the canopy like he didn't want to part either. So she asked him, "In your religion, do you pray for people?"

"Yes," he said, smiling in such a boyish way. "You don't even have to say it aloud. You can think what you want the Creator to hear, and he'll hear you."

"Then I'll pray for you," she promised. "I'll pray for you to come back safe."

At that, he took her face in his hands and kissed her again, standing there with the canopy open, somehow even more fervently than before. When he broke away, he stepped halfway out of the tent and said, "Good night, Brenna."

She replied, "Good night," and then he was gone, and she was standing there alone. It occurred to her that Katiel might have come by to sleep, seen them, and left to find somewhere to be in the meantime.

Brenna seriously hoped she hadn't, though. Because now that she looked at it, she realized that had been Katiel's sleeping pallet.

25

Katiel

When Katiel caught sight of the famous Halstat Station in the distance, she realized she had been blind. The black metal train station wove into the air in a pattern far too intricate for any smith to fashion. It was obvious it had been wielded of the ore. She wondered if one of her parents made it, or if there were others out there like her, creating magnificent things from the shadows. Considering the knowledge she now possessed, it felt like she had been blind to everything.

The group arrived in Halstat at dawn, and the mood was more mixed than ever. Sera was emotionless as always. Anton seemed ecstatic, like he was drunk on adrenaline, and Simeon seemed very annoyed to have to deal with a drunk person at this hour. Dakier was doing a horrible job of not acting guilty for fiendishly kissing her best friend in their shared tent, an event Katiel would never mention to them for fear of combusting in mortification. She did not mind them getting together, though they could have used Brenna's bedroll instead of hers. In fact, she enjoyed the idea of her two closest friends dating. She had seen it coming, and she now regretted not making a bet on it with anyone other than Alfien, since she could not claim her victory with him now.

Besides, she had used the time spent avoiding the tent to practice wielding. She had been unsuccessful once again, but she preferred practicing without an audience. Brenna seemed to mistake Katiel's frustration with the ore for frustration at her, though, because this morning she was being overly nice. She had offered to pack up everything for both of them and insisted they should ride Gunnel to the station together "for old times' sake," which Katiel was grateful for. Not only was it nice spending time with her best friend, but she did not particularly want to ride with Mara at the moment.

Ever since she had woken, Mara was frantic, like she could spiral into a screaming panic at any second. Katiel remembered her arguing with Master Larinne about coming. At the time, she had thought that was just the way their relationship was. But now, she wondered if it was something else. Katiel told herself she would talk to her right after they saw off Dakier.

Walking through the train station was like walking beneath a giant spider's web. A slew of black metal canopies shielded travelers from the elements as they waited, all spun with elaborate latticework that reminded her of the finishings on The Imperial's balconies. Katiel wondered how long it would take a seasoned wielder to spin the entire station out of nothing. Probably minutes.

Early as it was, the station should have been abuzz with activity. Instead, only a few people milled about the large atrium, the war having postponed most people's travels. As she surveyed the timetables and paid her fare, Katiel realized a bit too late that they were lucky to get seats at all. There was only one train leaving today for Ballynach, and the single train to Jinensin left in just a few minutes.

After everyone purchased their tickets, Anton, Simeon, and Sera ventured off to the marketplace at the far end of the station to sell their steeds, while Mara offered to secure temporary lodging for Gunnel so Katiel and Brenna would have time to send off Dakier before their own train departed. Though Katiel hated leaving her horse, she did not want to bring Gunnel into Bar Kur. She gave the horse's neck a tight squeeze before Mara took her, with a promise that she would be back soon to bring her home.

Dakier walked Kranich through the station, since he was bringing him to the fort as Father had suggested. They waited while he loaded him into the livestock car before heading to the passenger cars. As she read the sign *Departures for Jinensin*, Katiel surprised herself by tearing up before he'd even gone.

"Goodbye, Katiel," he said, and before she had time to recognize what he was doing, Dakier enveloped her in a tight hug.

Katiel sniffled as she squeezed him back. "Promise me you will come home to us. To your family."

"I will." It was a promise he could not possibly guarantee, but hearing it helped somehow. Perhaps if he promised, he would try even harder to come back to them.

He turned to Brenna, and they hugged and said quick goodbyes, and then he was off. Right when he set foot on the steps leading into the car, the steel box began to crank along the tracks, thick smoke billowing overhead.

Dakier held tight to the rail and waved at them from the top of the stairs, and Brenna was smiling her biggest smile, with one fat tear rolling down each of her flushed cheeks. "You could run and go kiss him one last time," Katiel suggested, "if you want to. There's still time."

But Brenna shook her head, watching as he crept out of view. "No, I don't want to." At Katiel's inquiring expression, she explained, "I don't want it to be the last time."

Katiel was about to ask what she meant when the clattering of running footfalls distracted her.

"We are about to miss our train!"

They turned in the voice's direction to see Simeon running toward them, flailing his arms in the air, with the others not far behind.

Brenna and Katiel wasted no time rushing after them. Brenna panted from the back of the group, "It wasn't supposed to leave for over an hour yet."

"The time listed for this ride was in Barkurian time," Mara explained. "This week, while we were traveling, the clocks turned back for the summer solstice."

"I hate this Continent," Sera grumbled.

Thankfully, the platform for Ballynach was close, and they all scrambled into the passenger car and down the hall to the last cabin. But as she was about to slide into the cabin behind Brenna, Katiel noticed Mara was no longer behind her.

She rushed back down the hall to find Mara frozen on the steps, visibly shaking. The train would start moving at any moment, but it looked like she was considering jumping off. Katiel placed a hand on her shoulder and asked in her calmest voice, "Mara, what's wrong?"

"Just nerves," Mara said unconvincingly.

"It's not too late to change your mind," Katiel told her. "You don't have to come with us."

"Yes, I do." She looked down dejectedly, sounding almost pained when she said it. "I need to be with you to tell the Barkurian Cabinet what I heard."

Brenna popped her head around Katiel's, seeming to have noted the absence as well. "Are you sure you're all right? You seem sick or something."

Katiel nodded her agreement. She really did look sick, and she only faced the return to Bar Kur because of her. Because Mara was a keeper, and she was a wielder, and Master Larinne had instructed her to.

"It's your choice," Katiel reassured her. "You don't have to continue along with us if you don't want to."

It obviously was not the right thing to say because Mara's quick breaths somehow became even quicker. The train started rolling, achingly slowly as Dakier's had, and Mara's eyes darted frantically between Katiel and the exit. It seemed the choice terrified her even more than whatever awaited her in Bar Kur.

She looked back at the platform, like she was picturing the jump, before turning back to Katiel as if a thought had suddenly occurred to her. "Katiel, I should've told you earlier. Your thoughts are too jumbled to wield. I watch your eyes. Your mind flickers all over. You must single-mindedly focus on creating something new when you wield. Focus on what you are trying to create."

"You'd better leave if you're going to," Brenna said in a rush. "We're leaving the platform."

It seemed Brenna felt just as bad about luring Mara out of hiding as Katiel did, especially since they both knew they needed Mara to convince Jay that the assassination was actually a treasonous plot. But what she still did not understand was why Mara had gotten so panicked, so suddenly. Why she had left Bar Kur immediately, instead of trying to warn the authorities about the plot, and why she had not told Master Larinne earlier about General Taregh and Ellis Fallon.

Wait. Ellis Fallon—that had to be it. Katiel had been blind about more things than just the ore. She should have recognized it sooner.

Mara had said she left home because she was dating someone in the government. She heard Taregh's voice, but she recognized Ellis from his shoes alone. She was protecting him. And now she was terrified of turning him in.

"Mara," Katiel breathed. "Is it Ellis?"

Mara tightened her white-knuckled grip on the metal handrail. "What about him?"

"You love Ellis," Katiel ventured. "You're panicking because we're heading back to Bar Kur, and you don't want Ellis to be tried for treason."

Brenna gasped from behind her.

Mara's eyes now darted in every direction except for Katiel's, and she gulped before saying, "Yes."

Brenna gasped again. "But you must turn him in! It's the right thing to do."

"I know," Mara said, then paused like she was about to argue before deciding against it. "I know."

"We need you to tell Jay what happened and what you saw," Katiel told her. "We need you with us. But Jay and Ellis are friends. Maybe he will go easy on his friend, somehow."

Mara nodded, moving closer as if to follow them to the cabin. "You are right. It's about ending the war, not about

Ellis." When she said his name, the corner of her mouth turned up the tiniest bit, and Katiel was certain that it was the first time she had seen Mara looking genuinely happy.

That look was all Katiel could think of as they made their way into the cabin. The journey to Ballynach would take all day, placing their arrival well after sunset. Katiel, Brenna, and Mara sat along the bench facing the others, with Katiel directly across from Anton, and stowed their belongings overhead. The only belongings they kept with them were Katiel's stores of the ore—tied to her waistband and tucked out of sight—and the letter, which Katiel knew Brenna kept on her person.

Brenna, naturally, had brought a set of playing cards and said they ought to play Wielders, "for obvious reasons," even though they had six people and Wielders was a four-player game. None of the Drezchy had ever played before, but after only a round, Anton and Sera caught on and annihilated everyone else to the point that it was almost not fun anymore. Except it *was* fun, because Anton wanted to be Katiel's partner, which had both the benefits of winning repeatedly and getting to send silent signals to Anton.

After playing for hours, they finally called it quits. Anton and Simeon pulled out textbooks to read, Mara took out a knife to trim her nails, and Sera took an unsettlingly cat-like nap where she slept while sitting straight up. Brenna dozed off, too, in a decidedly less graceful position. She leaned against the window, her face emitting the faintest squeak as it slid down the glass.

Katiel was in no mood to read or sleep as the nerves coursed through her. She believed in Brenna's plan, and she believed they could make a difference, but Ballynach was the heavily fortified capital of a nation at war. They could not predict the risks they were facing.

As the others rested, Katiel watched the mountains beside the window. This portion of the tracks cut into the mountain, evidenced by the vertical rock face only a few feet from the train.

Suddenly, Katiel heard a commotion farther up in the train. She shook Brenna awake. "Do you hear that?"

A symphony of high-pitched screams bellowed through the car, and everyone's heads snapped to attention.

Sera peered out the window and said matter-of-factly, "The bridge is out up ahead."

Brenna's hands flew up to her hair. "The bridge that has the tracks on it?"

"Yes," said Sera, but everyone was already craning their necks out the window to see for themselves.

Visible now as they rounded the bend, the bridge ahead marked the border between A'slenderia and Bar Kur. It was an intricate metal latticework that had almost certainly been wielded from ore, a structure that suspended the railroad tracks high above a deep gorge. By the far edge of the gorge, the tracks cut off in midair.

The train's brakes screeched with all their might, but it was futile. From their place between the cliffs, the conductor did not have enough time to see the damage and stop a train this size. The vehicle would go over the edge.

"We could jump," Simeon suggested.

"We would hit the cliff faces," Anton argued.

Simeon amended, "We could jump *into the water,* once we are above the river."

Anton shook his head. "It's a hundred-foot drop."

Sera said nothing, instead opting to slide open the window and fling herself out of the train car, somehow aiming her body upward through the narrow gap and landing atop the cabin. Several loud clangs sounded from above as she sprinted across the metal roof.

"Is she running on top of the train?" Brenna shrieked.

"Yes," Anton yelled back. "She'll jump onto the tracks once she reaches the last car." The screaming from the other cars grew louder.

Brenna cried, "I cannot do that!"

It might have been comedic were they not hurtling toward their impending doom.

"Katiel, wield the missing tracks across to the other side," Simeon said, the panic rising in his voice.

She hesitated for only a second, and Brenna said, "You can do it. I know you can do it. Metal is the easiest."

She knew she could not do it, honestly, she knew, but there was no time to waste. She flicked a piece out from under her thumbnail and blew, guiding a vast silver dust cloud out of the car. They were over the gorge now. This was her only chance. The shrieks of the other passengers grew as they caught sight of the strange formation gathering around the missing tracks. The dust took shape—it actually took the form of the tracks she wanted for a moment—before it fell into nothing.

"There's no time," Anton said as he hastily untied the curtains that blocked their train car from view of the hall.

"What could you possibly be doing?" Simeon sputtered.

Anton ignored him. "Can you all swim?" Everyone nodded, and he said, "Sit on the right-hand bench."

Unsure what else to do, Katiel followed the order, the others wedging in on either side of her, and in a quick motion Anton tied the group of them to the back of the bench with the rope from the curtain. He pulled it so tight that Katiel lurched forward, while deafening screams echoed across the gorge as the engine went over the edge. It would be mere seconds before they followed.

"Do not panic," said Anton. "When we make contact, the car will immediately fill up with water. You cannot panic. Swim out the window, look for the sky behind the water, and kick your feet off the car to reach the surface."

No sooner had he said it than the rest of the train went off the tracks, and there they were, suspended in the air between their countries, bracing themselves for a hundred-foot drop in a train car.

26

Dakier

From the outside, Fort Cajetan was exactly as Dakier had expected. The fort stood in the middle of a grassy field, with a single dirt path leading up to it. A massive wall of logs surrounded the compound, each log's end sharpened to a point to create a spiky rim across the top of the barricade. A Tibedese flag flung violently in the wind above the gate, where someone had sloppily carved the fort's name into a horizontal plank of wood.

The clang of metal against metal rang out from inside the wall, doing nothing to steel Dakier's frazzled nerves. He had ridden ceaselessly from Jinensin, but it hardly mattered. It was well past the date listed on his notice to report for the draft. He shuddered to think what the punishment would be before scolding himself. Tibedo was a peaceful culture. They wouldn't give out lashings or cut off fingers like the Drezchy forces were rumored to. Surely the officers in charge would understand once he explained how far he'd had to travel. At least, he hoped that would be a passable excuse—and that they wouldn't realize he was still days later than he'd had to be.

He dismounted Kranich as he approached the gate, where an armed guard checked his draft notice and wordlessly waved him on. Inside, the compound was massive, with expanses of raw dirt stretching between the long, rectangular buildings, dispersed across the space like matchsticks in a box. The soldier standing guard waved him toward a building to the right, and Dakier gulped hard as he approached the intake booth with Kranich in tow.

There were two men in drab brown army uniforms seated at the table, both of them with a copper skin tone and black hair, the same as everyone in Cajetan. The same as he had.

"Here to report for the draft," Dakier said in Tibedese, before recalling that this was a military establishment and adding, "Sir."

"Name," the man on the right said blandly.

"Dakier Mandia."

"Age."

"Seventeen."

"Draft notice."

Dakier produced the notice from his pocket, but the man did not so much as read the page. Rather, he shoved a bundle of fabric into Dakier's outstretched arm, crumpling the notice beneath it. Dakier could only assume it was an infantry uniform. That must be his dismissal, then. Brenna's advice about mentioning his skills was sound, but as the men at the table stared him down, he lost every bit of nerve he possessed and kept quiet.

"Wait," the first soldier said. "The last batch of draftees was due to arrive a week ago."

"That's right!" The other snapped his fingers. "Trying to evade the draft, were we?"

Dakier could feel his own eyes widen despite himself. "No, sir. Certainly not, sir. Sirs." His words came out all in a rush that did nothing to lessen how guilty he must seem. "I live in the Northern Mountains of A'slenderia, sir, and it is quite a far distance to travel."

Both men's brows furrowed as they glanced at each other and back at him. The one on the left wordlessly waved toward himself. After a second of hesitation, Dakier realized he wanted the draft notice after all and hastily shoved it forward.

The man read the address on the notice and showed it to his colleague before they both shrugged in perfect unison. Dakier was starting to wonder if they were brothers.

"He'll still need a punishment for the tardiness."

"Two days of Collection?"

The first nodded solemnly. "Fair. You're assigned to infantry, with two days of Collection."

It seemed he was being dismissed again. Dakier debated moving on, but he didn't know where to go next or what Collection was, and he did not want to risk not serving his punishment when he was already reporting so suspiciously late. "Collection, sir? My apologies. I'm not familiar."

"Shoe collection." The man said it like his meaning should have been obvious, but the clarification only confused Dakier further. He impatiently waved Dakier on, despite having no one in line behind him, when someone interrupted.

"Seventeen, but you brought your own horse?"

The man addressing him was standing off to the side of the table, and it unnerved Dakier to ponder how long he'd been standing there silently enough to remain unnoticed. He might have been thirty, but he didn't wear the same drab garments as the others. His featured a small-brimmed, flat-top hat, and bronze medallions dotted the shoulders of his jacket. A captain's uniform.

"No, sir," Dakier replied, hoping that was the correct way to address a man of his rank. He was taller than all of them, so he ducked his head on instinct. "This is my employer's horse."

The man raised an eyebrow so high that it nearly touched his cap. "Your employer let you bring their horse to war?"

"Yes, sir."

"And you're only seventeen?"

Dakier wasn't sure where these questions were going, but he said, "Yes, sir."

"It's a shame when lads this young get drafted." He looked at the men at the table, like he expected them to nod along with him. "Might I ask, do you have any specialized skills?"

"Yes, sir." Dakier tried not to seem too excited at the possibility of escaping the infantry. Brenna was right, though. He would need to be assigned to another faction if he wanted to remain true to pacifism and still serve Tibedo. "I am fluent in Tibedese and Endran, okay with Aslen, too, and I am a skilled farrier and blacksmith. It's what I do for work, sir."

"Fluent in Endran and Aslen?" the man repeated. Dakier fought the urge to correct him, since his Aslen was only passable, but it did not matter. "I tell you what, if you'll allow me the use of your horse, I'll have you in the stables for unit twelve, tending to the cavalry. Let's see if we can avoid the young lads on the battlefield yet, though you'll still need to serve in Collection. But let's see if we can't make it one day instead of two." He extended a hand to him, asking, "How does that sound now, Mandia?"

"Excellent, sir." Dakier's new uniform occupied his right hand, so he shifted the cumbersome package under his elbow as quickly as he could and extended to shake. "Thank you, sir."

On the way to the bunks for unit twelve, the captain showed him where to stable Kranich and the rest of the cavalry's area. "The Cajetan units saw our first battle yesterday, right at the border," he said as they approached Dakier's assigned barrack, "with more coming."

When the captain left him in the doorway, Dakier realized he was still uncertain how to address his newfound unit leader. He waved a hand and yelled after him, "Sir, I didn't catch your name."

With a tip of his hat, the man hollered a quick reply over his shoulder. "Captain Pereira."

Dakier tucked the information away and made his way to an open bottom bunk, asking around to check if anyone had claimed it. When he felt confident that no one had, he changed into his new uniform and flopped onto the paper-thin mattress. The shoulders of the uniform jacket were tight, and the waist was far too loose, but the long day of travel had exhausted him too much to care.

Absentmindedly, he took Brenna's hair from his old coat and held it between his fingers. He was about to move it into the inside pocket of his new jacket when someone dangled himself from the top bunk, hanging his head upside down as he looked at Dakier.

Dakier flinched away in surprise, shoving the lock back into his pocket. He hadn't noticed anyone on the top bunk when he'd selected this one. He sat up straighter and introduced himself, trying to salvage the interaction into something less odd. "Dakier Mandia, unit twelve, farrier. I just arrived today."

The guy swung off the top bunk and into someone else's bed on the lower bunk opposite Dakier. "Farrier, no kidding? Same here. Just got in today, myself. The name's Salvedor Sousa, but you can call me Sal." Sal was heavyset, with a youthful, round face, close-cropped black hair, and a sparse black mustache. "I'm surprised they put you in here with me. I thought they were reserving tasks like this for the younger blokes."

Dakier raised an eyebrow. "I'm seventeen."

"No kidding?" Sal quipped, rubbing his hand on the back of his neck. "Some blokes get all the luck."

Dakier seriously did not know how to respond to that, but it turned out he did not have to, as Sal was already on another subject.

"Is that red hair?"

"No," was Dakier's feeble denial as he reflexively pushed his jacket shut.

"Do you have a Barkurian girlfriend?"

"No," Dakier said again, considering telling him to mind his own business.

"Then why do you have someone's hair in your pocket?" He shook his head. "That's just plain gross."

"Fine, it *is* a girl's," Dakier said. "But she isn't my girlfriend."

"Oh, I see. Unrequited love situation, then?"

Dakier bristled, not wanting to think back to his and Brenna's last night together around this talkative stranger. "No."

Sal went quiet for a second before giving his verdict. "Seems like a girlfriend to me." As Dakier's cheeks burned profusely, he went on. "Listen, man, I'm just impressed you have a girlfriend, period. But I'd get rid of that if I were you. Some people around here might not take too kindly to your girl being the enemy."

Sal might be overly friendly, but he wasn't wrong about that. There was no chance Dakier was going to get rid of it, but he could play along, if for no other reason than to avoid a target on his back. "Yeah, you're right."

Sal shook his head with his mouth curled into a funny shape, like he might burst out laughing at a moment's notice. "You must really love this girl to still think about her while fighting against her country."

Dakier said nothing more about it, instead making an excuse that he needed to go wash up after his journey.

But the more he thought about it, the more he realized how right Sal actually was.

27

Brenna

Brenna fought the urge to scream as water poured in the window, filling the train car. Instead, she clamped her mouth shut, conserving the air. Anton's improvised restraint had worked—they all survived the impact, at least—but now they were tied to a vessel that was rapidly submerging.

Anton yanked on the end of the rope to free them with enough speed to suggest he had tied a slip knot. Simeon slung himself out the window instantly. Brenna tried to follow, but when the water rose up her legs, she could not move. The fear froze her in place. In what felt like less than a second, she was completely underwater, swimming inside a train car.

She opened her eyes to view the murky shapes of the car through the clouded river water. She saw Katiel's blue dress swirling ahead of her, saw the flowing shape disappear through the white rectangle that had to be the train car window. Brenna attempted to follow, but she couldn't move—except it wasn't fear this time. Her shoe was wedged under the bench, trapping her ankle in a twisted position. She tugged hard, a searing pain shooting up her calf, but her foot refused to move.

Everything was fuzzy. She was losing the last of her air. It took all her strength to grab her ankle in her hands and yank it free. But that was when she saw Mara.

In the hazy water, she couldn't tell for certain, but it looked like Mara was unconscious, her foot and calf caught up to the knee. Brenna yanked on Mara's leg, but the effort was too much for her. The car was sinking, and she couldn't hold her breath any longer. She had to get out.

Sweeping her legs and arms in a large diamond-shaped motion, she swam out the window, following the glimpse of sunlight overhead. She placed her feet on the edge of the car by the window, swimming as close to the car as she could, and pushed off.

The water burned the edges of her eyes as she flew to the surface, but she kept them open, not daring to let the surface out of her sight. The next moment, she was in the air again, shoulders surging out of the water as she gasped for breath. She noted the direction of Bar Kur and swam hard for its bank, grasping the rocky outcropping as tightly as she could to avoid being sent downstream.

Brenna couldn't believe it. She had made it. That harrowing drop, and they were fine.

Well, *she* was fine.

But Mara was still down there.

And she didn't see the others.

Brenna dove into the water again and opened her eyes, searching for any sign of Mara, but it was no use. She wasn't a skilled swimmer, and she could barely make out the shape of a train car in the depths below. The car was far beyond her reach, and she didn't know if the one she saw was theirs or one of the many other cars.

Swimming to the surface again, she clung to a rocky outcropping as she twisted in search of her friends. She could only pray that Mara freed her leg before the car went too deep.

Upriver, a waterfall billowed over the cliff's edge. A'slenderia was mountainous where Bar Kur was flat, and it seemed even the river felt the sharp contrast as the water beat unrelentingly on the rocks at its base. It was a miracle Brenna had made it to shore, with the speed and fortitude of the rapids pouring from the waterfall's base.

Anton stood on a rock behind her, his suit jacket discarded as he searched over the water, as frantic as Brenna.

"Where are they?" she shouted up to him. "Where are the others?"

"There," Anton said at the same moment that Brenna saw them, Katiel and Simeon both, tumbling fast downriver—right into a group of sharp, jagged rocks.

Katiel kicked furiously, her face surfacing for a second before the rapids yanked her under again. Simeon did not appear to be moving at all, as if the crash had knocked him unconscious. Upon seeing them, Anton raced down the bank. Brenna followed him as fast as she could, but with the slick ground cover beneath her, it proved difficult to keep up.

"Take Simeon," Anton shouted, but the command did not seem directed at her. She followed his gaze to see Sera making her way down the steep cliffside of the A'slenderian bank, flitting down the inch-wide outcroppings on the vertical surface with the agility of a mountain lion. Simeon was veering closer to her bank, and the moment she was near enough, she plunged in after him.

Brenna was almost far enough downriver to dive in herself when an enormous surge of water crashed into Katiel. Katiel fought against it, but it proved too much for her as she slammed head-first into a boulder protruding from the river's center. Brenna gaped in horror as Katiel went limp, and the water peeled her friend's body off the rock and back into the rapids. She started sinking instantly, and her head disappeared beneath the rapids.

Out of nowhere, Anton was beside Katiel in the river, pulling her to the surface. He swam with an arm around her waist, paddling violently with his free arm. Brenna was close enough now to reach them from the shore, and within seconds, she had Katiel by the shoulders, dragging her onto the flat gravel cover of the Barkurian bank. As soon as Brenna had her, Anton went back for the others.

She heard Sera screaming something to Anton, but to Brenna, the words sounded as muffled as if she were still underwater. Katiel was not waking up. Frantically, she pressed her clasped hands against Katiel's chest, and on the fifth try, her friend coughed as water poured out of her mouth. She looked up at her with glazed eyes, as if slowly waking from a dream.

"Brenna," she strained to say. "What happened?"

Before she could answer, Brenna heard a sharp intake of breath behind her and whipped her head around. Where she expected to see Sera and Anton paddling over with Simeon and Mara, she only saw the two of them, with Sera telling Anton, "We try again," before they both dove back under.

Katiel pushed onto her elbows to watch, her face mimicking the horror Brenna felt.

A second later, Anton and Sera were back, wading in place despite the tumultuous rapids. "It's too deep to reach them," said Sera. "The current is too strong to pass below."

"We try again," Anton said, mimicking Sera's words, before they dove again.

In a wink, Anton and Sera surfaced, Simeon slung between them. They hauled him onto the rough shore, flinging him onto his back. Sera pressed on his chest, and he shot up, coughing up water and panting hard. Anton clapped him on the back with a strained expression. It was obvious Anton had thought they'd lost him. Simeon stared at Sera with a peculiar look on his face, and then down at his forearm. It was clearly broken, with the bone snapped in the center and the section closer to the wrist hanging limply at a grotesque angle.

"Mara is still down there!" Brenna shrieked. When she heard her, Sera dove back under.

Brenna pressed a hand to her chest, trying to calm her pounding heart as she waited. Peering into the depths, Brenna could see no shape of a person and no shape of the steam engine that had now fully submerged. The gorge must be incredibly deep. If any survivors sank down far enough to be out of sight, it was unlikely anyone could dive deep enough to retrieve them. Brenna would dive in again if she were a stronger swimmer, but Sera had already gone farther down than she could. No matter how deep Mara was, Brenna hoped Sera could reach her.

As she looked around the gravel shore, Brenna took notice of all the people sobbing, holding each other, and looking longingly at the water. Several others hadn't made it, she realized. The passengers were weeping for family and friends who didn't survive the crash.

After what felt like hours, Sera surfaced and hung her head in defeat.

Brenna choked down a sob. She could not believe it.

Mara was gone.

Her chest tightened as she imagined Sera deep under the surface, swimming into the dark. Swimming toward a figure sinking deeper and deeper down. Her eyes filled with tears at the thought. She reached over to hold Katiel, who pulled her into a tight embrace. Her friend's shoulders shook beneath her soaked frock.

"This is my fault," Katiel said. "I should have been able to help earlier. It should have been easy to repair the bridge."

"Oh, no, it isn't your fault, Katiel," Brenna assured, salty tears streaming down her cheeks. "You did great. You did more than anyone else could have."

Behind them, Anton watched Simeon with a desolate expression. Seeing how distraught he looked, Brenna pulled away from Katiel and placed a hand on his shoulder. "You did all you could."

He nodded and looked back at the river, the way one might look down a city street when they were hopelessly lost. Then he pointedly turned to the crowd that had gathered. Many people were eyeing their group with suspicion, and, even worse, one man was eyeing Katiel in particular. Brenna wondered if he had seen her conjure the ore from their train car in her attempt to help.

"What was that—that shadow we saw?" Brenna heard someone ask, though she couldn't tell who had said it.

"It was her," someone else said, pointing toward them. Pointing toward Katiel. "She did this."

Brenna recalled the crowd's screams as they saw the cloud of ore hovering over the gorge. She didn't know how they could blame Katiel, though, when they'd seen her go down with the car and almost die herself. Brenna considered firing off an excuse—saying it was a swarm of gnats, perhaps—but that would only make them look more suspicious.

"It was the smoke from the train," Sera said as she walked closer, positioning herself between the crowd and Katiel.

Anton ducked his head. "We need to get out of here."

Brenna helped Katiel to her feet, but none of them made a move to leave. For a few moments, or perhaps an eternity, the five of them stood side by side, their eyes still fixed on the space where Mara went down with the train, as if hoping she would miraculously return. The young woman had already gone through so much and yet remained so brave. It was unbearable to think she was gone forever. Despite the intensity of the ache in her chest, Brenna felt too sorrowful to cry.

The image of the sinking figure crept back into her mind's eye, and Brenna couldn't help but wonder what she was doing here, and why. Ever since Bar Kur had gone to war, she had only associated with friends from enemy nations and with a fugitive who had fled to one. She had told herself it was for Henred, to stop him from fighting for a false cause, but she shuddered to imagine what Henred would think of her now. She hadn't even gone back in to help Mara once she had Katiel back. She could've at least attempted to dive in again, even if she was a weak swimmer. She could have at least tried.

Maybe Orla and Jay and everyone else in Fir Kelt had been right to sneer at her associating with foreigners. Maybe she *was* a traitor. Maybe she should have been loyal to her country and her family above her friends, and above her heart. If she had done all they wanted her to, perhaps she could have avoided this situation, this moment as she stood by the water's edge, this despair that was all her own fault. It was Brenna's idea to bring Mara back to Ballynach as a witness. Now they had no witness and no letter from General Taregh as proof. Yet the ordeal had cost Mara her life.

Brenna knew this was her fault.

She was finally back in her home country, but she had never felt less at home. Though she knew where she stood on the map, maybe that look Anton bore had only been an image of herself reflected in his eyes.

Because now, more than ever, Brenna was hopelessly lost.

28

Katiel

Gray skies reflected the grim mood as the five made their way to the nearest train station. The southern part of the country was like the Bar Kur that Katiel was accustomed to. Rice fields lined either side of the train tracks they followed, the rectangular bogs forming the jagged yet orderly pattern of a dragonfly's wing. The first station was in a town called Clon Killy—not too far from the crash site, according to the map Katiel carried. On foot, the trek was still taking hours.

She had awoken soaking wet on the banks of the river, sputtering water and struggling for air. At first, staring up at Brenna's red cloud of hair, she had no memory of what had landed her in the situation, but as she walked, the events came back to her in flashes. Each one filled her with more shame than the last.

First, there was Anton having to save her. She did not know how she had succumbed to the rapids, but she had, and then he was there, suddenly, pulling her, helping her. Their hair and her skirts swirling deep underwater was the image that stuck in her mind the most. She realized she had not properly thanked him, but she knew if she did, she would start crying again, so she decided to save it for later.

She had made such a futile attempt to help. Sending the ore to rebuild an entire bridge at the last moment—who did she think she was? Did she think herself a master wielder who could manage such a feat? She may have discovered she had magical abilities but, apparently, for her it meant nothing. If Mara's words in the safe house were accurate, her parents might have been legendary wielders. Meanwhile, she had the power to swirl dust around. Dust magic was not so useful.

Perhaps that was why her parents had never told her. Maybe they had noticed she could not do it correctly, so they had wanted to spare her the humiliation. A part of her was furious at them for keeping such a huge truth from her, but she had to admit she had been happy not knowing. It was a burden to be told she was powerful. People expected things from her now, regardless of whether she could do them. People trusted her now, and look where that landed them.

She dabbed at her eyes with her still-soaked shawl. Look where her supposed abilities had landed Mara, indeed.

Unfortunately, Simeon's memory was not faring as well as hers. He did not remember how he had ended up on the Continent at all, much less on a riverbank in Bar Kur, and he pestered Anton with questions throughout the walk. He seemed particularly concerned that Sera was there, asking about it again and again as she made him a tight splint from Anton's suit jacket. It made Katiel wonder what had happened between them back in New Drezchy, for him to be so shocked that Sera would be working with them now.

"Are you all right?" Brenna asked softly as she sidled up to her. Lost in her thoughts, Katiel had not noticed until then that she had broken away from the group.

"Yes." She attempted a smile, for Brenna's sake. "Are you?"

"Yes," Brenna replied.

Katiel knew the answer was not the truth, for either of them.

"Is the ore okay?" Brenna added. Katiel's eyes shot open as she felt for the pouch at the waistband of her skirt.

She pulled it out, and they both stopped walking for her to open it. To her amazement, though the outside of the velvet pouch was soaking wet, the ore inside was the same as it had been. It was as if the substance was completely impervious to water. Katiel wished Mara were with them to ask her more.

Suddenly, another thought came to Katiel's mind as she recalled another precious thing that water might destroy. "What about the letters?"

Brenna let out a staggered breath, as if she grew anxious at the mere thought of them being destroyed. She patted the chest of her shirt where she stored them before pulling out a sopping wet square of folded parchment.

"Mara had the one with Taregh's seal..." Brenna began.

Katiel could tell she avoided saying that the third letter was gone. It was too close to saying aloud that Mara was gone.

"And the others?"

Gingerly, Brenna pried open the folds. It was the one Brenna found in the candlestick, Katiel could tell. Half of the words were blotched beyond recognition, while some were still legible, albeit barely.

"This one does not look great," Katiel said. "How is that one? Is it enough to prove to Jay that Mara discovered the plot before it occurred?"

"The water smudged some words." Brenna hung her head. "Including the date."

Katiel released a staggered breath of her own. The date on the letter was the most important piece of proof they had, especially now that they had no witness. Without it, she did not know if they had enough evidence for Jay to take anything to his superiors in the government. Katiel hated to admit it, but the thought crept into her mind that at this point, they should return home.

"Do you think Clon Killy might have a post office that we could stop at on our way to Ballynach?" Katiel asked, overcome with the urge to change the subject, even if only for a moment.

From the hopeless look in her friend's eyes, she could tell Brenna was contemplating giving up as much as she was. And something in Katiel could not stand the thought of Brenna, who had always been the picture of hope, giving up on something she believed in.

"I wanted to write to my parents, in case they hear about the train crash. And tell my father where to go to retrieve Gunnel. I thought if word somehow got back to them that there was a wielder present at the crash, they would worry about me."

Brenna put an arm around her shoulder and gave her a squeeze. The silence between them conveyed everything Katiel had avoided saying—that losing Mara, and knowing that it just as easily could have been her, made her feel immeasurably guilty for leaving her parents.

Though she had not said the rest of what she meant, she knew Brenna understood.

Clon Killy ended up being less of a town and more of a train station with a few smaller buildings attached to it on either side. Luckily for Katiel, one of them was a post office. The others agreed to wait outside while Brenna and Katiel headed in to mail her letter.

"You better hurry with that, miss," the stout man behind the counter commented as she bought some parchment and an envelope with money Anton had lent her. Naturally, even though everyone else had lost their things, Anton had managed to save his satchel, so he still had his wallet and his papers. "Train's about to leave. Last one today."

Katiel flashed her best polite smile. "I will be quick." As she bent down to retrieve the bill from her waist tie, Brenna locked eyes pointedly and jerked her head to the side. There were a couple of men talking in the corner, dressed in the stiff olive-green uniforms of the Barkurian police. Katiel loosed a breath, glad she had tied a scarf around her head to hide her hair when she entered Bar Kur. If anyone was looking for the wielder from the train site, she imagined they would be searching for a girl with blond hair. Thankfully, the scarf had remained tied around her wrist when they had lost their other possessions to the riverbed.

"Thirty people dead," the tall policeman was saying to the other. "What a shame."

"Can you believe some kids ran from the scene of the crime instead of waiting for the pushcart?" the portly one replied.

"That's a crime, if you ask me."

"Might be. But practicing magic is a crime no doubt, if you believe those passengers going on about it at the scene."

The tall officer scoffed. "The crash must've addled them. There hasn't been a wielder seen around here for decades."

Brenna's eyes had widened into cheese rounds. Katiel tried to continue jotting down her letter inconspicuously, but it was of no use. The officers had seen them.

"Aye, you two," the lanky policeman called, stalking over to them. "Where did you get in from? Last train arrived hours ago."

"Oh, you know," Brenna gulped, floundering for an excuse, "some place."

Katiel fought the urge to clap a hand across her own forehead.

"Is this one A'slenderian?" the other officer asked Brenna, like Katiel was a horse rather than a person, and reached for her headscarf as if to pull it off.

Brenna smacked the officer's hand away.

Katiel did not have to wait for Brenna to tell her to run.

She raced out of the post office and onto the narrow swath of gravel that separated the buildings from the tracks. Anton, Sera, and Simeon were loitering under the awning for waiting passengers. When they saw her sprinting toward them, they all bolted in the opposite direction, wasting no time in getting away from whatever she was running from.

"You filthy traitor!" the portly officer shouted at Brenna as he chased after them. "A Barkurian aiding an A'slenderian when we are at war! You should be ashamed of yourself!"

Katiel stole a glance back to see him close in on Brenna's heels. He was surprisingly fast.

It was then she noticed the train was already moving, albeit slowly. Sera leaped onto the side of a cattle car and slid past the cracked door, Anton and Simeon following close behind.

Katiel quickened her pace and ran up beside the car, mentally preparing herself to leap in sideways.

"Jump," Sera instructed impatiently, like it was the easiest request in the world. Then again, it seemed to these Drezchy, it actually was.

She jumped and tumbled into the car, falling feet over head and slamming hard into the opposite wall. As Katiel righted herself to check if Brenna had caught up, her friend slammed hard into her, knocking them both back into the cart.

For a moment, Katiel thought they had gotten away.

"Nowhere to run now," the officer said, standing in the opening. He had kept with them all the way into the cattle car.

Without thinking, Katiel blew a speck of ore from her fingernail into a cloud around the officer. In shock, he stumbled back and lost his footing. Brenna seized the opportunity and kicked him in the chest, sending him tumbling out of the slow-moving car.

As the officer vanished from the doorway, Katiel knew it was the most foolish thing she could have done. She had not only outed herself as the wielder at the scene, but had confirmed the stories from the other passengers that the officers had written off.

Peering out the opening, she watched the officer stand back up, rubbing his backside with one hand and shaking a fist at them with the other.

Simeon slid the door shut before slumping his back against it. "You realize the ore is supposed to become something other than dust, right? You know, a weapon, an invisibility cloak, something like that?"

"The ore can become an invisibility cloak?" Brenna asked, looking at Sera, who only shrugged.

"How should I know?"

"I thought it was an ingenious use of resources," Anton chimed in, his smirk making her uncertain if he was serious or not.

"Agreed." Brenna clapped her on the back. "Our fearless Katiel, always saving the day!"

But she did not always save the day. She could not stop the train in time to save Mara, or the others they had just heard about. "We overheard the officer say that thirty people died in the train crash."

The others gasped at Katiel's declaration, and Sera repeated, "Thirty people?"

The keeper pulled up her hood to hide her face, but not before Katiel saw a single tear slide down her cheek.

29

Brenna

Ballynach was a massive city surrounded by an even more massive stone wall. Brenna was not sure why she had never come before, if for no other reason than to visit the historical sites. Ballynach was one of the oldest settlements on the Continent. Ballynach Gate alone had been keeping enemies out for over two thousand years, or at least that was what the man on the sidewalk claimed as he tried to persuade them to pay him for a guided tour.

The buildings looked like overgrown versions of the cottages in Fir Kelt—all thatched roofs and jagged upper levels that hung out precariously over the street, with brown crossbeams breaking up the tan façades. The group followed Katiel's instructions as she read the map, heading down a broad avenue to the center of town, toward Ballynach Castle. Their map didn't list the government offices, but it did list the castle, and it seemed logical that the royal cabinet wouldn't be located too far from the king's residence.

The part of town they passed through was unappealing, to say the least. Wet clothes strewn across the street dripped on Brenna's hair. Stables housing various farm animals were mixed right in with market stalls selling fruits and cheeses—all well past any edible state. The tiered upper levels of the buildings seemed to prevent rainfall from washing the buildings properly, because dark splotches of dirt covered most of the ground floor façades. In the distance, factories billowed smoke from tall stacks, forming a gray mist that seemed to cover the entire city.

"Which way?" Sera asked when they arrived at a fork, as Katiel unfolded the map again. Sera had been talking much more than normal since they had passed through the gate. Brenna wondered how she could be nervous to enter Ballynach, when she had run across a moving train and descended a cliff face on her tiptoes without uttering a word. The place wasn't clean, sure, but it wasn't *that* bad.

Katiel pointed them to the left, and as they kept going, the ground grew cleaner and the smoke cover thinned overhead. The buildings changed from the stacked cottages of the residential area to the newer-looking, orange-bricked buildings that seemed to signal some other part of town. The government district, Brenna supposed.

That meant they were close.

Continuing along the same street, they entered an open square that was void of people. It was like a park, but instead of trees, statues sprawled across the open area. Raised, orange-bricked platforms weaved between and around the statues, inviting pedestrians to have a rest.

Katiel seemed to accept the invitation as she perched on a curved section of the low brick wall and pulled out the canteen and the map. "I would have thought we would be there already," she said, cocking her head to the side as she surveyed the page.

Anton propped himself against the platform next to her. He mumbled something about the direction they should head and leaned farther in to place a hand on the map. Seeing the blush that crept over Katiel's cheeks and the nonexistent space between the two of them, Brenna decided to read the plaque in front of each and every statue.

There were fourteen statues, one for each of the fourteen King Stefans. This must be King Stefan's Square, a landmark she had heard of a thousand times. For such a famous place, Brenna had thought it would be less empty.

Brenna had made her way down the line to Stefan IX when she noticed Sera standing at a noticeboard. Simeon stood behind her, holding his sling with his good arm. His confused gawking made it clear that he was still shocked to be in Bar Kur and still had no memory of crossing the ocean to get there.

As she followed Sera's gaze, it took Brenna no time to recognize what she was looking at: a poster with a drawing of Katiel's face on it. Above her head was the word *WANTED* and below it, *for Practicing Forbidden Arts and for Assault of a Law Enforcement Officer.* Brenna knew instantly what the 'Forbidden Arts' portion referred to: wielding the ore.

When she saw Brenna there, Sera simply said, "They have wronged you."

Brenna blinked several times fast as she realized there was another poster next to Katiel, one that was evidently supposed to be her. It was a sketch of a girl with curly hair and round eyes, but also a huge, crooked nose and strange ears—one ear large and one small. It had similar words inscribed around the image as Katiel's—*WANTED for Assault of a Law Enforce-*

ment Officer—but the portrait couldn't pass for her. At least she hoped not.

"Aye," Brenna called to Katiel and Anton across the square. When they caught sight of her, she impatiently waved them over. "Come here."

They hurried over, following her eyes to the noticeboard. Katiel immediately grabbed her own poster and yanked it off the wall. Anton yanked Brenna's down after her and took in the image with a raised eyebrow. "What exactly did you say to that police officer?"

Brenna looked at the page again, noticing in the small print that there was even a bounty listed. "Three hundred leaguemarks a head? That's a pittance."

"It's good," said Katiel, crumbling her poster and stuffing it into her satchel. "It means they do not want us that much."

Katiel started walking away from the board and out of the square, and the rest of them followed.

Brenna said from behind her, "For the record, I think we're worth more than that paltry sum."

Anton said, "You aren't supposed to want a higher bounty on your head."

Brenna couldn't help but add, "How about a more accurate sketch?" to which Katiel laughed outright.

"No, you are not supposed to want that, either."

"Enough, imbeciles." The vein in Sera's neck looked like it may well burst from the restraint it took not to call them more names. "Put your wanted posters away. Which of these buildings is the Office of the Secretary of War?"

"It's in this plaza?" Simeon asked.

The plaza they entered was wide, larger than the square, with several orange-bricked rectangular buildings that all looked alike, and one ancient-looking stone structure that stretched tall above the rest. It had to be Ballynach Castle.

"Yes," Sera replied with an odd lilt to her voice, "I believe so."

"There." Katiel pointed across the plaza, in the direction Sera had already been facing. "The Office of the Secretary of War is ahead of us."

Brenna fought the urge to cry out in triumph as she caught sight of it. Not bothering to wait for the group, she rushed across the courtyard and up the few steps to the oak double doors. They had come so far, and being this close, she would not waste another moment.

She turned the latch on the brass doorknob, but the door did not open. Locked.

"It is too late today," Sera said from behind her, gesturing to the sunset behind them. "The office is closed."

Brenna hadn't noticed the colorful skies until then, but Sera was right. Brenna didn't know where Jay stayed when he was in Ballynach either, so they would have to secure lodging and return tomorrow.

She unfolded the poster again as they walked away, needing something to do with her hands to stay busy. That was when she noticed an additional charge that hadn't been on Katiel's: *And For Harboring The Enemy.*

Something in her heart broke to read those words because, in a way, it was true. But there was no time to worry about it now.

A few more hours, and everything would be over. The war would end, and Henred and Dakier would come home.

This was going to be the longest night of her life.

30

Katiel

That night, Katiel could not sleep. The anticipation of the coming day—of finally telling Jay of the contents of the letter and all they had found—was too much to allow her any rest.

They had secured lodging at a hostel near the Secretary of War's offices. Bunks filled the large corridor, men and women alike in the same room. She peered down at Brenna below her, and Simeon on the top bunk next to hers, both out cold. It appeared she was the only one with a problem sleeping.

She inched down the rickety ladder, hoping she did not wake anyone as she made her way to the hostel common area for some water. Though she was not all that thirsty, it would be nice to stretch her legs after staring at the ceiling for hours.

She made her way to the water cabinet and downed a full glass, and she was about to head back to bed when she noticed Anton by the window. He sat on a forest-green velvet chaise, watching the rain trickle down the glass with his chin in his hand.

Something in her wanted to bolt and avoid any conversation, but this time she actually did have something to say, so she sat in the armchair opposite him. "Thank—" she began, and coughed despite herself. She did not know why she was nervous about speaking with him now, after everything they had been through. "Thank you for saving me in the river. I meant to thank you earlier."

He jerked upright, like he had not noticed her there. "Katiel." He smoothed down his collar, even though it was not ruffled. Though it was the middle of the night, he was still wearing a high-collared shirt under a vest and slacks. She was still wearing her day dress, too, since she had not wanted to change in the shared quarters. "It was nothing."

A candle flickered on the table beside him, the surface splayed with papers. It took her a second to make out the ink blotches and swathes of black as Anton's blueprints, the ones she had glimpsed in his suite in The Imperial—plans for bifocal eyeglasses, a mechanical leg, a device that measured the distance a wheel traveled. All of them ruined from being submerged in the river, all of them unreadable. What had to be months and years of work, erased.

"Your inventions," she breathed.

"They're just papers." He sighed. "I came up with them once. I can do it again."

Unsure of what else to say, but not wanting to go back and lie there alone, Katiel tried to reassure him. "You'll remember what you created."

"Katiel, I was worried about you," he said, abruptly changing the topic. "When you were trapped under the water, I didn't think before diving back in. I couldn't bear the thought of you getting hurt."

She did not know what to say. The sudden intensity startled her, though some part of her did not mind it.

"I know I'm being strange, since we've only just met," he went on, his dark eyes boring into hers. For once, he sounded almost awkward. "It's strange for me to feel this way about anyone."

"Feel what way?"

He shrugged, looking back at his papers. "To care about what happens to them. Care if they're alright at the end of the day." When he looked up, his eyes went far beyond her, like he was remembering things she did not know about. "I know that makes me sound horrible, but in my culture, caring is a weakness."

"You rarely care about what happens to people?" It did not sound possible. Besides, he did not act like he did not care. "Not anyone?"

"Not most people." He paused, peering up at her through his thick eyelashes. "I care about my sister." His slight smirk faded as he continued watching the rain. "And Simeon." It was clear his friend's current state weighed on him. Simeon's arm was healing fine, but his memory of the past several months had not returned. "He didn't want to go into Bar Kur. I pushed him to come. He thought it too dangerous, but he came with me, anyway."

Katiel placed a hand on his shoulder. "What happened was not your fault." It hurt to see him blame himself, especially when she was the one to blame. "Those people who passed away, and Mara—" She winced, pained to say the name aloud. "They didn't have to die. I could've restored the bridge. It was a metal bridge. It should have been easy."

Anton scoffed, not unkindly, but in a way that suggested he could not believe what he was hearing. "That was an impossible ask. We were all terrified. No one in their right mind would have expected you to do that."

She felt a bit of relief to hear it, even if the words did not ring true. "You did not seem scared."

He said drily, "Seems I'm a talented actor."

"Your acting helped me." She did not know why she would reveal her feelings to him, but it was true. "I truly am sorry about your blueprints."

"They were nothing special." Anton gazed beyond her again, like he was still thinking about something else that he did not mention.

"Are you trying to remember what you invented," Katiel ventured to ask, "when you look off that way?"

Anton raised his thick eyebrows, like he had not noticed he was. "No, not that." He waved it off. "Thinking about things I would like to forget, I suppose."

With that, they sat in silence for a while, both watching the rain. To her, it felt comfortable, but she wondered how he felt. She wanted to help him like he had helped her—reassure him about his worries or fix his blueprints somehow—but sitting so close to him distracted her traitorous mind. The dim flicker of candlelight cut across his sharp features, and his rolled shirt sleeves exposed rough, heavily veined forearms. Wavy, dark hair framed his thick neck, which pulled taut his high collar and the silk tie that was tucked into his tapered vest. She wished she could see him without all that on.

"What are you thinking about?" he asked, slicing back into her mind.

Anton had a way of seeing through her completely, of seeming to sense exactly what she was thinking. Being around him was to be constantly seen at the core. The sensation was intoxicating—and terrifying.

A deep, bold facet of herself overcame her again as she said, "I would like to forget, too."

The boy with the face of a statue held her gaze for far longer than was proper, his eyes laced with knowing. The wisps of her bangs curtained her vision, but she did not look away as he blew out the candle.

Gently, he took her hand and guided her from the room. He led through the darkness to an alcove at the end of the hallway, ensuring they were well and truly alone. Her eyes adjusted to see the harsh edges of him again.

He had her pinned in place, her back nearly touching the wall and her chest nearly touching his. "Katiel." He said her name and nothing else, waiting for her, asking everything and nothing.

"Anton," she whispered, his dark eyes narrowing when she said it, "Make me forget."

And it worked.

He laughed—a dark, unfriendly sound. He placed his palm above her, spreading his fingers on the wall, and stepped closer, pressing her back against the surface. When he kissed her, her head spun. The touch was sweet, soft, different from his rough voice. Different from how it was before. He moved unhurriedly, pulling the sleeve of her dress aside, feathering his lips on her collarbone, across her shoulder. A small sound escaped her throat at the contact, and he returned to crush his lips against hers once more.

Spinning in the blackness with Anton, the war felt so far away. The deaths and the letter and the draft, forgotten relics.

They remained that way for a while, kissing all the flesh that was already exposed. Katiel wanted him to do more.

When he pulled away, grazing his nose against hers, she lunged for the contact again without thinking, and he smirked down at her as he held back. With the tiniest of movements, she had made it obvious how badly she needed him. A mistake, she thought.

"We should go back," he said, and she nodded her agreement. Before she made another mistake. When they did, Katiel could finally calm herself enough to sleep.

It was good he ended it when he did, after whatever amount of time they had been together—it could have been a minute or an hour for all she knew. She would have stayed with him all night if he had wanted. She would have done anything he asked.

The way she felt when they were together, swimming in a mind without worries, it was like nothing she had experienced.

She wished it could have lasted forever.

31
Dakier

Collection ended up being much worse than Dakier expected. Two days after he arrived in Cajetan, his unit was sent to offer their support to a unit stationed at the border. They were still another day's travel from their destination, but once they got close enough to the Barkurian border, the group made camp for the night, and Pereira informed Dakier that he was to break away from the group for shoe collection.

His assignment as a shoe collector was to scour the empty battlefield for deceased horses, then remove their iron shoes and saddles to take back to the fort. His unit set up camp a fair distance away from the site of the battle, so Dakier ventured out alone for his assignment just before sunset. When he got close enough, the raw stench of death hit him before he saw anything.

The plain field before him was the sight of the first battle so far in the war—one Tibedo had lost badly. Medics had carried away the wounded, but the dead remained—men and horses alike—and it was nothing less than horrific to walk among them. Foot soldiers had shut the men's eyes as a last respect, but the eyes of the horses were still open, full of life, and terrified.

Later that night, Dakier lay in his tent with no chance of sleep as he tried to put the sights and smells of the battle site far from his mind. He wished he hadn't brought Kranich here now. The horse had no way of knowing what he was walking into. In truth, Dakier wished he hadn't brought himself here, either. Tomorrow, he would lead his group in whatever support Pereira's cavalry needed during the battle, and he shuddered to think about what he might witness then.

Feeling a fresh surge of panic, he unwrapped the prayer beads from his wrist and twiddled them between his fingers. The familiar shapes brought him a wave of comfort. The tiny clay beads were a small taste of his soul that he could carry anywhere, even into battle.

It occurred to him that he hadn't recited prayers for several nights now. He didn't even remember how many nights he had missed. It was the strangest thing to forget when he needed the Creator's help and protection more than ever, but deep down, he knew why. Because how could he ask for their success tomorrow, when that meant asking for the deaths of countless Barkurians? People not so different from him. People who believed themselves to be defending their nation against a serious threat.

He closed his eyes, silently asking for safety for his unit, for his countrymen, for Brenna and Katiel to be successful in their efforts. When he thought about her, Brenna's big smile that last day at the train station flashed through his mind, like nothing could—

A whinny trilled from outside, from where his unit had hitched their horses to a post beside the tent. It was Kranich, unmistakably. Something about the tone of it was worried, frantic, off.

Dakier debated ignoring it, another small noise on a quiet night, but since he was awake, he may as well check on the creature. This area didn't have any large predators that he was aware of, but checking would at least provide comfort to himself, if not the horse.

Outside, Kranich's eyes were strained as he stood by the post, mimicking the look of the other horses stationed beside him. Dakier followed his gaze, squinting in the dark. The horse was looking at the tall field grasses sprawled in the distance.

Dakier strained to see with the moonlight all but gone, but then he saw it. Several figures, unmoving, hiding there in the brush.

Barkurian soldiers.

"Ambush," he said in Tibedese, but the word did not come out as a scream like he'd intended. He tried again and found his volume. The voice sounded like it belonged to someone else. "Ambush!"

A gunshot fired in his direction, close enough to send his ears ringing. But he wasn't hit, and neither were the horses. The gunman had missed.

He ducked behind the horses and dove back into the tent to get his rifle. He could feel himself still shouting, and the others were waking and reacting and grabbing guns of their own.

The situation was a blur. He could hear shouting now all around the camp, and he hoisted his gun in front of him and ran out, the firearm positioned to shoot at a moment's notice.

More shots rang out around him, and the smoke and ringing were merging into a terrifying cacophony. His senses blurred together like Katiel's cloud of ore when she bathed the campsite in magic.

"Fall back," he heard one of the Barkurians say in Endran. "They've seen us. Retreat! Fall back!"

Beside him, a rifle fired from the Tibedese side, assailing his ears again.

"They're falling back!" Dakier shouted to the group in Tibedese, suddenly aware that he was the sole man among his comrades who could understand what the other side was saying. "They said they are retreating!"

As the smoke cleared, they could see the small group of Barkurians keeping to the command and running back into the tall grass.

"Hold fire," Pereira said.

Dakier watched the four men running away from them, Barkurians who would do anything to destroy Tibedo. An ambush broke every code of civilized warfare outlined in the Kerafin Pact, and these men had ambushed their camp in the night as they slept. It probably counted as a war crime, or it should if it didn't.

Dakier felt a sheet of anger wash over him—a once-common occurrence that had become foreign since moving away from his stepfather. For a moment, he did not recognize it. But it was there anyway, covering him. The enemy had framed his countryman for an assassination. Now they were coming to kill soldiers while they slept. If Barkurians would do anything to the Tibedese, maybe it would not be so bad to disregard pacifism in this instance. Maybe the ends justified the means, if Barkurians were like this.

No, Barkurians are not all like this, and that line of thinking is not helpful, he scolded himself. How could he think that, when he had Brenna in his life? When he knew Mara, who told all of them the truth, or Henred, who had defended him that day at the festival?

A shot rang through the silence, coming from his side, and the bullet met its target, landing squarely in the back of the head of one of the Barkurians retreating.

Pereira yelled at his units to hold their fire. The fallen soldier's comrades looked back before registering the casualty and running again for their own lives.

Dakier watched the man go down, falling slowly as if time melted around him, and tried to keep himself from thinking the man deserved it.

32

Brenna

Brenna was sinking deeper, falling through a world made of water. Her foot would not move. She reached for it, trying to free herself from whatever had caught her, but the more she reached, the farther away her own foot became. It was running away from her, a piece of herself stretching to spite her.

She screamed. The air she had held swirled in a horrific flurry around her face. Her lungs betrayed her, catching on the release and trying to draw in a breath. But there was only water—pouring in her mouth, in her nose, down her throat—

"Brenna," a voice called to her. Katiel's voice. "Brenna, wake up." She half-wondered how she could hear Katiel underwater when she jolted awake, sitting up and drawing in a huge breath, her forehead slamming painfully into the bunk above her.

"Oh, my gracious," Katiel said at Brenna's reaction. If she realized Brenna had been having a nightmare, she did not comment on it. "Brenna, listen. This is important. Anton and the others are gone. They left in the night, and the ore is gone."

"The ore is gone?" Brenna blinked as her eyes adjusted to the dim light of dawn. "Do you think they swiped it? I thought you kept it on your person."

"I did." The frustration was evident in Katiel's tone, though it seemed directed at herself rather than Brenna. "Anton must have taken it when we were kissing. That must be the reason he followed us all this way, just waiting for an opportunity. I should have known not to trust him."

Despite the serious nature of the conversation, Brenna felt a stupid grin spreading across her face. "You and Anton kissed?"

Katiel's eyebrows fell into horizontal lines. "Yes."

"Good on you." She truly could not contain her grin. Katiel looked like she wanted to strangle her.

"Yes, except for the part about him only doing it to use me and steal the ore."

"Right, right, right." Brenna nodded furiously, rubbing at the back of her neck. "Sorry. Are you sure they're gone?"

"I think so." Katiel motioned toward the three bunks fully made. It looked like no one had stayed there. "And when I woke up, in my hand, there was this note."

She handed the note to Brenna. It was a tiny corner of parchment that looked like someone had ripped it from the corner of a page. Etched in a stately hand, the note consisted of an outline of a heart followed by *"f. A"*.

"Wow, too lazy to spell out the word 'from'." Brenna shook her head. "In that case, you're better off without him." She passed the scrap back to Katiel. "I'm surprised they didn't sell us out to get that reward."

Katiel shrugged, the faintest sign of a smirk tugging at her lips. "Well, you *did* say it was a pittance."

Brenna was so glad to see Katiel even slightly happy that she ventured a joke to keep up the good spirits. "Which would be even more of a pittance to your rich boyfriend."

"Stop," Katiel said, rolling her eyes. "We must go talk to Jay."

"Right." Telling her brother-in-law her information about the framing certainly put a damper on Brenna's good spirits. "I have to know, though, how were you so sneaky? Where did you go to kiss? I didn't even notice you two were gone long enough."

"Stop."

"Right."

KATIEL WAITED OUTSIDE WHILE Brenna swung open the heavy oak door to the Offices of the Secretary of War. The lobby was stately, a room covered from head to toe in dark wood wainscoting and emerald velvet draperies. The decor reminded her of Galvey.

A young woman in a tartan suit jacket and matching skirt sat behind a wooden pillar, intently filing through a stack of papers. She did not so much as look up as Brenna walked up to her, leaning her forearm on the pillar. "I need to see Jacoby Donnell, please."

The receptionist's features did not move an inch. "The purpose of your visit?"

"Personal visit," Brenna said. "I'm his sister." She decided she needn't mention the *in-law* part. After all, a sister-in-law was a type of sister.

The lady's eyes showed the faintest hint of surprise before she said, "Very well." She stood from her post and started walking straight back, deeper into the offices.

Brenna hoped she was supposed to follow, because she did.

The woman stopped at an unassuming door on the left that looked like all the others, curtly saying, "Mr. Donnell." She knocked twice before opening the door.

When he saw Brenna standing in the doorway, Jay dropped his papers onto the desk.

Hurriedly, she stepped in, and the receptionist clicked the door shut behind her.

"Brenna?" Jay came over to where she stood, sounding angry already. "What are you doing here?"

"Jay, I have the most important thing to tell you," she said, the words falling out all in a rush. "You had better sit down."

"Where have you been?" he demanded, ignoring the promise of her news. "The Salzbrucks wrote to us to say you girls had run away. Your mother and Derenta have been worried sick about you."

"They have?" They were always so preoccupied with their own lives, it surprised her to hear it. After sending her off to A'slenderia, she hadn't thought they would care where she was.

"Yes, of course they have!" His consistently thin patience was even thinner than normal. "But look, this is a government office. Leave. Go home."

"No, I can't go," she argued. "I know something about the war. I came to tell you. The assassination of the king was a framing. It wasn't Inigo Farro. It wasn't a Tibedese person at all! We don't have to be at war anymore."

Jay pressed his index finger and thumb to the bridge of his nose. "Stop, Brenna. Just stop. You need to get out of here."

That was not the reaction she had been expecting in the slightest. This was the single most important revelation she had ever heard, and he hadn't so much as flinched. He mustn't have heard her correctly. "What? Why?"

"You are wanted," he ground out through his teeth, "for assault." It was obvious he was struggling to keep his volume low. "This is a government building. You need to leave."

"You already saw those wanted posters?" It had only been a day since the event in question. The image of the girl with the huge, crooked nose and the wonky ears flashed across her mind. "You recognized me?"

"Actually, no," Jay admitted. "That likeness was horrendous. But when I saw a poster of another girl with curly hair right next to a wanted poster of Katiel, it took little effort to put two and two together." Brenna had to admit she was relieved, because that meant the authorities might never find her. "Did you actually assault a law enforcement officer?"

"No, no, just knocked him off balance," Brenna assured. "He was fine."

"Does Katiel practice the forbidden arts?"

"Sort of," Brenna said, "I can explain. But later. That isn't what's most important right now."

Jay's jaw ticked. "You're lucky no one will know it was you. Now leave this place at once. Better yet, leave the walled city altogether before someone else sees you with her and puts it together themselves."

"No, Jay, no. Listen to me." Brenna lifted her palms in protest. "I know who killed the king. But it wasn't Inigo Farro. It was someone here, in this office. It was a planned conspiracy to eliminate the rightful ruler and take control of Bar Kur."

Jay's widened eyes betrayed him as he appeared to steel his features back into cool indifference. "Preposterous. Why would you think so?"

"This letter," Brenna said, whipping the letter out from the neckline of her dress. "It's in Tibedese, and it's a little smudged, but it's here. It was someone warning Inigo Farro about the framing. I had it before the assassination took place, but I didn't know I had it or what it said. Once I figured it out, I came all this way to find you."

Jay reached out like he was going to take the letter from her, but Brenna jerked it out of his reach. She wasn't sure why she had done it, but when she saw the angry look in his eyes, she was glad she had.

"We met a woman named Mara Quigley, who worked in this office. She told us she knew you." Brenna could hear the desperation in her voice, growing fiercer with every word she spoke. "She was dating Ellis, and she overheard him speaking to General Taregh about this plot. The general planned the assassination of the king at Bar Kur Day, so he could frame the Tibedese and start a war."

For a moment, Brenna thought Jay might be considering her words. But a heartbeat later, he scoffed. "Why would you believe any of this? And where is Mara to tell the other members of the King's Cabinet? Why wouldn't she warn them ahead of time?"

"She thought she was protecting Ellis!" Brenna rushed out, far louder than she had intended. She dropped her voice an octave. "I found Mara and convinced her to return with me, but there was a train crash, and she passed away on our way back into Bar Kur."

Jay sighed. "Do you honestly expect anyone to believe that?"

"Yes," she spat, with unwavering ferocity. "Because it's the truth."

But her brother-in-law did not seem to believe it. He was staring daggers at the letter still clutched tightly in her hand. "Give that to me," he ordered. "Now."

She moved the note back behind her, farther from his reach. "We've journeyed across the Continent to find the information for you. To find the truth. It was General Taregh. We have to tell the Cabinet. Together."

"Give me the letter," Jay repeated, "and leave."

Brenna leaned away from him, her brow furrowed in question. "Not if you don't believe me. Do you?"

He said nothing.

"I came all this way looking for you! We did all this to bring you the truth. I thought you could stop the war!"

"Keep your voice down," he warned.

She didn't care who heard her. "Arrest me for all I care. Send me to the front lines with Henred and Dakier and everyone else who is risking their lives for this while you sit here doing nothing!"

Still, he did not reply.

The worry in the back of Brenna's mind slammed into the forefront. The situation was worse than him doing nothing. He *had* done something. She hated the wheels as they clicked in place in her mind. Jay had been there that day when Mara overheard the plot. Jay was responsible. Jacoby Donnell had worked with General Taregh to eliminate their king.

He might have been the one who tried to chase Mara the day she had risked everything to get the truth out. The day she had sent the letter that changed everything for them, that lent hope to the hopeless situation that had wrecked Brenna's world and threatened countless lives.

If Jay had been working with Taregh, conspiring to kill their king, she did not know the person she was standing in front of. The local leader that the people of Fir Kelt adored. The husband to her sister and the father of her nephew, baby Stefan. Named after the king.

She had to know.

"Do you believe me?"

Her brother-in-law watched the parchment she held away from him, his jaw clenched in fury. "No, Brenna, I don't. Now give me that false letter and get out of here."

"Never," she spat, shoving the letter back into her bodice before he could grab it. He would probably burn it if he could. "Henred is out there, risking his life because of you. He looked up to you." The tears were flowing now, but she didn't care. She didn't dare look at her brother-in-law's disgusting face as she continued. "He loved you. Henred wanted to be just like you!"

"Brenna." Jay's tone was softer. "Leave."

"Henred was willing to risk his life for the cause." She looked down, away, holding her hand across her chest lest he was that desperate to retrieve Mara's letter. "Henred loved King Stefan, too. He loves Bar Kur. He was willing to die for them both."

Tears flowed down her face as she placed a hand on the doorknob, but she didn't bother looking back.

"And you were willing to kill them."

33

Katiel

In the alley beside the Secretary of War's office, Katiel fidgeted with the knot on her headscarf. She pulled the tie closed for the fourth time since she had been waiting, as if it could get any tighter.

The longer she stood here, waiting for Brenna to come back, she realized they should have added some sort of contingency plan in case they got separated or in case Brenna ran into trouble and did not return.

To steel her nerves, she turned to look at Ballynach Castle, visible from her hiding place. Bulky stonework made up the façade, a stark contrast to the wrought iron latticework of the government buildings in A'slenderia, buildings she now recognized as being wielded of the ore. Barkurian culture had never tolerated wielders, even back when other nations accepted it. The castle might have taken a year or longer to make, while the wielded equivalent would take only minutes.

She had always taken it for granted that wielders were legends of the past, but now she wondered if there were others out there like her, creating magnificent things from the shadows. There might be others like her in this very city, if only she could recognize them—

An arm wrapped around her neck from behind, wrenching her off her feet. Her hands clawed at the arm in a wild panic, a mangled screech escaping her throat as she grasped for breath.

"Bring her in," a second person said.

The grip loosened, and she fell to the ground, but the person holding her grabbed her wrists and tied them together behind her back before she could wriggle free. The captor hauled her to her feet and pushed her forward by her wrist binding, toward the stoop and the oak double doors—leading her inside the Secretary of War's office.

She cut a glance over her shoulder to see who held her, but it was only a nondescript Barkurian man in military uniform, not anyone she recognized. She could not see the person whose raucous footsteps sounded behind them.

The man led her down a hallway to an unmarked door, but just as he reached forward to open it, the door swung away from them to reveal Brenna standing in the doorway. As Brenna registered them, she jumped back in shock. Jay stood a few feet behind her, gaping at them.

The man with the loud footsteps sauntered past and took a pointed stance near the center of the room, his feet spread wider apart than was natural. He was short, with a ruddy, pockmarked complexion and a bushy red beard flecked through with white. He grazed his eyes from Katiel to Brenna and over to Jay. "Interesting company you keep, Jacoby Donnell."

"General," Jay said hurriedly, giving an awkward salute.

Katiel sucked in a breath, taking in the title. It was General Taregh, the one who had framed a man to start a war. The man who had killed King Stefan XIV, his own king. The traitorous murderer, standing right in front of them.

Brenna locked eyes with her, expression ablaze, checking that Katiel had recognized the same thing. Her lips parted slightly, like she might be about to say something, but Katiel gave a fierce shake of the head to warn her against the idea. They needed to avoid speaking lest they reveal what they knew. There was a chance that General Taregh did not know why they were here, and this was merely about the encounter with the policeman.

Though she had a feeling it was not.

"Take them away," the general said, flicking a disinterested hand in their direction.

Katiel did not have time to react before a white cloth pressed against her face, the sting of chemicals filling her nose.

That was the last thing she saw.

34

Brenna

Brenna awoke lying on a damp stone floor without the slightest idea where she was. Katiel was lying on the floor face down next to her, her limbs splayed as if she had fallen, wearing the same dress she'd been in earlier. Brenna looked down to find herself clothed the same as well. Stone walls surrounded them on three sides, and the fourth consisted only of metal bars. A jail cell.

They were in a prison. A wet, underground prison, from the looks of it. The only light streamed in from tiny square windows near the ceiling, not even large enough to fit a hand through.

Jay had done this. The last thing she remembered before the chemicals took over in Jay's office was the sight of him, standing there, doing nothing as Taregh's lackeys drugged her and Katiel. He let them drug her. He let her go to prison.

"Katiel," she said, rushing over to her friend and flipping her onto her back. She shook her frantically, and, within seconds, her friend coughed and sat up, blinking and dazed.

"Brenna?" Katiel asked, looking around and taking in her surroundings just as she had. Her hand darted to her neck, her fingers prodding her collarbone. "My necklace. It's gone."

"They must've confiscated it when they brought us in," Brenna said, heat rising to her cheeks. Jay had let this happen to them. "Are you feeling faint?"

"No, I feel fine."

"How?" She had thought Katiel needed to be in contact with the ore at all times, though she didn't fully understand why.

Katiel drew her voice quieter. "I have some, under my fingernails and between my teeth."

Brenna released a breath she didn't realize she'd been holding. "That's a relief," she said as she stood up to look out the cell bars. There were other cells perpendicular to theirs on both sides, but she couldn't see anyone in any of them. That didn't mean they were alone, though. There was plenty of space hidden in the back of the cells that she could not see. "At least we're in a cell together with no one else, right? That could've been awkward."

"It's not funny, Brenna."

Brenna turned to her, stricken by the sudden tone. "What does that mean?"

Katiel steeled herself before she spoke. "It means I don't want to hear your jokes. This is not funny. It is serious. We're in a prison cell."

Brenna reeled back. She couldn't comprehend why Katiel would quarrel with her right now. She knew it was serious. That was exactly why she was joking. To put some semblance of lightness in the bleak situation. Taregh could torture them for information—press them for what they knew, and even worse, for what they didn't. If this was the last place she ever saw, she didn't want her last memory to be wringing her hands in fear.

"I know it's not funny," she snapped back. "I was trying to make the best of it." She briefly considered against it before adding, "That's more than you are doing."

Katiel took a long pause, like she was trying to calm herself before she said, "This is your fault."

Brenna's breath hitched at the sting of her friend's words. That sentence pierced deeper than anything, because Brenna knew it was her fault. Not even deep down, right at the surface. She already knew it. This whole mess they were in was her fault.

"I never would have gone if it had not been for you pushing me so hard. I never would have done any of this if it hadn't been for you. You misjudged Jay's loyalties and insisted we go to him, and now we are here. In prison. In a foreign prison, for me." She looked right at Brenna, her eyes melting like she was sorry for what she was saying even as the anger seethed. "So no, I do not want to hear about making the best of it."

"I make the best of it for you!" Brenna's voice rose to a bellow. "Are you kidding? I make the best of it for all of you. You, and Henred, and Derenta, and my mam, and even Dakier! I am always willing to make you laugh, even if people think I'm stupid for it. All I ever want is for all of you to be happy."

Katiel crossed her arms. "Well, leave me out of it. That is a burden neither of us needs. You should find things to make yourself happy and stop worrying so much about other people."

She knew what she wanted to say: that other people's joy made her happy, and other people's sadness made her sad.

It was what she wanted to say, but some stubborn part of her couldn't let the argument drop. "How can you pin this on me with how you acted with Anton? Losing the ore and all that?"

Katiel's nostrils flared. Brenna tried to ignore the tears that were forming on Katiel's lashes now, and on her own. "He was nice to me and reassuring. I thought I could trust him."

Brenna knew the second she brought up Anton, she had gone too far. But hadn't Katiel gone too far as well, blaming her for everything? She couldn't help it anymore, as the words came tumbling out. "I am nice to you and reassuring! You can trust me!"

She had practically shouted it, but Katiel didn't look like she was being shouted at. She looked like she didn't understand, but wanted to.

Brenna quieted a bit. "It happened with Alfien, too. You meet a new boy and forget about me. I'm here for you, too, but you shut me out." She felt her tears falling now, salty and hot. "You didn't even tell me about the stuff with Anton. I could've been there for you. Or just had fun talking about it." She paused and looked up at Katiel. "Do you think I would've judged you or something? Because I wouldn't have."

Katiel turned her back to her. "I do not want to talk about this."

Brenna was finished talking about this, too, so she said, "I'll be on the other side of the cell," and sauntered to the opposite corner by the bars. Not the damp stone corner where she was fairly certain two rats were communicating with each other. She could never be mad enough for that.

The tension was palpable as it spread in the space, growing thicker the longer they sat in silence. It was like there were a hundred yards between them, despite sitting only a few feet apart. Brenna wanted to say something nice to fix it, but everything she thought of only stretched the space between them further. Time slowed, or maybe it raced by. Brenna was no longer sure.

Maybe the rats were having their own dumb argument, she thought drily. But the silly thought did nothing to halt the shame that overcame her as the fight played back in her mind. Each unnecessary remark filled her with remorse as she recalled it. It was foolish to waste time on a petty disagreement when they should be working together to escape.

Wait. They should work together to get out of here. Katiel had a power that could create anything—including a key.

"Katiel, you can wield us something," Brenna said as she turned back to Katiel, slumped on the stone ground with her skirts billowing around her. "Something to help us escape."

"You want us to break out of jail?"

"Yes, of course!" Brenna nodded animatedly, crouching down to Katiel to make sure no one heard. "I might stand a chance of getting the charges dropped, but I don't think you do. Not as an A'slenderian. But it's okay—you can wield a key and we can run out." She looked over each shoulder, through the bars and into the empty room beyond. "I don't see any guards."

"I cannot wield anything, and you know it." Katiel hung her head, seemingly speaking to herself as much as Brenna. "There is something wrong with me. Even if I supposedly have the ability, I cannot do it."

"Yes, you can!" Brenna clasped her hands on her friend's shoulders, forcing her to look at her. "You can. I know you can. In my heart, I know it." Katiel searched Brenna's face, like something there might let her know for certain that it was true. "There has always been something special about you, something different from everyone else. Maybe this is that thing." Katiel looked like she might object, like she still didn't believe in the ability, so Brenna went on. "And anyway, I don't see many other options, unless you think you can fit through that apple-sized window. Now is the time. You have to."

"Okay, you're right," Katiel conceded. She wasted no time before flicking a speck of ore out from beneath her fingernail and breathing it in as she had countless times now. Only this time, nothing happened. No cloud of shining dust.

"Are you sure that's the right stuff?" Brenna asked. "Maybe that was actually just dirt."

"No, Brenna, it's the ore," Katiel said, her tone ripe with frustration. "I can feel it."

"Okay." Brenna nodded her encouragement, though she had no idea what that meant. "Okay, that's okay. Keep trying."

So she did. She tried and tried, so many times that Brenna took a seat opposite her while she waited. Nothing happened, not even the first step that she had seen Katiel complete with ease before. To her credit, Katiel did not stop trying until the sunlight coming from the window had all but disappeared, even when nothing seemed to happen.

Brenna had her arms wrapped around her knees, halfway losing focus on the wielding attempts, when Katiel abruptly stopped, dropped her elbows to her thighs, and pressed the palms of her hands into her eye sockets. Her shoulders started shaking, and Brenna realized she was sobbing. Silently bawling, on the floor of this wet prison cell, alone.

Brenna had really made a mess of things. "I know this is all my fault," she said, wrapping her arms around Katiel. "I know. I've been thinking about it for days now. That's why I got so mad. I didn't want to admit that we never should have left. I'm sorry I pushed you to come." Her face was soaking wet now, so she made a futile attempt at drying it with her sleeve. "And I'm sorry for all the stuff I said earlier. You didn't have to—"

"No, I wasn't fair." Katiel cut her off in her soft tone, letting her hands drop away from her face. "Blaming you for everything was just an excuse. I wanted to come all on my own. Without you, I never would've left home." Her voice hitched on the word 'home,' like she would give anything to be there now, before she swallowed it. "But I also would have never discovered that I wield the ore. I would have listened to what I was told forever, and I never would've found out what I could do, and I wouldn't know what it was like to go after the greenest grass for myself. I never would have done any of this if it had not been for you—but that's the best part. I'm glad we left, for these experiences and, mostly, for knowing that we did everything we could do. We tried to tell the world the truth about Inigo Farro being framed, we tried to rely on the people we thought we could trust, and we tried to stop the war. We tried as hard as we could and we didn't quit, even when it seemed impossible. And that's worth something, at least in my heart."

Brenna pulled her tight, stuffing her face into Katiel's hair and the back of her shoulder. Brenna would find a way to get them out. She had to. She couldn't let them die here.

"Even if we died in here"—Katiel picked up, as if reading her thoughts—"I would die at peace knowing that when something was wrong, we did everything we could to fix it. So I should not be angry with you, and you shouldn't be sorry. Because I'm not sorry for leaving. I am not sorry at all."

Brenna nodded, slowly but firmly. Katiel was right. When they knew something was wrong, they really tried, even with the odds stacked against them. "I'm not sorry we left, either."

"Pardon me."

Brenna's head shot up at the pained rasp of a voice. By this point, she had concluded they were alone down here.

"Hello?" she called into the rest of the prison.

"You said you wanted to help Inigo Farro," the rasp said. Hesitantly, Brenna walked up to the bars to look toward the words. "You said someone framed him."

Brenna glanced back at Katiel, unsure what to do. But they had been standing up for the truth so far, and the person in the other jail cell could not get to them anyway, even if what she said angered them. So she said, "Yes, we found evidence that he was. This war started because of a lie—that's why we're in here."

In the cell perpendicular to hers, she saw a figure there, struggling to its feet. When the person finally stood, they crept up to the bars. She could not see any features within the shadows, only the silhouette of a person. It appeared to be an average-sized man, or perhaps smaller than average.

The man tried to clear his throat and ended up coughing uncontrollably. "Why would you care about that man?" The coughing had lessened the raspiness of his voice, revealing a thick Tibedese accent.

Brenna looked at Katiel again, unsure she should talk to him. Katiel shrugged the tiniest of shrugs. Maybe they were both foolishly hoping he could help them escape. "He's a person, like anyone," Brenna said. "It's unjust to frame someone." She didn't know why she was going on, but something in her wanted to. "My closest friends are from A'slenderia and Tibedo. I don't want our countries to be at odds."

"Hmm," the man said, like he was poring it over. Despite the hoarseness, his voice did not sound old, likely that of a man in his thirties. She wondered how long he had been down here. "Did you ever wonder what happened to Inigo Farro after the parade?"

She honestly hadn't, but she didn't have the chance to consider fully before the man stepped into the light. Dim as it was in the twilight prison, she could make out his face now. He had a thick, dark beard and unkempt, filthy hair, but that was not the startling part. His face was bloodied and scarred, with thick welts rising on his temple and jawline. He should have been beyond all recognition and yet, he looked oddly familiar.

He was still looking at her gently, waiting for her answer. So she said, "No, I supposed they killed him, honestly. I guessed the Barkurians at the parade killed him right after the assassination."

The man shook his head. "They took him to be interrogated, to find out what he knew. They kept him in the old dungeon under Ballynach Castle. Where they keep political prisoners."

Brenna cocked her head, about to ask him why he was telling her this, when the realization slapped her across the face. The eyes, so round and unusually close together. The long, thin nose, same as the picture in the newspaper.

In front of her was the stranger whose plight had started all of this. The reason they left home.

He seemed to see the recognition on her face before he said, "I am Inigo Farro."

The name that was more than a name. The name that symbolized nationalism for so many people now, for the Tibedese and the Barkurians alike. The name she could never forget, down to the font used that first time she saw it in the newspaper. Or the way Mara had written it.

"We found a letter for you," Brenna explained as Katiel rose to stand beside her at the bars. She couldn't help how fast the words spilled out, still in shock that they were meeting someone who, in her mind, was only a legend. "Someone tried to warn you about the framing before it was too late. Someone from Bar Kur was trying to warn you not to attend the parade that day."

The edge of Farro's mouth dipped forlornly. "If it wasn't me, it would've been someone else."

"But you were a lead keeper, right?" Brenna clarified. "That's why they targeted you. And that is how Mara recognized your name."

"It's true I was a lead keeper," he said, "but other than that, I was nobody. No one knew my name outside of the business. I'm ashamed to say, I don't even recognize anyone by the name Mara. But I must've led a meeting she attended at some point. On Bar Kur Day, I was just another traveling merchant at the parade, there to sell the handicrafts my wife and daughter make. They weave little charms to hang above the bed at night, to ensure sweet dreams." He smiled a little as he remembered them. "They're very talented, you know."

"Had you ever met General Taregh before?" Katiel asked. "Were you ever involved in politics with him?"

"Oh no, I would have never wanted to be a politician. I hate attention, and I loved my life as it was." Inigo Farro's shoulders slumped. "I started off on a rough path, in a bad part of my hometown. When I was a boy, I stole food for my family and got sentenced to prison for so long that when I got out, I was a man. At first, no one would hire me, but I found a calling as a keeper, and I met my wonderful wife, whose business helped get us on our feet. We had a good life together with our daughter. That life was all I wanted."

Brenna felt a lump form in her throat. It hadn't occurred to her that he might have a family, waiting for him and missing him. She hated Taregh for doing this, but she hated Jay more. He knew what it was like to be part of a family. He should have cared about Inigo's family, too. "Do you know what happened to them? Your wife and daughter?"

Inigo hung his head. "I wish I did. I haven't heard anything. Since they aren't in here with me, I hope that means they made it somewhere safe." He leaned against the bars, meeting Brenna's eyes across the narrow corridor. "I am thankful that your friend tried to warn me, even if I never received it. But I don't quite understand, why would Taregh want to target a keeper?"

"We don't fully understand either," Brenna said with a shake of the head, "but we know he's after the ore."

"Of course," Inigo said. "The ore is power. Power starts wars. It is such a shame to lose lives over that. First the king gone, and now the rest of the royal family gone with him."

Katiel turned sharply to Brenna. She had been listening intently throughout the conversation, not saying a word. But now she asked, "What do you mean, 'the rest of the royal family'?"

35

Katiel

"What do you mean, 'the rest of the royal family'?"

As quickly as Katiel asked, she knew the answer. Something she had not considered at all—a foolish thing to overlook in retrospect. Killing King Stefan XIV alone would do nothing to give Taregh power because the throne would go to the king's heir. Katiel knew the king had children, though she could not remember how many. There had been no word about them lately in the news.

"The royal family of Bar Kur," Farro explained. "I've been down here for weeks, but I hear things. From the guards. And from General Taregh. He said they took King Stefan's children and the queen in order to, as he put it, 'eliminate' them. Said he planned to pin those murders on me, too." He shook his head. "Since it was days ago when he said it, I assumed they were gone by now."

"There have been no reports about the rest of the royal family," Katiel said, surveying Brenna's reaction. She had to be thinking the same thing Katiel was— that the royal family could still be alive. "Why would he tell you?"

"Taregh has typically been the one down here"—he paused as darkness flashed across his mangled face—"*dealing* with me. He said it to taunt me, I suppose, but I've been trying to get him to talk. I found if you can get him talking, he talks a lot. Anything that challenges him. He'll get threatened and go on rambling."

"We have to save them, then," Brenna said. "If we can save the queen, she'll have to believe us about Taregh being the culprit, and she would have the power to end the war."

"But we don't know where they are," Katiel pointed out.

"I don't know, either," added Farro. "Taregh never mentioned a location."

Brenna looked down at her boots as she shuffled them on the damp ground before whipping her head back up. "Wait! Yes, we do," she said, snapping her fingers in triumph. "In the letter from Mara. It read, *'the others will be at the mill.'* I think I had it all wrong when I read it before. Maybe it was about the other royals. Maybe he's keeping them at a mill."

Farro gasped. "A mill. I think you might be onto something. Once when Taregh came down here, he smelled vile, but I couldn't place the scent. Now that you say that, though, he smelled exactly like a paper mill. The sulfuric scent is pretty distinctive."

"Oh, that's—" Brenna started, when boot steps thumping in the distance cut her off.

Without delay, Katiel slunk back into the shadows, waiting for the guard to pass. She sat back against the wall and closed her eyes, pretending to be asleep. She hoped Brenna was doing the same.

The metallic clang of keys echoed off the walls as the steps drew closer. She could tell that the person was in the prison chamber now, circling. Then they stopped—just outside her and Brenna's cell. A thousand worst-case scenarios rushed into her mind, and she bit her lip hard as she fought to avoid shaking. She did not dare open her eyes, no matter how badly she wanted to see.

She hoped, somehow, they might get lucky, and it would be Ellis. He had known Brenna since she was a baby. Perhaps seeing Brenna down here in the dungeon might make him reconsider what he was doing. He might go easy on them and let them leave. If it was General Taregh, on the other hand, they may soon be as bruised and butchered as Inigo Farro. Even a rogue guard might want to hurt them, too.

Please let them leave, she willed to the Creator, something she never did. Sheer desperation was the only reason she was doing it now. *Please, please, let them leave us.*

She wished so badly that she could reach out and grab Brenna's hand, but she stayed still. She wished she had never fought with her. They needed each other now more than ever.

If only she could have sent that letter to her parents when she tried. If she did not make it out of here, that discussion at dinner might be the last conversation she ever had with them. Tears swelled against her lashes at the bleakness of it. Their last conversation, about something random and forgettable. It should have been her telling them she loved them.

With a terrifying *thunk*, the footsteps started again. But no one opened the cell. The steps grew softer and softer until all that remained was an unsettling stillness in the air.

She did not move for a while after that, and neither did Brenna.

"If you're going to get out of here, now would be the time," Inigo Farro said from his place in the shadows. "Taregh comes by this time of night, and then there's a night guard who keeps a vigilant watch in here until dawn."

Katiel grabbed Brenna's hand. It was shaking as much as hers.

If only she had seen the guard's keyring on his belt as it jangled past.

Wait, that was it.

Mara had told her to concentrate while wielding, but she was concentrating on the wrong things. She had been focusing on the type of object, but she could not expect to wield a key she had never seen. Keys were all different. They each served their own purpose. A nail, a chain, a watering can, everything she had practiced—it was all the same. She had been concentrating on the essence of the subject she was trying to wield while ignoring the details that informed how to craft the subject precisely. She had been going about it all wrong.

The hairpins she used to secure her braid crown were gone, taken with her necklace, but she knew exactly what those were like. She saw them every day, and the details remained clear in her mind. She could wield them. And if she could wield two of them, Brenna could pick the lock and get them out of there. This lock might be more complex than the ones at Galvey, but Brenna *did* always say she could solve any puzzle.

Katiel placed a fleck of ore in her palm and squeezed her eyes shut as she lifted her palm to her lips. Everything else brushed away. She only needed to imagine a hairpin. Not just any, but her own. The kind she used every day. Her hairpin, the sole image in her mind.

She blew out, and nothing. Not even the dust.

It was truly hopeless.

No, she could not think this way. She could do it. She had to try.

For Brenna, for herself, for everything they had done together. For Henred and for Dakier, bravely fighting on each side. For her parents, for trying to protect her.

For the royal family, if they were still alive. If they could get to them before it was too late, perhaps it would change things. The queen could arrest General Taregh for ordering the murder of her husband. If they found them, the war could still end.

And if they did not, and Taregh pinned those killings on the Tibedese as well, the Barkurian people would never forgive them. The peace of their Continent might never recover.

She closed her eyes again, not squeezing this time, but shutting them gently instead. Softly. Full of peace. The peace that always existed deep down rose to the surface.

This time she visualized not just the hairpin, but pulling it out of her braid after a long day. Securing her favorite hairstyle in the morning before she did her chores. Brenna smiling at her when she clicked the lock open, when they ran out of here together.

Katiel drew another fleck and blew. The cloud appeared and ensconced her and Brenna. Shimmering dust surrounded them, filling the cell, illuminating the space, and blocking out all else. This time, she held onto it. This time, she would not let go.

The image of Brenna's triumphant smile stayed in her mind as she molded it. First, to shrink the amount. It was too much for a hairpin. And as she thought about it, the cloud shrank. Shrank to a tiny puff, hovering above her hands.

Now she only had to shape it. Her fingers worked fast, like they had a mind of their own, spinning and shaping the dust that filled the air.

And suddenly, there it was. Her hairpin. No longer made of ore, but of the same metal as hers had been. She never knew what type of metal hers was, but she could recall the way it felt in her fingers, and that had been enough.

The second it became its own substance, gravity took over. Katiel reached out, clasping the creation in her outstretched palm as it fell.

Brenna was staring at the hairpin, mouth agape. Katiel shot her the briefest of smiles before wielding a second, afraid the ability would somehow wear off if she waited.

"You did it," Brenna breathed as Katiel offered her creations up to her. "I knew you could."

"Can you pick the lock?" Katiel asked, willing Brenna to believe in herself like she believed in her.

Brenna looked hesitant, but she said, "Yes."

Her hands shook as she took them.

She reached her arms through the gaps in the bars, feeling for the lock that she could not quite see. She stared up at the ceiling while she moved the first pin, waiting, listening for a click. And then another one.

Click, click.

The padlock loosened, dipping slightly, and Brenna grabbed onto it, yanking open the clasp.

The lock clattered against the stones as it fell to the floor. It was the sweetest sound Katiel had ever heard.

Brenna opened the cell door, and they both rushed out. "I don't know where to go," Brenna said, hushed and frantic. "We didn't see how we came in."

"Let's just run," Katiel said. "We can find the way as we go."

She was on the tips of her toes, about to take off, when Brenna said, "Wait." She was standing in front of Inigo Farro's cell, looking at the ruined figure resting on the cell floor. Seeing him this close, it was obvious why he did not stand for too long. "What about him?"

"I don't know." Katiel pursed her lips tightly.

Suddenly, Farro's eyes shot open, and he rose to his feet, decidedly nimbler than he had been earlier. "Go on," he said. "Get out before the general comes."

"Wait, since you hear things," asked Brenna, "do you know who the general is working for? Have you heard of someone referred to as the 'boss'?"

Inigo looked down as he tried to remember. "No, I haven't heard of anyone. Now go, get out."

Katiel's mind raced with the decision. They could not release a war criminal—not them, these random girls. And if they let him out, she was not sure he could keep up with them and escape. But they also could not leave any innocent man here in this cell to die.

"Free him and let's go."

Brenna reeled on her. "You think we should?"

Katiel nodded before she could change her mind. "He is innocent."

A hesitant look came across Brenna's features, but she stepped closer to the lock on his cell. She waited while she thought. While she wrestled with herself.

"He's the enemy of Bar Kur," Brenna said at last. "But he didn't do it. And that's what matters."

Without so much as looking over her shoulder to check for the guard, she set to work. And in doing so, she set him free.

"Brenna, one second," Katiel said. Honing in on her new-found concentration, she wielded a knife, and then another. Not any knife but Dakier's pocketknife, the one he kept with him for chores at the farm. Something she knew, and something they could use if they ran into anyone on the way out. "Here, take it."

When she placed it in Brenna's palm and closed her fingers around it, her friend shot her a desperate look. A look that conveyed how terrified she was at the thought of having to use it.

"Just in case."

"Wait," Farro said as he stepped out of his cell. "You're young. You shouldn't have to resort to violence." Despite his words, he made no move to take the knives from them. "While I've been down here, I have been listening closely to the footsteps of the guards. I can lead us out. Stay behind me, and if anything goes wrong, I'll distract the guards so you can run."

"But I've honed my ability now." Katiel held up her palms. "I can make something. I can help us."

Farro shook his head. "There are grave consequences to wielders using their abilities for violence. And grave consequences for being discovered by the authorities as a wielder. You two wound up in this fight because you were trying to help me, and you've helped so much already. If it comes to it, I will delay the guards, but you must promise you won't wield, and you'll run instead."

Brenna swallowed hard. "We promise."

Katiel nodded, but she hoped it did not count as a promise on her part. They had made it so far, and she did not want to give up now, no matter what.

36

Brenna

Brenna flew down the dark pathway of the maze-like dungeon, her shoes scraping against the rough stone. Katiel and Inigo Farro's footfalls echoed through the corridor as they ran in front of her. Inigo took the lead, dashing past doorways and darting around corners at an amazingly fast pace given his injuries. He must've been planning his own escape, Brenna realized, since he'd listened for a way out so closely.

Katiel took a sharp left and, before Brenna knew what was happening, Katiel grabbed onto her arm, hauling her into the passageway after her. Footsteps that Brenna had not registered were approaching them, two sets coming from different directions. It had to be the changing of the guard. They had barely made it.

Inigo waited, still as a rabbit as he listened. Brenna knew what he was doing—he was focusing on the guard who was leaving, waiting for the sounds of someone ascending a staircase. They were underground, so to get out, the only way to go was up.

When the footsteps faded into the distance, Brenna sprinted away, not daring to look back. She kept running, the sound of their breathing filling the passageway, until they reached a spiral staircase. Inigo winced as they climbed, slowing a bit, his injured leg catching up with him.

They halted at the top of the stairwell and peered out.

Before them was a short hallway, ancient-looking with walls of stone, a place nothing like the modern government building that held Jay's office. At the end of the hall was what appeared to be a guardroom, with well-stocked rifle racks lining the walls.

A shrill whistle shattered Brenna's ears, reverberating off the stone. The guards must have figured out that they were missing.

At the sound, Katiel set off in a sprint down the hallway. But it was too late. A swarm of guards gathered at the opposite end, blocking their path. Behind them, another guard blocked the way out.

The guards had them surrounded. Breaking out of the cell had been of no use. For a moment, Brenna thought it was all over.

But then Katiel pulled her hand to her mouth, and Brenna's breath caught in her throat. Katiel was going to wield—and reveal her ability to the guards.

Inigo shouted, "Don't!" as he lunged for the guard behind them. In a flash, he grabbed the guard's gun from his belt and ran toward the other guards. Brenna knew what he was doing. He was sacrificing himself to save them. Like he said he would.

"Run, now!" he screamed at them. A guard tackled him to the ground, sending the gun sliding across the stone floor. "Save the children! End the war!"

Katiel's eyes flashed as they locked with Brenna's. Inigo was right that they had to save the royal family, but he had a family, too.

Inigo staggered to his feet and turned back to the guards, like he might try to take them on unarmed, when Katiel huffed. A fast-moving cloud of ore filled the chamber, encircling the guards. They cried out in shock as the ore temporarily blinded them, and Brenna saw her opportunity. She couldn't hesitate this time. Turning on her heels, she took off in the other direction, darting through the narrow passage the guard had been blocking.

Two sets of boots thumped behind her as she swerved past the stairwell and down another hall and then another, both identical to the one they had come from. Blindly, she ran for the double doors at the far end, hoping for a way outside. She clutched the brass handle, and the door swung open, sending her tumbling out. Katiel and Inigo were close enough behind to fall into her, and they landed in a heap on the rough pavement outside.

Outside.

It was a miracle. They made it out.

Brenna peeled herself out of the stack and was about to let out a cheer when she noticed the scene before her.

Jay was a few feet away from them, climbing into an open window on the outside of the castle. Registering who had tumbled out the door, he tried to step down and instead lost his footing, flailing his arms and landing on his back on the stone pavers. The second he landed, he sprang back to his feet on reflex.

"Jay?" Brenna did not know whether to run toward him or away. "What are you doing here?"

Jay shook his head in disbelief before he grabbed Brenna's wrist and pulled her toward him. "No time to explain. Come on."

She whipped her hand free. "We aren't going back to jail."

He clutched his hands to his head in exasperation. "I'm trying to help you get away. Now come on!"

Katiel met her eyes and shrugged, as if to say, *What else are we going to do?* And she wasn't wrong. The guards would surely find them if they tried to escape the city on foot. Brenna was amazed they had evaded them thus far.

Jay took off again, without grabbing her this time, and Brenna followed him as he darted past a building opposite the castle. Around the corner, there was a generic coach-for-hire with a young man who Brenna had never seen before sitting in the driver's seat. "A carriage?" she asked when she saw it.

"It'll be slower but more discreet," Jay said in a hushed tone. "There are a million in the city that look just like this. Now get in."

"What about him?" Brenna cocked her head toward Inigo, who lingered a few feet behind them.

Jay eyed him up and down, dread overcoming his features as he recognized who it was. For a second, Brenna was sure her brother-in-law was going to turn him back in, but all he said was, "I never saw him."

"I can make my way out of the city on my own," Inigo said, somehow not sounding the least bit afraid, "and reunite with my family in Jinensin. Words cannot express the great service you've done for me. And you," he addressed Katiel, "must be extra careful, now that you've revealed what you can do."

With those parting words, he disappeared before Brenna or Katiel had the chance to utter a word.

Jay opened the carriage door, his eyes frantically darting in the castle's direction. "*Please*, get in."

"Where are you taking us?" They had to get to the mill to find the other royals. She knew they were still there. Something in her could feel it.

"Why does it matter?"

"We have to find a paper mill." Brenna didn't bother to explain the connection to Mara's lost letter. There was no time, and the vague wording likely wouldn't be enough to convince Jay. But it was the only lead they had, and finding the other royals was too crucial not to try.

Jay shook his head. "There are loads of mills in this city."

Brenna thought back to the odd creases on the page that all led up to the upper left. She'd assumed it was from how the page had been folded, but now she wondered if it was a part of the message itself. "It might be in the northwest part of the city," she said, her instincts telling her she was onto something. "Somewhere your boss would keep something important to him. Very important."

"No, Brenna." Jay looked like he was about to wring his hair again. "We have to get you out of here."

"Yesterday you wouldn't listen to me." He had to know she was not moving if he wouldn't agree. "Listen to me now. Trust me."

A look of realization swept over Jay's features. "Wait, the northwest, you say?" Looking like he was going against the last of better judgment, he huffed, "Fine," before giving the driver an address. Brenna and Katiel poured into the carriage, Jay hurrying in after them. The door had barely clicked shut when the coach took off.

"So, you *did* know of a mill," Brenna said, her voice rising above the hoofbeats and wheels clanging against the cobblestone pavement. She and Katiel sat next to one another, across from Jay. "Were you in on the plot to kill the rest of the royal family, too?"

"'Plot to kill the royal family'?" Jay shook his head in dismissal. "Don't be ridiculous. I didn't plot to kill the king, either."

"Then start explaining." Brenna crossed her arms. "Why did we get arrested in your office?"

Jay dragged a hand through his short hair. "I knew Taregh wanted to go to war with Tibedo. I was behind it, even." A horrible admission, but at least he could admit it. Still, Brenna hoped he could see the disappointment on her face. "I thought it was the best thing for our nation, but I didn't know Taregh had an evil plan to achieve it. I didn't know he would kill King Stefan." He sounded sorrowful, and Brenna knew it was the truth. Jay had named his son after King Stefan. Jay backed Bar Kur, even if it meant starting a false war. But the Barkurian people relied on the steadfastness and the tradition of the monarchy for a sense of stability. Killing the royal family was like killing Bar Kur itself.

"Once the king was gone, I suspected Taregh had something to do with it," Jay continued. "He seemed almost happy about the assassination. But I didn't know for sure. I hadn't suspected Ellis, though—not at all. He never mentioned a word about it. When you came into the office with your letter, my first reaction was to deny it, because I didn't want to believe I'd had a part in it. But the more I thought about it, I knew you were right. Ellis stopped showing up to work a couple days ago. When you said he was involved, I knew his absence had to be related."

Brenna patted her chest reflexively, feeling the familiar crunch of parchment in her dress. She still had the original letter, the first one they'd found that started everything. She hadn't even thought to check in the prison if it had been taken along with Katiel's necklace. It was amazing she still had it.

Jay's eyes followed her hand, registering that she was indeed still in possession of the letter. "I didn't know he was going to arrest you. I don't know how he found out what you know, but it wasn't me. Did you tell anyone else about your letter?"

Anton, Sera, Mara, Simeon, Dakier, Alfien.

Brenna cursed herself for telling so many people.

Next to her, Katiel was biting at her cuticles, and Brenna knew she had to be thinking about who they had told. Dakier, Alfien, and Mara were the safe bets against telling Taregh, but the Drezchy—not so much.

"I'm sorry," Katiel mumbled from behind her hand.

Brenna knew she was blaming herself again for trusting Anton. "Don't be sorry." She reached over and squeezed Katiel's free hand. "What I said before was wrong. You can't just go your whole life never trusting people. If he was the one who turned us in, it was his fault for betraying us."

Jay was looking back and forth between them with a raised eyebrow, like he wanted to know more but had somehow discerned this was about a boy. He breathed in sharply through his nose, making it clear he had decided not to ask.

Brenna was glad he didn't as she thought back on Jay's admissions. Everything still wasn't adding up. "So, you didn't know about the plot to hurt the rest of the royals. How did you know where to direct the driver, then?"

"Taregh has some artillery warehouses out on the northwest side of town in a milling compound. If he had something important, he would keep it there." Jay paused, like he almost didn't want to ask what he was about to. "Do you truly believe he took the rest of the royal family hostage?"

Brenna nodded. "Inigo said that the queen and King Stefan's children were being held at a paper mill on the outskirts of the city."

"Inigo." Jay scoffed. "So we're acting on a lead from a war criminal. I hope you're right about all this."

"Me too," Brenna replied. Jay's eyes softened like they did sometimes, in the rare instances he seemed to care about her.

"I was stupid not to see that once he did what he did, he would go after the others," Jay said, clearly referring to General Taregh. His regret was evident, and almost heartbreaking. Brenna had never seen him so much as admit he was wrong, let alone beat himself up about his mistakes. "But I wasn't there that day you mentioned, Brenna. I didn't know he planned to kill the king. It hardly matters, though. Once I knew he planned to break the law, I didn't turn him in. Unlike you, when I found out the truth, I did nothing."

"There was nothing you could have done." Brenna wanted to reassure him, though she did not quite believe it was true.

"Look." Katiel motioned to the window. She pulled the curtain back an inch, and the stone wall surrounding the inner city came into view.

"We're leaving through the western gate. A guard may come up and question us. If so, let me do the talking." As soon as the words left Jay's mouth, they heard the creaking of a rusty gate lifting to let them pass.

"Lucky," Katiel said. Brenna nodded in agreement, thinking it unusual that no one stopped them to search the carriage. She supposed the wall was there to keep people out rather than to keep them in.

A few moments later, the coach screeched to a halt.

The footman opened the door with a curt bow of the head. "Your destination, sir."

Brenna thanked him as they stepped into the outer city, swathed in twilight. The buildings here were sparser than in the inner city, with gardens and unkempt lawns sprawling between them. A narrow, curving lane wound through the area, a dirt road with no gas lamps and chunks of grass growing over the path in patches.

Her eyes followed the road's length, but she smelled it before she saw it in the distance. A paper mill. It was part of a crop of large wooden buildings, all interconnected. There would be loads of nooks and crannies in there, perfect for hiding something. It had to be the place.

She was about to say as much to her companions when an eerie feeling came over her.

It had been too easy. Something wasn't right.

She sensed the presence behind her before she heard the voice.

"We have to stop meeting like this."

The hair on her neck stood on its end. General Taregh. He had found them. Or this had been a trap, somehow.

She had no more time to think. Something hit her in the back of the head, and everything went black.

37

Katiel

"Can you people not stay conscious for five minutes?"

General Taregh's voice grated against Katiel's ears before she opened her eyes. She felt for her surroundings before she dared to reveal that she was alert. She seemed to be seated in a wooden kitchen chair, and a light tug at her limbs confirmed she was bound with her ankles together by the floor and her hands together behind her back. No wielding then, not in this position. She shifted her weight, feeling the absence of the knife from where she had tucked it into her skirt pocket. Taregh must have taken it, and probably Brenna's as well.

"I can tell you're awake, blond girl," the general drawled.

Katiel opened her eyes to meet his.

So he did not know her name. That meant he did not know who her parents were. Inigo was right. He was already doling out valuable information without even realizing.

The general was standing over her, wearing his military uniform and his typical tar-eating grin. She was in a barn, with her chair tied to a wooden support beam. To her right, Brenna and Jay were trapped in the same position. Jay was out cold and covered in blood—Katiel had seen him put up quite a fight when Taregh had arrived—but Brenna was wide awake and unscathed, glaring at the general like the evil idiot that he was.

Behind Taregh, the night sky shone through the double barn doors he had inexplicably left open.

"What do you want with us, Taregh?" Brenna demanded, never breaking the icy stare she had fixed on him.

"Methinks you little girls know a little too much," he drawled.

"'Methinks'?" Brenna repeated incredulously. She was bold to mock him now, but she had always been bold. Katiel was glad to see her spirit still intact, even if they might not make it out of this. "What are you going to do, kill us? Like you killed the king?"

"Obviously."

A chill jolted down Katiel's spine. There was no emotion in that word. Not even a perverse joy. It was clear he could kill both of them and feel nothing. It was obvious from the second she saw his lifeless eyes.

She studied them again, now, and it was the same. The edges of his eyes did not expand and contract normally to show his emotions. She had seen a dead sheep with more feeling behind the eyes. Another shiver shot down her spine at the haunting thought.

"You think you could be a bit more creative than that," said Brenna. "Just killing everyone who gets in your way seems like a cheap shot to me."

"I'm plenty creative," the general snapped, his voice rising.

What Brenna was doing was obvious—stalling him until they could find a way out of this. And it was working. A grown man and government official was falling for the taunts of a teenager. He was pathetic, but that was something they could work to their advantage.

Katiel always let Brenna do the talking, but it was not fair this time. It was not fair to let her stick her neck out for both of them.

The only issue was, she did not know what to say. She tried to think of what Brenna would do. What Anton would do even, cunning as he was despite the betrayal. Strange as it was, she realized both of them would do the same—they were both very bold people, as she had said to him that first day in Heidel's. A day that felt like years ago now.

Both of them would try to make their lives worth something to Taregh, even falsely. Try to offer him something he wanted, the promise of information. Taregh had no empathy, but he had ambition. And that should not be too hard to manipulate.

"You do not know how much we know," Katiel told him, the sentence coming out weaker than she would have liked. "We know more than you think."

Brenna gaped at her, but she played along convincingly. "No, don't tell him. We told them we'd never talk."

"Shut up, both of you!" he screamed, surprisingly shrill.

Just then, Jay awoke with a sharp intake of breath. Upon taking in the scene, he immediately launched into his defense. "It was me, General. I was the only one trying to stop you. The girls are innocent. They knew nothing about it."

But Taregh said, "Quiet, Jacoby," and punched the side of Jay's face so hard that he lost consciousness again.

"You'll break his neck!" Brenna yelled, straining hard against the ropes on her wrists.

"That would be a pleasant surprise," Taregh said. "One less busybody around the office for me to deal with." He flashed an eerie smile, his mouth too deliberately shaped. His dead-sheep eyes still showed nothing. "And if you don't start talking, I'll break yours as well."

Do not be afraid, Katiel willed herself. *Do not be afraid. Keep him talking. Keep him talking.*

"We know you have the queen and the royal children here," she ventured, saying anything to heed Inigo's advice. Anything to keep the general talking instead of killing them. "We know about your idiotic plot to frame Inigo for it."

"It is a brilliant plot," Taregh seethed, slamming the back of his hand into her jaw.

The world slowed as she closed her eyes, reeling from the impact. She could have sworn she heard a crack, but she could not reach up to touch her throbbing face. She was in the blackness, but it was not the blissful blackness with Anton. It was a horrid, lonely place.

Katiel swallowed hard as she opened her eyes. She could do this. They would make it out of here. After everything, it could not end like this.

She could not let him win.

If she could get one hand free—

"Anyone would believe that poor, sniveling Farro did it. And I have him. I'll set him up at the right place at the right time, just like I did on Bar Kur Day." Taregh had taken the bait. Her flippant remark offended him enough to tell them more information. To defend himself, to them. "With no clear heir to the throne, there will be a power vacuum. And I have strong reasons to believe I will be chosen as the new king." Another bit of intelligence that Katiel tucked away. She assumed the boss had promised him the position, whether they intended to honor their word or not. All the while, Taregh sneered like he had won something. Like his criminal admissions should impress them. "I'll be at the helm of Bar Kur, one of the most powerful nations in the world. See, it's a brilliant plot, no?"

"You're a monster!" Brenna screamed at him. He had evidently struck a nerve with her. Katiel widened her eyes at her friend, willing her to focus on escaping, but Brenna was not paying attention. "The people fighting this war are good people who care about Bar Kur, who think our country is being threatened and needs defending! Good people like my brother!" That was the nerve. It was Henred. Who was out on the battlefield, who she had not heard from in weeks. "They trust you! How could you do that to them?"

"If they trust the government, that's their mistake."

Brenna looked like she was about to scream at him more. More things she felt with her heart, more words he could use against them. So Katiel cut in with the first thing she thought of. Something that meant nothing to her, something else to keep him talking. "What about the boss, the one you work for? Will they not rule above you?"

"No, it's Tibedo's mines they want," he jeered. "They couldn't care less about Bar Kur."

It angered him, then, the thought of someone else being above him.

Katiel meant to tuck the information away with everything else, hoping it would come in handy somehow, when her focus hitched on a word. Mines.

What sort of mines would be valuable enough to start a war over? More valuable even than acquiring the port city? The answer smacked her in the face. The ore.

Of course, it had to be true. This conflict centered on the ore—finding it, controlling it. Controlling those who could control it.

Mara had said as much about why the wielders had disappeared after the Ten Years' War. Why her parents had gone into hiding, why they had hidden her away. Not even letting those loyal to the wielders know she existed.

And she had undone all their efforts with one stupid decision. She had walked into the thick of the conflict in her futile efforts to help end the war.

She never should have left home.

General Taregh was glaring at her, contemplating. Finally, he drawled out, one word at a time, "How do you know about the boss?"

Neither of them answered. He drew back like he was going to strike her again. Katiel did her best not to flinch. Make him think she was strong and unafraid. Even if she was not.

"You were there that day, in the offices with the maid." He spoke unnervingly slowly, his dead eyes narrowing on her as he reached the erroneous conclusion. "You helped her evade Sera and escape out the window."

He got closer, screaming something. Perhaps it was a question that she was supposed to answer. Perhaps he was demanding to know how they had gotten in.

But she could not focus on that. All she heard was the name.

Sera.

Sera always wore a black cloak with a hood. The same thing Mara described the person she evaded that day as wearing.

The keeper who was new to the business, who had only recently met Master Larinne, and who did not hesitate to hold them at knifepoint and then join their quest.

Sera, with her uncanny agility, racing out of the train car like some kind of trained assassin while the others struggled.

Sera diving back into the water again and again, more desperate than anyone to save Simeon and Mara. The look in Sera's eyes as they left, the desperation for a woman she barely knew.

That had not been a coincidence that the bridge was out. It was a calculated attack, accomplished by someone trained to kill.

But that person had miscalculated. The attack was not meant for random civilians. It was meant for them.

Sera, who had a tremendous store of ore in her clutches right now.

Or in Anton's.

Katiel recalled the conversation she had overheard between Anton and Simeon. The one he said he wanted her to hear. Did that mean he had known the role Sera played, but he had wanted to warn her? Why would he bother?

An ungodly wealthy man, guileful and calculating enough to speak her language and notice her abilities, traveling in a foreign country with nothing better to do than join their dangerous endeavor. He had as much as said he did not want to tell her his genuine reasons for coming. Why warn her at all, then? Why pull her out of the water after the train wreck, saving from a death that could have easily passed for an accident? None of it made any sense.

"Are you even listening, you insolent girl?" General Taregh screeched at her. He must have been screaming more things for a while, then.

He reeled back as if to strike her, probably hard enough to go back out.

She flinched this time, but no pain came.

Instead, a flash shone outside, through the barn doors. A flash of red and orange, blazing against the night sky. And the next second, the sounds of firecrackers, gunshots banging one after the next.

Someone had set off an explosion in the artillery storage facility.

38

Brenna

Brenna watched Katiel lose focus as Taregh screamed at her. She dared not say anything, but as Katiel disassociated further from reality, Brenna desperately hoped that this was another part of her brilliant plan. So far, Katiel had shown even more cunning and valor than Brenna knew her capable of. She showed no fear when Taregh hit her—nothing like the terror that thrummed through Brenna, threatening to eat her alive.

Brenna willed her friend to come back to life, to say some other clever, brilliant thing, when the world outside exploded.

The heat rushed through the open door even from this distance, burning hot against Brenna's face. The artillery was popping, each setting off the next and adding to the fire roaring outside.

They had to get out of the barn, fast. Fastened with ropes to a wooden structure, they would burn alive.

A flicker of movement caught in her peripheral, and she whipped her head to it. A person hid among the barrels stacked by the doorway.

Not any person, but Sera, cloaked in her usual black. She pressed a finger to her lips, and Brenna darted her eyes away, praying Taregh had not followed her gaze.

She didn't have time to wonder how Sera had gotten here or why she had come before Taregh swore and raced out the door, heading in the fire's direction. Jay had said the general stored artillery here, likely enough that he would need to salvage any he could before it was all lost to the flames.

The second he disappeared, Sera emerged from behind the barrels. With a knife clutched tightly in her hand and the hot air blowing her cape behind her, she looked like someone from a legend. Like Queen Sylka, when she came to rescue her people in the sagas.

And that's what Sera was doing. She had set off the explosion. She had come back to rescue them.

She crouched down to Katiel first, examining the knot that tied her to the support beam. Deeming it too intricate to untangle, she sawed at the rope with the knife instead. It made sense she would go to Katiel before Brenna. Katiel had the power, and Sera served the wielders, at least in theory. Though if Taregh was to be trusted, it sounded like she was some sort of double agent.

"How did you find us?" Brenna whispered.

Sera glanced over her shoulder, slicing the knife back and forth at a mad pace. "It was easy. I followed you here from the jail." The first rope snapped in two by her hands, and the success spurred her on even faster as she moved to free Katiel's wrists.

"Why did you come back?" It took every bit of Brenna's willpower to keep her volume down. "You tried to kill hundreds of innocent people in a train crash!"

"I sent information ahead about you two and Mara—a report of your whereabouts so the general could capture you upon your return to Bar Kur." Sera's focus waned as she worked on the ropes, evidently admitting something she would rather not. "I didn't know what the general had planned, but knowing I had a part in the train crash, it's hard to live with myself. That's why I came back."

"Then why did you do it?" Katiel asked her, sounding more hurt than fuming mad, like Brenna felt.

"She heard too much," Sera replied, sounding pained to say it. "You *all* heard too much. I didn't want to. I was following orders."

"But why would you work for General Taregh?" Brenna eyed the feeble progress Sera was making on Katiel's ropes, despite sawing at a grueling pace.

"I don't." Sera shook her head. "I work for New Drezchy. Er, worked for. For my country. For the boss."

Brenna stilled as the words sank in. Sera had known who the boss was the whole time. She had been spying, working against them. She posed as a keeper in Linden to follow Mara and report on her whereabouts.

"Anton." Katiel breathed the name at the same time the thought occurred to Brenna. "The boss is Anton."

"No, it's not," Sera said sharply. "Anton knows nothing about my involvement with all of this. Neither does Simeon."

Katiel pressed her lips into a tight line, like there was something she was holding back. "But they ran off. Anton stole my ore."

"You really didn't figure it out, did you?" Sera shook her head, now making good progress on the last of Katiel's ropes. They had to be almost ready to break. "Anton has his own reasons for wanting the ore and for trying to find a wielder—for his research. That's why he had me swipe your necklace that day on the street in Linden. But he isn't the type to want a war."

For trying to find a wielder. Suddenly, everything that happened made more sense. Anton *had* been involved in taking Katiel's necklace off that day in Linden, to verify that she was a wielder. He had likely tipped off the innkeeper about them breaking into the wax shop, too, so Katiel would stay with him.

"If you knew who Anton was," Sera continued, "and knew why he took the ore, you would understand. He always has his reasons."

Brenna was tempted to say how ridiculous that was, that there would never be a good reason for him to betray Katiel, but the flames growing around the doorway distracted her. They hadn't reached the roof yet, but once they did, it wouldn't be long before the entire structure collapsed on top of them. "Hurry," she pleaded.

The last rope binding Katiel's wrists sprang free, and she seemed to forget the conversation. "Cut Brenna free from the post. I can untie my feet."

Sera moved behind Brenna, a panicked groan emitting from her lips. "Your ropes are thicker. This may take time."

"We don't have time." Brenna said it mostly to herself. She prayed Taregh would stay away, wherever he had run off to. She prayed she could make it out of here, that Jay would wake up, that neither of them would burn alive.

"There," Katiel breathed, sliding the loosened rope over her feet.

She turned toward Brenna like she was going to help her.

"Go, Katiel!" Brenna insisted. "Go find the royal family. Save them. Bar Kur needs them."

"I can't leave you here like this!"

"Better me than them."

Katiel's face twisted like she wanted to object. Brenna knew she did not agree, not at all, but because she was a good friend—because she was the best, truest friend any girl could ever ask for—she nodded.

And then she disappeared into the night.

39

KATIEL

KATIEL DID NOT BOTHER keeping to the shadows as she sprinted for the mill. There was no time to waste trying to find the royal family, not with the fire blazing throughout the complex.

She recognized the shabby exterior of the barn Taregh had tied them in. They were in the same set of buildings she had seen from the carriage before Taregh and his goons attacked them. That meant the paper mill that Inigo mentioned had to be close by. The smoky night air clouded her vision, though she hardly needed her sight in the reeking complex. The pungent stench of paper pulp rose above the sulfuric smell of the fire and guided her to the building—along with another horrible, unfamiliar scent.

She wished to never find out what could cause such a disturbingly human odor. But as she clasped the door handle, and the stench overwhelmed her, she knew whatever lay inside had to be horrific.

She pulled as hard as she could. The metal chains binding the sliding doors together caught against her effort, holding the doors in place.

"Hello," she yelled against the wood, "is anyone in there?"

The faintest sound met her in reply, little more than the squeak of a mouse. But she could have sworn the tiny voice asked for help.

"Are you in there?" she tried again.

This time, no reply came at all.

Desperately, she kicked at the wood in frustration, and the bottom of the door swung away with the force. It was loose on its hinges. That was enough. She dropped to her stomach in the dirt and slammed her shoulder into the bottom of the door. It barely budged, but it was enough to wrench her arm under it. As the rest of the door collided with her torso, the weight of the thing felt like it could rip her arm from the socket, but she gritted her teeth and pressed onward. She was small enough. If she pushed the door to the farthest point, she could fit under it. Clawing for purchase on the inside, she pressed her feet against the earth outside and—

She was in. She slid under as the door swung back into position behind her.

But the momentary triumph could not have prepared her for the horrific sight that awaited her.

It was a paper mill like any other, like the one they used to have in Fir Kelt that Brenna had persuaded her and Henred to sneak into years ago, "just to see what was in there." That mill had been a long room full of vats and presses, with pulleys and turnstiles to wear the paper thin.

This one was the same, except there were no windows, and along a long wall were four bodies, caked in filth and chained to large pieces of machinery that forced them to remain in a seated position on the stone floor. They were each secured far apart, too far to reach the others even with their legs, and it was evident from the disgusting stains and the smell that they had not left their positions for a while before they died.

Bile rose in Katiel's throat at the horror of what she witnessed, but she choked it down. The smell of smoke was growing stronger. She needed to leave before the fire made it to her end of the complex.

Then, out of the corner of her eye, she saw it. A flicker of movement. They were not dead bodies. The bile rose again. At least one of them was still alive.

She stepped closer. It was a woman, two little boys, and a girl who probably stood tall as Katiel but was rail thin. Queen Alva, the Princes Eoghan and Muiread, and Princess Stefana.

"Please, don't hurt us," the girl—the princess—choked out. "We will wait for Ellis. He'll help us."

"Ellis Fallon?" Katiel stammered. "Don't worry. I'm here to free you."

Katiel crouched down to get a look at the chains, but the girl jerked away, as if to shield her brothers despite her limited range of motion. "Don't touch us. Ellis!" the girl screamed.

"Be quiet," Katiel said, slamming her hand over the girl's mouth.

She screamed louder, the sound muffled against Katiel's palm. The smaller boy began to cry.

"Ellis is one of your captors, along with General Taregh. They trapped you here." Katiel could not fathom what was in the girl's mind, but there was no time for it. The flames were creeping into the far edge of the room. The building could collapse in moments.

"Ellis is kind when he comes," the girl insisted. "Not like the other man."

Katiel's head snapped up from where she had been looking at the chains, trying to think of what could break them. "What other man? Taregh?"

"Since Ellis stopped coming, the Secretary of War comes for meals," the princess said. "I don't know his name. But he doesn't tend to us properly. Mother died when Ellis stopped coming."

"Okay," Katiel said, trying futilely to process the information in the surrounding chaos. Gingerly, she reached for the cuffs again to see if she could pick the locks.

The girl looked like she might pull away again when a crash sounded behind them. A rafter caught fire and fell, sending sparks flying through the space.

"Let her, Steffi," the larger boy said. "Ellis isn't coming back. Let her try to free us." The smaller boy kept crying.

Katiel turned the shackle over in her hands gently to avoid hurting the tiny wrist within it. There was a seam and a keyhole. Interesting that it had a seam, since that meant it was an ordinary cuff rather than one fashioned by a wielder. That meant the general likely did not have any in his employ, then.

"Do you know where he keeps the key?" Katiel asked both of the children who had spoken so far.

"No, we don't know who has a key," the boy answered. "We didn't see who brought us here."

Katiel turned to the woman, meaning to inspect her shackle next to see if it matched, but the girl said, "Mother has been gone for two days."

Two days. And they had been here all the while. Katiel shuddered, unable to fathom the trauma of that.

"Hold still. Do not worry." Katiel was trying to say something to reassure them, but she needed the assurance herself as much as the kids. "I am going to free you."

But she did not know how she would manage. The fumes clouding the room sent the younger boy coughing. She needed to hurry.

She did not have the hairpins anymore, but this was not the sort of circular lock that clicked to let her know when it loosened, so the pins would not do much, regardless. Moving the metal machinery they were chained to was out of the question. The equipment was extremely heavy, far too heavy for her or the children to drag out.

Desperately, she scanned the space for anything she could use to free them. The vats for mixing pulp would be of no use, but the racks used to stretch the paper had a metal lever on each. If she could break it off, perhaps that could sever the chains—no, she was not strong enough to break chains with that. She could beat the chains all night with the lever and the thick iron would hold.

Smoke billowed into the room, coming from under the far door at the opposite end of the space, but the door she had come in remained clear. She had time before the inferno consumed them, but not much. She would have to wield something to free the children. But what, she did not know.

40
Dakier

"Mandia," was Pereira's first word to Dakier since the ambush. The captain said his surname sharply, speaking from his perch atop Kranich. Dakier walked on foot with the other farriers, keeping alongside the mounted cavalry officers. Not even an hour had passed since the attack, but the unit had already packed and set out, heading to the battlefield to assist the army units stationed at the border. "You really do speak Endran, then?"

So he *had* noticed earlier that Dakier had understood them. Dakier hoped it would not be an issue. "Yes, sir."

"Good." Pereira nodded. "In that case, you'll be with me today, translating. I have a few choice words for the Barkurian captains about the actions of their men this morning."

"Happy to assist, sir," Dakier replied, a statement that was only half-true. His Endran was perfect when speaking with Barkurians—he knew all of their subtleties and slang—but it was precisely because he was used to speaking with them that he possessed the skill at all. His Endran had been used in casual interactions with Brenna and playing cards with Henred at their family home. It was all wrong, being out here, using the knowledge he had of their culture to negotiate a war. Of Brenna's culture, with all she meant to him now.

It was later on the same day when they arrived at their destination, but to Dakier it felt like a week had passed since the morning's ambush. The battlefield was little more than a clearing, a flat expanse in the sparse grasslands that populated the border between Tibedo and Bar Kur. It was impossible to know exactly where the border lay since there was no road or river to mark it, but someone must have thought they knew, because there was a red flag stuck in the earth near the center of the clearing.

"That's our rendezvous point," Pereira said, following Dakier's eyeline to the flag.

The plan was to begin with the captains speaking together at the rendezvous point, trying to negotiate an outcome other than a bloody battle. At first, the prospect had excited Dakier, but according to both Sal and Pereira, it was a farce for civility. This was the way every battle began in all the wars of the Continent, and the talks never resulted in anything but both sides calling their lines to attack or setting a time for the next battle.

The negotiations started off contentiously, no hint of peace to be had. Dakier should have known better than to hope otherwise. There were three officers from the Tibedese side and three from the Barkurian, each standing side by side beyond the imaginary line indicated by the flag. Dakier was the only translator, as the Barkurians did not bring one. Strategically, it was a strange choice. Most likely, something had happened to theirs too recently to find a replacement.

In the distance behind them, a long row of Tibedese soldiers backed them—foot soldiers and cavalry officers bearing their rifles in the same orderly fashion. At the opposite end of the expanse was a hoard of Barkurian soldiers, armed the same but greatly outnumbering their Tibedese opponents.

The officers dismounted their horses before the negotiations began. To appear impartial, Dakier did not ride in on a mount, though his Tibedese army uniform ruined the illusion.

"Your attack this morning on our encampment was in direct conflict with the Kerafin Pact," was the first statement from either side. Pereira's words.

Dakier translated, matching Pereira's harsh tone to fulfill the captain's wishes, though he would have preferred to soften it.

"That *unsanctioned* attack," one of the Barkurian captains replied, emphasizing the word, "was conducted by only four men. And yet our side had a casualty while yours had none. I would say that makes us even for the initial break with the Pact."

Shooting someone in the back while retreating was also against the Pact, but no one needed to mention it. Everyone knew it. Pereira's strategy deteriorated further as the discussions went on, Dakier keeping faithful to each side's tones and inflections as best as he could.

Eventually, the deliberation turned to determining a proper time and place for the battle—to Dakier's shock, Pereira had explained that when the negotiation inevitably failed, they would schedule a battle that both sides agreed was fair.

The last thing he translated for Pereira was innocuous enough—"We need three days' time to prepare"—that Dakier was taken aback by the Barkurian's reply. The Barkurian captain announced that there would be no scheduling and shouted orders at the army behind him to attack.

Dakier translated for Pereira all in a rush, but it was hardly necessary. Pereira and the other officers were already back on their mounts, understanding a message that language was not needed to convey. The Barkurians had broken protocol again by initiating battle immediately.

Pereira whipped out a dagger from his belt and stabbed the Barkurian officer who spoke squarely in the chest, and it was all over.

And all beginning.

The Barkurian line broke out in a chant as they raced closer, and the Tibedese line charged forward to meet them.

The officers exchanged blows, alternating between retreating from the closeness required by the negotiations and firing at the other side at point-blank range.

Dakier was the only person in the center with no mount, facing the entire front line of the raging Barkurian army.

He was the sheep with a broken leg to the wolves that approached, the obvious weakling and first target. The translator role, the role he had thought of as an honor, was actually that of a calf first in line to the slaughterhouse.

Dakier shouldered his rifle, trying to prepare for the inevitable.

His inevitable slaughter.

He whispered a quick prayer within his mind—his last words to the Creator, he knew. At least this way, he could go with both his beliefs and honor intact. There was no way he would survive this position, and strangely, he could accept it.

Except for what he witnessed now.

A Barkurian soldier had peeled away from the line, faster than the others. His rifle was pointed right at Pereira. A few more paces, and he would be close enough to take down the captain, and maybe the others as well. With their leadership dispelled, the Tibedese would be defeated before the battle began. And besides, it was Pereira, the kind-hearted captain who believed in him.

The Barkurian soldier seemed to think himself too far away to make the shot, at least not accurately enough with his own officers so close to his target. But he wasn't too far for Dakier, not at all. The Barkurian soldier was alone, and Dakier was a capable shot even from a distance. He knew he could take out the soldier.

He knew he could. But not if he should. Who was he to take a human life? The Creator gives life, and the Creator takes away. The man cutting across the field was human. It wasn't right.

The soldier stopped running. He was going to shoot.

But Dakier fired first.

The bullet met its target, straight through the soldier's chest.

Straight through his heart.

He went down, and suddenly Dakier realized it.

Dakier recognized him—the wide mouth, the smattering of freckles, the close-cropped haircut.

It was Henred.

41

KATIEL

KATIEL STOLE A GLANCE at the children before pulling her fingernails up to her eyes, trying to think of anything she could wield that would aid her in freeing them. The kids watched her expectantly as they waited for their rescuer to do something, but the longer she took, the more she saw their expressions sag. Their confidence in her was clearly waning, but she could not blame them. She should have known finding them would be the simple part.

Her fingernails were perfectly clean, no traces of black under any of them. She swore to herself. The rest of what she had put there must have come loose or washed away.

She reached into her mouth to scrape at her gums, trying to find another morsel of ore. The princess eyed her skeptically. "What are you doing?"

Katiel pulled her hand in front of her, and, thankfully, she had retrieved one speck of ore. It would only be enough for one try, but that was all she needed. She could wield now.

"Brace yourselves," she warned them. "I am about to wield something to free you."

"You're about to what?" Stefana shrieked.

"She's a wizard," the older boy—Eoghan—breathed. "A wizard, come to save us."

"No, wizards have gray beards," the littlest one chimed in, the first time he had spoken instead of crying.

Katiel ignored them, drawing her hand up to her mouth. She could do this now. She could do it. Just exhale, expand, shape—

"Eo, wielders don't exist anymore," Stefana told her brother, "outside of fairy stories."

"Please, do not speak for a moment," requested Katiel, as gently as she could. "I need to concentrate."

Honestly, it was good Stefana had said something. She had not been concentrating like she needed to. She had not visualized what she needed to create this time. It should be easy to wield again since she had succeeded in the jail, but it was not. There was something wrong with her, some reason she could not do what she should.

She wished she were as smart as Brenna or as inventive as Anton. Or Simeon—he had suggested she make an invisibility cloak, his mind immediately going to a unique place beyond what she could imagine, beyond what she assumed her power could do. Any of them could create something to get out of this, something to break the chains. But they were not here, and Brenna was still out there, possibly getting hurt, and she needed to hurry—

Her mind raced with the panic and the urgency of the situation—she could not concentrate.

"Queen Sylka was not just a fairy story," Eoghan whispered to his sister. He must have thought Katiel was too preoccupied to notice, beyond listening. He was brave to say anything now, to act so nonchalant. Katiel hated to think of what all these children had gone through to speak so casually in a situation like this. "Queen Sylka and Oskar Spyri were real."

Katiel's breath hitched in her throat.

Of course—Oskar Spyri. When she heard the name, the memory flooded back to her. Oskar was the hero in his story, saving Queen Sylka in a time of need, but he had to hone his emotions to succeed. With his magic focused on what he truly felt, Oskar conjured an arrow that was always true to his aim. It was part of him, so it could not miss if he was the one who loosed it.

Mother had a reason for all her stories. Katiel knew that now. Her parents' actions made little sense before, but now that she was out in the world alone, the story's message became clear. The ore was part of her. It was why she could not be without it. Why she felt like she was sprinting alone through the dawn when she wielded it. Why she felt so alive.

It was a part of her mind. She could will it to do anything. She could will what she created to be sharper than the finest blade, will it to be stronger than she was on her own.

It was not about what someone else would do. The ore was hers to wield, even into something that could move on its own, if she could hone herself into something tangible. Something living, like the ore felt alive in her.

But she did not know which emotions she felt in order to focus as Oskar had. When she felt anything too intensely, she tried to put it out of her mind. That was how she always handled feelings—she tried to forget.

Now, all she felt was terror. Terror that the children would die if she could not save them, as so many people had died from the train crash when she had failed. Terror that Brenna would die, too, if she could not get back to her, and terror that Henred and Dakier would both perish in battle before they could end this war. If it was possible to end it at all anymore.

Suddenly, the answer became obvious, as if Oskar Spyri himself were guiding her. As if Mother's story was for this exact moment, meant to stay locked in her memory until it would matter most. The fears that she wanted to push away and forget could help her. Her fears showed her what she cared about, what was important to her. The fear was what she had focused on in the jail when she morphed her worries into a visualization. A visualization of them succeeding.

It all seemed obvious now. She knew what she would make.

She expanded the ore, and the children went silent, staring in awe at the small, sparkling cloud before them. With the slightest motion of her hand, it formed into a sword, crafted as she imagined it, before falling gently into her palm. The weapon was light as a feather and sharper than should be possible, but able to strike with the force of an ox despite its weight. It did not obey the laws of physics, but that was purposeful. She could create something new, something that bowed to her own laws.

"Stretch out your chains, please," Katiel requested of the three children. "Place them flat against the floor so I can break them."

Prince Eoghan was the only one who complied, spreading his wrists as instructed, and she struck, aiming for the point on the links that looked the thinnest. She met her target with precision, the precision of wielding a sword of her own making. In her arms, the weapon felt like nothing, but at the contact, the blade sliced through the iron links like they were made of butter.

The chain broke in the center, allowing it to slip out of the ring that held it to the machine. The prince cheered, and Katiel struck again by his ankles.

"Can you stand?" she asked, but Eoghan did not bother answering. He bounded to his feet and wobbled a bit before righting himself. He was strong to do so after what might have been days without walking.

"Hurry, do the others," he urged, "please."

"Of course." Katiel nodded, moving to free the other two. It was quick work, her blade striking true with each swing.

Stefana stood, wobbling a bit herself before taking Prince Muiread by the hands and helping him to his feet.

"We should go," Katiel said. The fire had held back thus far, but with one rafter already collapsed, the roof could go at any second.

"What about Mother?" Muiread asked, looking at his elder sister.

Stefana shook her head, grabbing his hand to lead him to the door. She had given up—a thought too practical for a child.

A thought too heartbreaking for Katiel to bear. Never making it out of her prison was not a fitting end for the queen, not a fitting end for any person. Her subjects would want a proper burial for her, and she deserved as much.

"Wait for me outside and stay out of sight. I will get her," she told the children, suddenly confident in her strength, in the time she had, in the ability of the remaining rafters to hold. Hope was all they had gone by this whole time, her and

Brenna, and she should not give it up now. Not when they had made it this far.

The children did as she ordered, slipping out the same door she had come in. Quickly, she broke the chains that held the queen's corpse to the wall and averted her eyes as she dragged the body out of the building.

Even with the grim situation before her, she could at last breathe some manner of relief. The rest of the family was free now. The Tibedese would be spared from further implication in the conflict. At least something good had finally happened in all the chaos.

The body was heavy, but she managed to drag it out of the mill with no time to spare. The queen's feet had scarcely crossed the threshold when flames engulfed the building.

42

Brenna

Brenna knew it would do no good to urge Sera to hurry, no matter how much she longed to. Sera cut into the ropes with all her strength, but there were several holding her in place, each one thicker than Brenna's own forearms. The barn was halfway engulfed in the inferno already. Brenna could hardly catch her breath in the thick air, and the unrelenting heat was becoming uncomfortable on the exposed skin of her face and hands.

But Sera had more skin exposed, she realized—all of her arms and her chest above her tunic. Her flesh had to be scalding, besides the knife that was surely scathingly hot. Hoping it might help her relax enough to cut through the last of the ropes, Brenna said, "Thank you for coming back for us."

"You made yourselves easy to track," Sera said wryly. "I would expect nothing less from you two."

A joke, Brenna realized, but the thick air prevented her from even forcing a chuckle to show her gratitude. Sera had nearly killed her, but something in Brenna found it hard to hate the girl. She was an assassin for the New Drezchy government, so she had defied orders to come back and help them. In doing a good deed, she made herself a traitor to her country. It was so backward.

But she risked everything to save their lives now, and that had to count for something. Brenna tried to say, "You did the right thing," but the sentence came out too forced, and she launched into a coughing fit. There would be no more talking.

The fire was spreading closer. It covered every surface now, save for the posts she and Jay were tied to. There was no hope anymore. She needed to tell Sera to leave, to get out of here before the place collapsed—

Her wrists sprang free.

Instantly, she reached for her feet, meaning to loosen the ties there, but the world blinked in and out in black splotches as she tried. She needed to steady her breathing, take shallower breaths. She pinched her eyes closed.

One second, two seconds. Inhale. One second, two seconds. Exhale.

She could do this. She reached for her ankles again, her vision steadying, and untied her feet. Sera had already gone over to Jay to cut him loose, with a cloth from her waistband pressed against her mouth and nose.

In her peripheral, Sera straightened and stilled for a second before she turned on her heel, panic flashing across her eyes.

She had seen him before Brenna.

General Taregh, standing in the open doorway of the barn. The flames flickering across his pockmarked face were the only thing keeping him from blending into the night.

A smirk crept across his face as he reached into his jacket.

No, no, no, he was—

He whipped a pistol from his pocket. Sera lunged for him, trying to take the weapon, but he was ready for her. He lashed the pistol across her face, her neck whipping to the side with a sickening crunch. She crumpled to the ground, still as death.

Brenna could not breathe.

Sera—

No, it could not be real. It could not have happened. Sera did the right thing and came back for them. It couldn't be over for her.

Sera was not moving. Something in Brenna broke as it registered that another member of their traveling party might be gone from this world. She should pray for her, pray that she recovered—

But Taregh was still there. Standing there, waiting, crueler than any demon.

Brenna turned, hoping to run. She would break through the burning wooden planks of the walls if she had to, even if it scalded her. She had to get away.

The second she set off, he was there, gripping hard at the top of her shirt. She couldn't scream, couldn't waste the precious air left in her lungs for it.

The fabric he gripped gave a soft crunch, and she suddenly felt overly exposed in her square-neck blouse. But as Taregh's eyes lowered, she could tell his focus was on one thing only—the exposed corner of the letters peeking out from the edge of her neckline.

She tried to steel her eyes lest she give away how important they were, but as he swiped the parchment with his left hand, it was obvious he had already figured it out.

"What have we here?" Taregh purred, a sickening sound, as he scanned the words. Brenna tried to use the distraction to wiggle free, but his grip on her shirt didn't loosen. "Letters addressed to Inigo Farro. Hmm. How you wound up finding out the truth, I don't know. And I don't care. But we can't have this getting out once I am king."

He lifted the letters out to the side, reaching them toward the encroaching flames. Brenna knew what he was doing immediately. The flames licked at the edge of the letters, and the papers rolled inward and blackened. Before her eyes, the last pieces of evidence were reduced to ash.

Without a second thought, she swung at him, making contact with his ear. It did not faze him. A spark fell from the rafters and caught her hair, singeing a chunk of curls right next to her temple. The reek of burning hair and skin filled the space. The haunting smell was worse than the pain, somehow. Still, she couldn't scream.

Her lungs were tight—far too tight—in her chest. She was faring little better than the parchment. The blaze was sucking the last of the oxygen from the space, and she had no strength left to fight off the general.

She wouldn't last much longer in here.

It shouldn't have been Sera who died. She came back for them. And it shouldn't have been Mara. Brenna was the one who dragged her back into this when she had already made it out.

It was all her fault, and she didn't want to be the one to survive when the others didn't. She didn't want to live with the guilt of the deaths she caused. She should never have left the Yule Valley. She should have listened to Henred and never left home.

Kill me, too.

"Now, what would be the fun of that?" General Taregh drawled. She must have said it aloud, then. "Why would I kill you when you are the perfect thing to make my dear, traitorous Jacoby suffer?"

Without loosening his grip on her, Taregh reached over and slapped Jay hard across the face. Jay's eyes blinked open slowly, and then shot open wide as he took in the sight. "Let her go!" He thrashed against his bonds before launching into a coughing fit. There wasn't enough air left for either of them.

"You and Ellis are the traitors," Brenna ground out.

"Ellis?" Taregh scoffed. "He was spineless. To force him to do anything, I had to tell him I'd captured some maid he liked."

Mara, Brenna realized. He was talking about Mara. "But she made it out alive!"

Taregh shrugged, his grip on Brenna's throat tightening with the movement. "Ellis didn't have to know that."

"You're a monster," Brenna spat. "Now she is dead because of you."

"Yes"—Taregh nodded—"and it's a shame Ellis found out. He tried to free the royal kids after he heard she'd died." The way he said it, it was as if this proved Ellis was a horrid person, rather than proving to Brenna that he had been good. "At least the girl is gone, though. She was useless."

The blood rushed to Brenna's ears. He had ordered the murder of the king and of Mara, someone Brenna had come to call a friend. Taregh would kill anyone and do anything to rule Bar Kur.

Brenna swung her arm from behind her, mustering all the energy she had left, and smacked the general hard across the face.

He reeled back and slammed his head forward, the granite plane of his forehead colliding with the bone at the top of her nose.

A crack sounded. The crack of bone—her bone. The room spun, a swirling orange space made entirely of fire. Jay was screaming, thrashing, but she didn't hear the words.

Stay awake, stay alert. Eyes open.

The copper tang of blood hit her tongue. Her blood, she realized, trickling down her face.

She swallowed it.

She swung at him again.

The flickering, orange world was blurry, so hot and so blurry—

He picked her up by the front of her shirt, the place where his hands still gripped the fabric, and slammed her onto her back, onto the dirt ground cover of the barn.

"Don't hurt her!" Jay screamed.

The general was above her, reaching for her neck.

"Just kill me," she breathed.

He gripped her neck with both hands and wrung it. The difference was hardly noticeable in the thin air. She hoped she could pass out before anything else happened.

She hoped she could die.

43

KATIEL

KATIEL'S EARS RANG AS she crossed the threshold of the paper mill, her heart threatening to burst out of her chest. She barely registered the cloud of soot that billowed out of the building as it collapsed behind her. Her mind could only focus on heading back for Brenna.

"Wait here," Katiel hastily told the children before she dashed off in the barn's direction.

It was not too far. She could make it shortly. She willed Brenna to be all right. Surely, she had made it out already. Sera had been right there with the knife, ready to free her.

Surely, they had—

Katiel rounded the corner and caught sight of the barn, the doors flung wide open, the structure engulfed in the blaze.

She could see the figures, so far in the distance she could hardly make out the shapes. General Taregh, standing, dangling Brenna above the ground. Jay, still tied up. Sera was not there, or at least, not visible in Katiel's view.

She watched the general strike Jay and then slam his forehead into Brenna's.

Katiel was running as fast as she could, but she was still so far away.

Without even thinking, without worrying if she had more, Katiel flicked out another piece of ore as her feet ground to a stop.

If she had a gun, she could stop Taregh even from a great distance. She knew the mechanics of one—the pistol she sometimes kept with her in the valley in case wolves came for her sheep.

Katiel's first instinct was to ignore the chaotic scene around her, but this time, she let the chaos feed her instead. Let the intensity and the panic and the adrenaline overcome her until she could not think at all. Her eyes did not leave her friend's tiny form in the distance as her mind emptied completely, and in her sudden burst of clarity, she wielded.

She moved fast and thoughtlessly, expanding the ore and shaping it in two swift motions. She was no longer thinking, only acting, and within seconds, a loaded revolver drifted into her hands.

Brenna hit the general again and staggered. The thin air from the fire must be getting to her.

Katiel raised the revolver out in front of her, lining it up with the target. Just a few more yards, and she would be close enough to aim. Close enough to shoot Taregh.

But he held Brenna less than a foot away from him. A wielded weapon was supposed to have perfect aim for its wielder, curving the path of a bullet if it had to. But what if she hit Brenna instead? She could not risk it. She would have to wait and get closer.

General Taregh lifted Brenna and slammed her down on her back, the shapes warping in the distance.

No, no, no, that was not supposed to happen.

He reached out his hands, strangling Brenna. He was going to kill her.

She could not wait. She would have to trust her ability. Trust her connection with the ore to guide her aim. Trust something inside her before Brenna was gone.

The world stilled to nothing as Katiel pulled the trigger, her breath and her mind focused on nothing but the bullet. Time no longer existed as it flew, willed by her for the general.

The bullet sailed cleanly through his head.

He fell away, off to the side.

She was sprinting fast for Brenna and Jay, but, for Katiel, time remained halted.

She had killed a man.

The Secretary of War of Bar Kur.

She wielded something, something that came from her soul, and killed with it.

The warmth left her body, left her chest, despite the flaming complex around her.

She had taken a life with her deepest part of her, her ore—the soul, the lifeblood she had always possessed, even before she knew it.

And she would do it again for Brenna.

44

Dakier

It was Henred.

The man Dakier had shot.

The man he had killed.

He saw his face clearly, his hat flying off as he went down.

Dakier had not yet lowered his rifle.

As if on legs that belonged to someone else, he ran over to him, past and among the others, soldiers on both sides convening down the line.

Maybe it was not really him. Many others looked like Henred. It could be the trauma of the situation playing tricks on Dakier's mind.

But as he looked down at the unmoving body, there was no mistaking it. It was Henred.

He pressed his fingers to Henred's neck. No blood pulsed in his veins.

That was when he saw it, on the inside of Henred's coat. When Dakier reached for it, time stilled despite the frenzy festering around him. A lock of red hair, tied with yarn in a four-leaf-clover knot. Green yarn for Bar Kur—the mirror to the blue yarn tied around his own.

War was a cruel twist of fate, and they were all pawns in it.

As he tucked Brenna's lock into his own coat with the other, someone shouted at him in Endran, demanding to know what he was doing. Gunshots rang out in every direction. Sparks, cannon fire. The surrounding madness caved in on him, pressing in every direction. Several Barkurian soldiers reeled on him, but he was quicker. The promise of pacifism vanished as he reacted to the questioning, stabbing the Barkurian soldiers who stood closest to him with the sharp tip of his bayonet.

Two, three, four men went down at his hand. Young men, red-haired men, more Henreds with more Brennas at home waiting for them. But he had no choice. They would kill him the second he hesitated. Everything about it made him sick.

He had made it farther into their lines, a lone force to be reckoned with, as he aimed and fired on adrenaline alone.

It wasn't like he had imagined in books, where all the bad guys had masks over their faces and wore steel armor forged in spite. They were boys he was killing, whose faces he watched as they contorted in pain.

Like him, they were boys. None of them deserved to die.

But the thought cost him.

The butt of a rifle collided with his temple, knocking him off his feet in splitting pain.

His vision snapped to black, and then his mind with it.

45

Katiel

Katiel raced into the burning barn, the acrid smell of ash filling her lungs as she ran toward her friend. With a heave, Katiel yanked Brenna from the room, her body limp from oxygen deprivation, before going back in for Jay. She freed him as swiftly as she could manage in the thin air, and in a blink, she was back outside, kneeling before Brenna.

She was breathing better now, and she sat up when she saw Katiel.

"I was so scared," she choked out, the words breaking into a sob, "I thought I was going to die. I thought he was going to—"

Katiel wrapped her in a hug, pulling her tight before she could finish the thought. "It's okay. It is okay," she said as Brenna sobbed against her chest. Katiel stroked her hair, something inside of her breaking to see her dearest friend in such pain. "Nothing happened. Nothing happened. I'm here. It is over. He's dead. It's over."

It was as if, by saying everything twice, she might convince herself of it as well.

Brenna sucked in her tears long enough to push back and look Katiel in the eye. "You killed him?"

"Yes," Katiel answered, nodding. Saying it aloud made it more real, somehow. She had killed him.

"He burned the letters, Katiel," Brenna said, a fat tear rolling down her cheek. "They're gone."

"Don't worry about that," Katiel shushed her. "What matters is that you're safe."

The fire had singed Brenna's temple, revealing a bright red swatch of raw flesh where freckled skin should be. Brenna reached her hand for it, but Katiel nudged her wrist away. She should not touch it. And Katiel should not have left her there to go for the royals. She had made so many mistakes.

As if reading her thoughts, Brenna asked, "Were you able to save them?"

But she did not have to answer. The children were already walking up to them. Brenna's eyes widened as she took in their filthy appearance. "The queen was already dead," Katiel whispered to her, hoping the children could not hear. "Where is Sera?"

"She"—Brenna gulped—"she didn't make—" Brenna looked back toward the barn and gasped, like she expected to see something that was not there. "She was lying there, on the ground! Her neck snapped. I thought she died."

The only body lying on the ground was General Taregh's. Katiel averted her gaze, instead surveying the surrounding complex in the dim twilight. "She must have run off."

It would stand to reason, now that Sera had revealed herself as a spy for New Drezchy, that she would run off as soon as possible, and she was tough enough to get away even while injured. Katiel's feelings were mixed about the girl after everything that happened, but she had come back for them. It was a miracle that she had, but it was something.

For Anton, on the other hand, her feelings were anything but conflicted. She did not care why he had tricked her and taken her ore, because nothing could be a good enough reason. The crumpled note in her pocket was reminder enough of his betrayal.

"Katiel, you need to leave," Jay said from where he stood above them, cutting into her thoughts. Katiel had not registered that he was there. "You should leave the country. We don't know who else was working with General Taregh, who else might be on his side. We have to take the children back to Ballynach Castle right away for medical treatment, but they won't let an A'slenderian go with the information you know about the war—not one who practices the forbidden arts as well."

"What?" Brenna exclaimed. "How can you suggest she flee, with all she did to help?"

"Even if the war ends—" Jay started.

Brenna cut him off. "When."

"*When* the war ends," Jay amended, "the higher-up government officials might try to keep her here or execute her because of all that she knows. And besides, she's still a wanted criminal who broke out of jail. I think we can get the charges dropped for you, Brenna, but I'm not sure about Katiel. No matter how much you did to help. I'm just trying to keep you both safe."

Brenna's lips parted to object again, but Katiel stopped her. "He's right, Brenna. It is risky. The easiest thing will be for me to go back to A'slenderia."

Brenna raised a brow. "Is that really what you want?"

Katiel opened her mouth and then closed it again. Honestly, she hardly knew what she wanted at this point.

She wanted the war to end. She wanted Bar Kur to call it off in light of the information about the framing and the rescue of the royal children.

A part of her wanted to head home to the Yule Valley. She could return to her parents and go back to the life of peace she had known. But she feared those who sought to silence the truth about the war would follow her there and find her parents as well. Or the authorities of A'slenderia might discover they had broken the Kerafin Pact and given birth to a new wielder, and she feared the punishment would be severe.

Besides, the person she was now had never been to the Yule Valley. This person had broken a war criminal out of jail and killed a government leader. She was not sure her parents would recognize her.

Who she was now owed her protection to the world, to the ore. The gift that her father sent to protect her. The gift she had already lost.

That was what Katiel wanted most—to get the ore back. Sera had claimed Anton was not the one Taregh was working for, but Katiel was not convinced. After all, the spy had defended Anton's thievery and tried to kill them, so she couldn't fully trust Sera's assertion.

Anton always has his reasons. Sera had sounded sure, but the words seemed unlikely, considering his thoughtless note.

♥*f.* A

Why put a period after the 'f' but not the 'A'? It was careless—

Unless it was intentional. Unless it was a message.

The realization struck her fiercer than a winter wind. It was a message, only backward. Simeon said they had docked at Afdot Harbor. Anton must have been telling her to meet him there. Now that she knew where he was, Katiel knew she had only one choice. She needed to retrieve the ore from him.

Katiel scrambled to recall what else Sera had said. *If you knew who Anton was.* Was that not yet another indication that he might be the boss?

Deep inside, Katiel believed her intuition over Sera's assertions. Anton was the boss. He had to be. And she needed to recover her ore from his hands.

Her confidence swelled as she stood to leave. "Yes, it's what I want."

"Okay." Brenna stood as well with a bit of effort. "Then I'll come with you."

But Jay interjected, "Brenna, please, stay here with me in Ballynach. With all you did here, I can get you a role in the government." His look was so earnest, so unlike his usual smug expression, that Katiel could tell the offer meant a great deal to him. "I still don't know if anyone else was working with Taregh, and I need someone here I can trust. Right now, the only person I trust in the capital is you."

"He's right," Katiel said before slipping Brenna the letter she had written back in Clon Killy. "Please, mail this to my parents. I want them to know I'm safe."

Brenna must have noticed her earnestness, too, because she did not argue. "Are you sure you'll be all right alone?"

"Yes," Katiel said, and she meant it. She never had been confident on her own before, but now, she felt she could do anything, even alone.

She understood better now why her parents had hidden her away like the goat in the grandfather clock. But she could not hide anymore, not with the strange, otherworldly taste of the ore on her tongue reminding her what she had to do. She would go to Afdot Harbor and retrieve her ore from Anton.

Before it was too late.

46

Brenna

"May I present her candidacy for ladyship, for her bravery, Miss Brenna Malley of Fir Kelt."

Brenna heard the announcer's words as if through water, the garbled sounds of a near-forgotten dream. It felt as if she were living someone else's life. She'd stayed in the capital long enough to receive her ladyship, but she hadn't decided if she would remain in Ballynach to serve as the queen's lady-in-waiting. Standing before the throne, she was almost certain she should return to Fir Kelt with her family, who had arrived for her ceremony but were heading home immediately after. As for how she would explain her rejection to the queen—hopefully, she could figure that out before the evening's end.

Ballynach Castle's throne room was a luxurious space with emerald draperies edging gray stone walls. The room contained very many people and very little furniture, save for the illustrious set of thrones on a raised platform opposite the grand entryway—three thrones carved of stone that may well be older than Bar Kur itself. The ancient chamber looked like something from the sagas, a relic of the past, not something that should still exist in Brenna's time.

On the center throne, the largest of the set, sat the tiny, newly crowned Queen Stefana I, twelve years old and looking younger than ever as the throne dwarfed her in size. The smaller thrones beside her were both conspicuously empty.

The people were all watching her. Shoving her timidity aside, Brenna stepped up to the thrones and into the wide gap that the crowd had left for her.

"Brenna Malley," the queen said, rising to her feet. Still in mourning, she wore an elaborately pleated black gown, with a black-and-green tartan shawl draped over one shoulder.

Brenna dropped to a knee and bowed her head as the queen rose. She knew not to lift her gaze until the monarch commanded her.

"Your valor is unmatched," Queen Stefana I continued in her high-pitched voice. "Let it be known to all that you have saved my life and the lives of my brothers, ensuring the continuity of the esteemed monarchy of the sovereign nation of Bar Kur."

At her side, Queen Stefana held a sword with a jeweled hilt. As she finished her proclamation, she raised the sword into the air and touched the tip to each of Brenna's shoulders, the right and then the left. "Rise, Lady Brenna Malley of Ballynach."

Brenna did so, and the queen made the smallest of hand motions that sent a servant scurrying over. When he pinned a tiny bronze medal to Brenna's dress, the crowd erupted into applause, and Brenna did her best to force her wide smile.

It should have been the best day of her life, but it wasn't.

It had been less than a week since she'd faced General Taregh in the flaming barn. And it had been only one day since she'd heard what might have been the worst news of her life.

Yesterday, Brenna had wrung her hands as she waited outside the double doors in Ballynach Castle. Beyond those doors, the newly minted Queen Stefana I had called a meeting in the war room. A meeting to discuss what the government would do once they knew the truth about King Stefan XIV's assassination.

A meeting to discuss how they would end the war.

When the doors at last opened and the slew of statesmen began pouring out, Jay was among the last to leave. Brenna grabbed his sleeve the second she saw him and pulled him aside.

"Well?" she prompted, barely able to contain her excitement. This would put an end to it, now that the queen knew the truth. Henred would come home. Dakier would come home, too. And she could visit Katiel again, whenever she liked, their countries allies again.

Everything would go back to how it had been.

But Jay's expression was sullen. "Brenna, they're not ending the war."

The world slowed. She must have misheard him. "What?"

"Wars don't end this way, Brenna." Her brother-in-law placed a kind hand on her shoulder. "Bar Kur can't reveal the truth, especially not to Tibedo. It would weaken our position globally."

The disappointment that swept over her was unbearable, the reality of the world sinking in. Even when the truth was out there, it had not made a difference. But she didn't bother to ask why they would make this decision. In only a moment, she had grown up. She was no longer the same naïve, hopeful girl she had been, who had thought the mistaken knowledge of the assassination was the only thing keeping the war going. It was logical that Bar Kur would be unwilling to reveal the conspiracy to other nations. She could see how it would make their nation look.

She hated herself for understanding it.

"But there is good news." Jay said it like he expected her to ask what it was, but she didn't bother. The war hadn't ended. Their efforts hadn't mattered. "During the meeting, Queen Stefana requested you personally as her lady-in-waiting. She said you're the only one she trusts to do the job after everything you did." When Brenna did not reply, he went on. "This is a tremendous honor, Brenna. This is the greatest way you can serve the crown."

That honor was how she had wound up here, standing unmoving in a sea of celebratory people. Applause continued. Noblemen she did not recognize came over to offer their congratulations. Throughout it all, she did her best to smile and curtsy, but when Mam and Derenta and Jay filed up and hugged her, she couldn't help the tear that rolled down her cheek.

The trouble was, she didn't want an honor. She didn't deserve it. While she was being rewarded for bravery, the war continued. The people of Bar Kur did not know the truth. They still blamed Tibedo for the fall of their beloved king, and now for the death of the queen as well. The people she had wanted to protect were still out there on the front, risking their lives for a false cause.

And if she must receive it, Katiel should be with her, receiving her own award. Unlike her, Katiel actually deserved it. Katiel was the wielder. She was the navigator. Katiel was the one who had freed the royal children, but while Brenna was being awarded the highest honors, Katiel was out there alone somewhere, fleeing like a common criminal. Brenna hadn't even heard yet if she'd made it home safely.

"Imagine what Henred will say when he hears I'm a lady now," Brenna said, trying to lighten the mood before she broke into a full-out sob. "I can rub this in for ages."

Mam smiled—a sweet smile so familiar yet forgotten that Brenna almost teared up again. But before her mother replied, she gave a slight, uncertain glance at Derenta that sent Brenna's world spinning.

Because she knew that look.

"Brenna..." Mam started in an overly gentle voice.

Brenna's breath hitched. The look and that tone combined had her fearing the worst. "What happened to Henred?" she asked. But inside, she feared she already knew the answer.

Derenta reached for her shoulder. "We didn't want to tell you until after you got your ladyship."

No. Absolutely not. Nothing could have happened to Henred.

"We should step outside," Jay said, "into the hall."

Perhaps he was injured and getting discharged, Brenna told herself. That had to be the news.

Jay led the way through a set of oak double doors into a narrow hallway with tall windows punctuating the stone along one side. Brenna followed her family out, feeling the sensation of being underwater again—of everything happening too slowly, and yet too fast.

"We received the news the day before we left for Ballynach," Mam said in a whisper, "that Henred passed away several days ago in combat while fighting at the Tibedese border."

Derenta grasped her shoulder again. "We didn't want to tell you like this..."

The world tilted on its side, the wall of windows sliding up until they spanned the ceiling. Brenna thought she might have fallen over, until the wall righted itself again. It was only her vision, stranding her along with her heart. A shrill ringing made its way from her left ear to her right and back again, echoing through the passage that was now void of thoughts or feelings or anything at all.

"Brenna," Derenta whispered, her frantic tone poorly hidden. "Say something."

But Brenna shook her head, biting back the sob that threatened to come out if she dared speak.

Because what was there to say, anyway? That nothing mattered now? That this couldn't be true? That no matter how much good a person tried to do, the world was just too evil and too corrupt for the efforts of those who cared to make a difference?

Finally, she squeaked out, "I should leave." She would miss the end of the evening, when she was to accept her role as lady-in-waiting, but she could try to explain to the queen in a letter. At least she wouldn't break down in front of all those people.

"Wait, Brenna," Mam said, "before you go, Henred wrote you a letter. He sent it to Galvey, since we didn't know where you were once you left the Yule Valley." Her mother removed an envelope from her clutch. "At least read it before you decide for certain to return home."

Brenna took the note in her hands, a familiar material with a familiar filigree around the edge. Henred had stolen some of Brenna's own stationery to write it. That was so like him that she laughed, albeit the smallest of sounds.

Brenna,

I have literally never written anyone a letter before, and I never want to again. But I know you love them, so I hope this proves how sorry I am that we never made up before you left.

Mam and Derenta wrote me yesterday to say that you had run off with Katiel to stop the war. They asked me if I had any ideas of where you might've gone, to get you back home. I couldn't blame them; they were so worried. But I wasn't worried. As far-fetched as it sounds, the second I heard that, I believed you would end it. Sitting here in a war camp, writing you from my bunk before someone yells at me to turn off this lantern, I still believe you will. Because I know you. And if anyone can make a difference, it's you.

I know I don't tell you enough, or show it enough, but you are the best little sister a brother could ever ask for. And I can't wait to hear all about your adventure.

The Supreme Best Brother to Ever Exist,
Henred

Brenna wiped at her eyes again, teeming with emotion. She had this last letter from him, a token of her brother's love, and a validation that he knew about her mission and believed in it. He believed in *her.*

Because I know you.

That sentence meant the world to her. It reminded Brenna of what she said to Katiel in jail. From the first second she heard Katiel was a wielder, she knew it was true. She had believed in her friend regardless of if anyone else had, because she knew deep down that Katiel could succeed. Now it was time for Brenna to believe in herself just the same.

She was a lady now—a lady who had earned the queen's trust when no one else had. She'd helped rescue the royal, had helped defeat General Taregh, and had freed an innocent man from prison to return to his own family. She *had* made a difference.

And suddenly, she knew how she would make even more of a difference. She would stay in Ballynach and accept the queen's offer to be a lady-in-waiting. She would stay in the monarch's ear, closer to her than anyone, and convince her to call off the war.

The conflict was not over yet, but every war had to end.

And Brenna would not stop fighting until it did.

Continue the Journey

Get the Bonus Epilogue (told from Dakier's perspective) sent to your inbox when you subscribe to my newsletter at hayleywhiteley.com/subscribe.

Dawn and Dust, Book Two of the Kerafin Chronicles trilogy, is coming March 10, 2025, and is available for preorder at hayleywhiteley.com and amazon.com.

To find out what Anton has really been up to, preorder now to get the first two chapters of Dawn and Dust delivered right to your inbox!

Acknowledgments

First and foremost, thank YOU, reader, for being willing to pick up this book and give it a chance! I hope you enjoyed reading it even half as much as I enjoyed writing it. I sincerely appreciate the opportunity to share my love of books with you.

Emily Lawrence, thanks for being a great line editor. Thank you for refining the novel beyond what I could do, for thwarting many sneaky commas, and for teaching me that I have been using British English words my entire life without realizing it. Kim Long, thank you for your developmental edit. I have you to thank in particular for the title change, for the addition of more letters and clues, and for making Brenna work harder to earn her victories. Stefanie Saw, thanks for the gorgeous cover. It's hard to describe how exciting it was to see my work represented with such beautiful, professional art.

Thank you so much to my beta readers, Angela, Rachel, and Kari, for being such quick, thorough, and kind readers. Your feedback had a huge impact on what I kept in the developmental edit and on the final product of this work. Also, thank you sincerely to all the social media Street Team members. I so greatly appreciate you being willing to sign up for my team and share my book with potential readers out of nothing but kindness and support for indie authors.

Thank you very much to my family for supporting my interest in writing from a young age. Thanks in particular to my Aunt Beth for being willing to listen to me go on and on about story ideas (even very questionable ideas), read my terrible drafts from middle school, and always encourage me. Even though they can't read, I also owe a ton of gratitude to my cats Maui and (the late) Rainbow for keeping me company day and night while I drafted and edited this book.

Nick, my wonderful husband, I really can't live without you, much less write a book. I never would have (finally) finished one of the many books I've started without your constant encouragement and support. Thank you for letting me run every random detail of the story by you, for knowing all my characters by heart, and for saving all the maps I tried to throw away.

Hollis, my baby son, thank you so much for being the light of my life and shining so brightly in my heart. I was praying for you throughout the drafting process, pregnant with you throughout the editing process, and taking care of your little newborn self throughout the publishing process—and you brought so much joy to each step. Being your mom has given me more confidence and happiness than anything else in the world.

And finally, I have to thank God most of all—for (literally) everything, and for allowing me to have the opportunity to write and publish a novel.

About the Author

Hello! I'm Hayley Whiteley, author of *The Kerafin Chronicles*.

As a lifelong reader, I always dreamed of creating the type of stories that inspired me. After receiving my Mechanical Engineering degree from Auburn University, I worked for a few years in engineering before deciding I wasn't ready to give up on my writing dreams. I then revamped Brenna and Katiel's story (one of my many, many scrapped projects) and started from scratch on a new draft, which eventually became *Ink and Ore*!

Outside of reading and writing, I love baking, photography, spending time with my family, and doing nearly any activity outdoors, especially if it involves a beach. Though I'm from Alabama originally, I now live in Florida with my loving husband, my adorable baby son, and my sweet calico cat.

Made in the USA
Columbia, SC
01 November 2024

45318706R00219